Archer didn't want to argue with Rita

So instead he offered his hand in friendship. He'd have done the same after an argument with his little sister—if he'd had a sister.

Wrong. He'd reached for her because he'd been wanting to since the first time he'd seen her. He'd done it because he hadn't been able to resist any longer.

Maybe he just needed a woman. Well, that could be taken care of; he was a free man. What he didn't need was a relationship.

Archer didn't even know if he could *have* a relationship. The part of him that had trusted people had been pretty well blown to hell. The part of him that could care— He didn't even know if that part of him still existed.

Yet he'd wanted to reach out. Not to anybody. To Rita.

LISA HARRIS
is also the author
of this novel in
Temptation

UNDERCURRENT

TROUBLE IN PARADISE

BY

LISA HARRIS

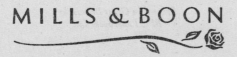

MILLS & BOON

MILLS & BOON and the Rose Device are trademarks of the publisher. TEMPTATION is a trademark of Harlequin Enterprises Limited, used under licence.
This edition published by arrangement with Harlequin Enterprises B.V. First published in Great Britain in 1995 by Harlequin Mills & Boon Limited, Eton House, 18-24 Paradise Road, Richmond, Surrey TW9 1SR

© Lisa Harris 1994

ISBN 0 263 79286 2

21 - 9505

Printed in Great Britain by BPC Paperbacks Ltd

1

SHE WAS OUT IN HER yard again this morning, taking photographs of weeds.

He couldn't figure her. He pretended to concentrate on measuring the lumber. He measured each piece twice before cutting.

And, although he didn't want to, although he *tried* like crazy not to, he kept watching her, just as he had from the start. She was a hard woman not to watch.

Not that she flaunted herself. She spent most of her days in faded cutoffs and T-shirts so baggy they hid all but her most obvious curves. Often as not, she was barefoot.

He knew her name from the rural mailbox: Margarita Elena O'Casey. It fit her; there was something exotic and unexpected about her with her long black hair and gypsy earrings.

What did he need with exotic? he asked himself bitterly. What did he need with unexpected? Calm, impersonal, predictable—that's what he wanted his life to be.

He kept his distance from her; he kept his distance from all of them—the few neighbors whose houses stood on the shore of this secluded cove. He'd made no gestures of friendship, he'd accepted none.

He didn't own the house he stayed in. He'd taped a temporary sign over the owner's name on the mailbox, put up his own name for the summer: A. Smith. It seemed a suitable, anonymous name, and it happened to be real.

All that Archer Smith intended was to keep the deal he'd struck with Patterson. He would stay in Patterson's lake house rent-free. In exchange, he'd put the place in repair. He would do simple, honest work. He would build a new deck.

He would restore the dock. And maybe he'd even figure out how to start over.

The summer alone, unburdened, would give him time to think, to heal.

But the woman disturbed him, for more reasons than he cared to admit. One troubling thing was clear. He wasn't the only man watching her.

Only six houses stood on this isolated shore of the lake. One was his. One was Margarita O'Casey's. One was empty for the summer. The other three held single men, like himself. He'd met the redhead at the mailboxes once. The redhead had whiskey on his breath, and he'd nodded in the direction of Margarita O'Casey, working in her yard.

"How'd you like a piece of that?" the redhead had asked with a sly grin. "I would. Hell, we all would."

Sometimes he saw them watching her with naked desire in their eyes. He didn't think she realized it. But that was insane—how could she not realize? Was she only acting innocent, just teasing them all?

One of these watchful neighbors was even newer to the tiny community than Archer Smith. Although the newcomer was the eldest of the men, he was the one who made Archer most uneasy.

His name was precisely stenciled on his mailbox: George M. Peavey. He had arrived three days after Archer. Peavey had descended on the cove in sound and fury, with a moving truck and professional movers whom he'd loudly commanded, scolded and bullied.

Peavey was sixtyish, short and squarely built with burly shoulders. He had the word *trouble* written all over him. He'd already argued with the redheaded man—something about a property line. Archer had overheard part of the disagreement, then deliberately tuned out. He wanted no part of it.

Of all the men, it was George Peavey who watched Margarita O'Casey most constantly, most furtively—and most hungrily. What did the old man see in her? His lost youth, his lost hopes and desires?

Oh, hell. What did he see in her himself? She had a natural, vital, carefree air about her—did he see her as a symbol of the sort of freedom he'd lost forever?

What's gone is gone, he told himself. He told himself that again and again.

Still . . . one single, attractive woman isolated on the shore of a backwoods lake with four lone men. Archer could sense trouble approaching, the way one can feel a thunderstorm brewing, even before the clouds gather.

RITA O'CASEY MARCHED purposefully into her backyard. She was barefoot, wearing ragged cutoffs and a gray T-shirt that said Arkansas—The Natural State.

From the lake came the muted roar of a speedboat at full throttle, and the querulous whine of jet skis. This afternoon the June air was especially sweet with the scent of mimosa.

A hummingbird whizzed by her on its way to the flowering mimosa. Cardinals and jays bickered in the trees, and from the shore came the harsh cry of a heron.

I love it here, she thought with an almost fierce delight. *I love being free again.* She took a deep breath, savoring her independence.

Somewhere in Midtown Manhattan, her ex-husband, Sterling, was devoting himself to the gods of advertising and the life-style it financed. Bitterly she remembered how devoted Sterling was to going to the right clubs, wearing the right clothes and running with the right people. And now he was free to play Duddly Studdly and sleep with all the women he wanted. She was happy to have escaped him and his pretentions and lies, and even happier to be barefoot and living in the country again.

THEY HAD BEEN DIVORCED for almost a year. She'd moved back to Arkansas to her grandfather's old vacation cabin, and she made her living working in stained glass.

Sterling's life was complex, competitive and full of clandestine affairs and intrigues. Hers was serene and soothingly celibate.

Still, she gave a sigh. If Sterling's world of commerce had its wars, so did hers. And she was just about to wage one.

She carried a huge spray gun, and it made her feel like a character in an animated cartoon. Soon she must madly pump the gun and make clouds of insecticide billow forth. *Foosh-whoosh! Foosh-whoosh!*

Grimly she clenched her teeth. Along with the cabin, she'd inherited her grandfather's battle: the Great Apple Tree Campaign.

Her grandparents had planted the dwarf apple tree fifty years ago, when they'd bought the land and built the cabin. It had grown and prospered, and it bore tart, juicy apples that were ambrosial. But there was a price, and the price was spraying against bugs, blight and rust—all summer long.

Defending the tree was no job for a wimp—or a wimp-size spray gun. So Rita constantly hauled out her grandfather's industrial-size weapon and militantly pumped spray. Family tradition was at stake. Also, the finest pie apples in the world.

She approached the tree, closed her eyes against the sting of the spray, held her breath against its fumes. Anxious to get the job done, she pumped as fast as she could. She turned her head over her shoulder to steal whiffs of untainted air.

Suddenly she felt a finger stabbing into her back—painfully hard. She gasped in surprise.

"Stop—poisoner," hissed a man's angry voice. "Stop... *stop!*"

She was stunned when the man grabbed her arm and wheeled her around to face him.

Dumbstruck, she stared into the face of George Peavey—the man who'd recently moved into the house behind hers.

He was new to the little lake community, but he already had a reputation as a crank and a troublemaker. He was short, bullnecked and had a thick head of gray hair and glasses with wire rims. Behind the lenses, his eyes glinted a pale, cold blue.

"Give me that," he almost spat as he tried to wrench the sprayer from her hands.

This man is crazy, she thought, almost panicking. If she hadn't been barefoot, she'd have kicked him in the shins.

"Give me that," he repeated with a zealot's wrath. "You won't poison *my* air, *my* environment."

He grunted and tried to wrest the sprayer away. Rita hung on with all her might, then almost jerked it out of his grasp.

"This is my yard," she said, furious. "And my property! Who do you think you are?"

The more she resisted, the colder his eyes grew, the harder the lines in his face.

"You're polluting my air," he accused. "You're shooting toxic substances at my house. Straight into my lungs."

She tossed her head angrily. "You can't charge in here and manhandle me." She hung on, and so did he, engaging them in an absurd but grim tug-of-war.

"The birds," he snarled. "You'll poison the humming-birds."

Rita gritted her teeth. "The hummingbirds won't come near this tree. It's already blossomed. I'm killing *bugs*, dammit, and I—"

He lunged in a sudden feint. At the same time, he twisted the sprayer and triumphantly ripped it from her hands. She glared at him in anger and disbelief.

"You're upsetting the balance of nature," he charged, his voice dramatically pious.

He raised the sprayer above him, as if it were the trophy from some holy war. "We'll have no more of this!"

"What are you going to do?" she demanded.

"I'll break it over my knee like the sword of a dishonored soldier," he returned. "My God—won't people ever learn?"

"It's mine." She clenched her fists. "It was my grandfa-ther's."

"Barbarians," he snorted. "You and your grandfather, both."

But he was going to do it, she saw, feeling sick at the thought. He was going to break it. He raised it higher in the air to get more power into his thrust. He took a deep, vic-torious breath and started to bring the sprayer down.

Then a tanned hand clamped around Peavey's wrist, immobilizing him. "Give it back," a voice said, dangerously quiet.

Peavey's cheeks flushed, his exultation vanished and a poleaxed expression came over his face.

Rita was astonished. Her attention had been so focused on Peavey, all other reality had been blocked.

Now the rest of the world rushed back. The hand that pinioned Peavey's wrist was attached to an arm, the arm attached to a man, and the man was her mysterious neighbor, A. Smith.

He wore faded jeans, torn at the knees. His white T-shirt was smeared with sawdust, and his unruly blond hair spilled across his forehead.

She'd seen A. Smith around before, of course. He was striking rather than handsome, and aloof. He'd seemed mild enough, but always kept his face an expressionless mask, as if determined to hide all emotion.

She was surprised to see that now he radiated a sense of menace. The mask had dropped.

He twisted Peavey's upraised arm so that Peavey stood, motionless and stiff, like a naughty child fearing greater punishment. Resentment showed in Peavey's eyes, and fear, as well.

A. Smith frowned, and his frown was formidable. "Give it back," he said to Peavey.

Peavey did nothing, said nothing. He seemed frozen.

Smith's upper lip curled. With his free hand he wrenched the sprayer from Peavey. He handed it to Rita.

"Thank you," she said, clutching it to her chest. She eyed him warily, her heart beating hard. *This is not a man to mess with*, she thought.

Smith jerked Peavey's arm down but didn't release him. "Now," Smith growled, smiling malevolently, "tell her you're sorry."

Peavey shot Rita a rebellious glance. He remained silent.

With startling swiftness, Smith's hand flew to the back of the man's collar. He jerked so hard that Peavey gasped.

Smith's smile hardened. "I said," he challenged softly from between his teeth, "tell her you're *sorry*." He shook Peavey by the neck, only once, but emphatically.

Rita winced. She didn't want violence, and she was sure that Smith could shake Peavey insensible if he so chose.

She almost said *"Don't"* to Smith, but something stopped her. Instinct told her he understood the situation better than she.

Peavey refused to meet her eyes. He stared with cold concentration at the lake. "I'm sorry," he muttered almost inaudibly.

Smith's smile disappeared. So did the softness in his tone. He shook Peavey again. "Say it so she can *hear* it," he snapped. She saw something dangerous flash in the depths of Smith's green-blue eyes.

"I'm sorry," Peavey almost shouted. But he kept his icy gaze trained on the lake.

"Better," Smith said, his teeth still clenched. "Now I'll warn you. Don't bother her again. Leave her alone. Or you answer to *me*. And stop watching her."

Peavey's chin jerked up. "I don't know what you're talking—"

Smith yanked the collar hard enough to silence him. He leaned close to Peavey's ear. His voice went ominously low. "I said, Stop watching her. Let her alone."

"All right, all right," Peavey said querulously.

The words were hardly out of his mouth before Smith thrust him away. "Get out of here," he said evenly.

Peavey scurried back to his own yard. Once there, he turned and scowled rebelliously at Smith. He shook with fury.

"You're a bully!" he shouted. "I'm an old man. I . . . have allergies. You'll pay for this. . . ."

Rita felt a dart of fear. Peavey, thinking himself safe again, was already making threats.

Smith's face was taut with distaste. "Come on." He took Rita by the arm. "I'll walk you inside. It's best if he thinks we're tight."

At his touch, conflicting responses swarmed through her. She wanted to resist his take-charge attitude, but at the same time she appreciated it.

He set a swift pace and marched her to her door. She hesitated. She wasn't sure she wanted this man in her house. The emotions he kept so carefully buried were frighteningly strong when he let them out.

He seemed to sense her anxiety. "Don't worry. I'm not going to try anything."

His hand on her arm gave her a sense of both security and subtle danger. Yet his expression was so stolid, so distant, that she believed him.

Wordlessly, she opened the door, led him inside. As soon as she shut the door, his hand dropped away from her. He took a step back, as if to give her space.

It didn't seem space enough. She sensed such energy pulsing through him that it did something odd to her nerves. The normally cozy, comfortable room seemed charged with electricity and too small to contain him.

Unconsciously she rubbed her arm where he'd touched her. "Thanks," she said. "I guess."

His eyes met and held hers. "You're welcome," he said. "I guess."

Something inside her shuddered into unwilling life. It startled her. *What is this?* she wondered. *What's happening here, and why?*

She studied him warily. He had a complex face, an arresting one. His jawline had arrogance in it and his mouth was bracketed by deep lines.

His eyes were an intense green-blue—a strange color, clear and piercing. Although he couldn't be much over thirty, his eyes had lines around them, as if he'd seen too much. She felt the shudder within her again, stronger and more irresistible.

Yet he was the first to glance away, as if he were more uncomfortable than she was. "I'm sorry," he said. "I probably came on too strong-arm. But I only hurt his feelings. Did he hurt you? I saw him grab you. . . ."

Her hand tightened on her arm. "No. He . . . startled me, that's all. But he wouldn't leave me alone."

"I saw." He frowned and stared at her big window overlooking the lake. From top to bottom, the pane's edges were hung with sun catchers. The stained glass gleamed like jewels in the afternoon light.

Her worktable was covered with her tools and a half-assembled glass panel she was making. The place was a mess, she supposed, and supposed that, like Sterling the Terminally Tidy, A. Smith would disapprove.

Still frowning, he glanced around her living room at its paneled walls, its rag rugs and the homely old sofa strewn with pillows her grandmother had crocheted.

The walls were hung with family pictures, posters and cluttered bulletin boards. Smith stepped closer to a photo of her as a child. In it, she wore a Minnie Mouse T-shirt and stood between her two older brothers. She'd lost her two front teeth and was grinning like an idiot.

He looked at it, his frown more pensive, then turned his attention back to the window. He nodded toward the sun catchers. "Is that what you do?"

"That's the little stuff," she said. "I do them for the stores and craft fairs. I like big pieces best. But I don't have any up."

He turned to face her again, his expression withdrawn, restrained. His eyebrows, darker blond than his hair, were so straight that their line was severe. Yet—and perhaps it was only a trick of the light—his mouth looked surprisingly gentle. His gaze was careful, almost nervous.

He's trying to put his mask back on, she thought, puzzled, and wished he wouldn't. *He dropped it for a moment, and now he wants it back.*

He frowned again. "I told him to stop watching you. He's been watching you—Peavey has. Did you know?"

"No," she said, not wanting to believe such a thing. "Why would he watch me?"

He looked her up and down. She felt that strange, lively shudder rush through her again.

"Are you *kidding?*" he asked, his mask dropping again. His lips curved in such mockery that she wondered how she ever could have thought his mouth looked gentle. For the first time she realized he had a sense of humor, and probably a wicked one.

Her face went hot because he was appraising her as a sexual being. For the past year she'd tried to forget she was one. After Sterling, she'd never wanted to feel vulnerable that way again. Up until today, she'd succeeded.

Sterling had said he'd fallen in love with her because she was spontaneous, frank, free-spirited and warm. After they were married, he'd decided she was too spontaneous, embarrassingly frank, free-spirited to a fault, and her affectionate nature smothered him.

She was not a quitter; she might have borne it, she would have struggled to work things out. But she discovered one thing about Sterling with which she could not cope: He was unfaithful. He seemed addicted to infidelity, committed to a lack of commitment.

The discovery of his adultery hurt her deeply and filled her with bitter irony. Sterling wasn't even *good* in bed. He was the wham-bam-thank-you-ma'am sort, and it amazed her that so inept a lover could be so accomplished a cheat.

But now, A. Smith was looking at her as if she were a desirable woman, and saying that old George Peavey watched her. She found the idea ludicrous.

"Me?" she protested, holding out the front of her shirt to show him how tentlike it was. "I'm a slob."

She believed it, because Sterling had said it so often. She was never careful about her clothes, she liked the feel of her hair swinging wild and free, and she seldom wore makeup because she never got it on straight.

But Archer looked her up and down again, one eyebrow lifting. "Some slob," he said.

His gaze, his low voice rattled her. "I just can't believe it," she said. "He never even spoke to me before. I avoided him— because you could tell he was trouble."

"You got that right."

"I mean, this is a complication we don't need out here. The neighbor from hell. We've all gotten along fine up to now."

He nodded. "Up to now."

"And you've made an enemy. I'll bet he's not the forgiving type."

"That's all right," he said. "Neither am I."

"Maybe he'll leave us all alone now," she mused. "Just stay at his own place and sulk."

"Maybe. Maybe not."

Maybe not. The prospect disturbed her. The cove was her slightly ramshackle Eden. Now Peavey had slithered into it, cold-eyed and ready to strike at anyone. He'd even come after her at the apple tree, which was a little too symbolic for comfort.

Smith seemed to understand her uneasiness. He reached into his back pocket and pulled out a dog-eared notebook and a stub of pencil. He must use them for his carpentry calculations, she thought irrelevantly.

He scribbled something. He tore off the sheet and thrust it at her. "My phone number," he said. "If he bothers you, call. I mean it. I saw this coming, and I wasn't going to get involved, but what the hell."

She took it, almost reluctantly. He had written his name beside it. "A. Smith."

"What's the A. stand for?" she asked.

"Nothing. Just call me Smith. And keep your blinds shut at night. Like I say, he watches you."

She shook her head stubbornly. "Then why would he act so hostile?"

"Who knows? He's not Mr. Average."

"And how do you *know* he's been watching?" she challenged. She wanted proof, not just scary speculation.

The corner of his mouth twitched, but he didn't smile. She thought she saw hunger, carefully controlled, deep in his eyes.

"I watch you, too," he said.

The words stunned her, even frightened her a little. She gripped the piece of paper more tightly.

Then his eyes turned blank, unreadable again. He moved toward the door. "So long."

"Wait," Rita said with more bravery than she felt. "What do you mean? *You* watch me?"

"Nothing," he said. "It's academic. I'm an observer. You're around. I observe you."

"Why?" She didn't understand. Ever since he'd arrived at the cove, he'd been unfriendly, as remote as if she didn't exist.

He allowed himself a minute portion of his sarcastic smile. "I don't know," he said. "Maybe it's those big earrings."

"Oh," she said, stung. She loved the gypsy earrings, but Sterling, of course, thought they were tacky. To keep him happy, she hadn't worn them through the two years of their marriage. But the day she walked out of their apartment for good, she'd put them on again.

She lifted her chin. "I don't take off my earrings for anybody," she said. "No matter what they think."

A. Smith let his smile grow a quarter of an inch. He gave her a look that made her stomach take a tumbling little pitch.

"Good," he said. Then he left.

She stood a moment, still clutching his phone number, her heart beating hard. On impulse she moved to the window and watched him walk back to his house. She reached up and touched one of her earrings absently.

What a strange man, she thought. And again she wondered what the A. in A. Smith stood for.

She was in her paradise, and she'd met a serpent. Could A. stand for Adam? She almost smiled.

But she didn't. When Adam and Eve got together, sex, pain and betrayal came into the picture, and Paradise was lost.

She wanted no Adam. Sterling had taught her enough about betrayal and unhappiness. She wanted only Eden, and and she wanted to be in it safely alone.

A. SMITH WENT BACK to his carpentry, angry with himself. He hammered until his very marrow throbbed and his ears rang.

He tried not to think. He kept thinking.

Why did you do it? Haven't you learned your lesson? Don't try to be a hero. There aren't any heroes, stupid.

He hadn't intended to meet the woman, talk to her. He hadn't wanted to do it.

Lies. He'd been lying in wait, like an animal of prey. He'd even flirted with her—reluctantly, as if he couldn't help it.

He hammered until his arm ached to the roots of his shoulder. He could pretend he'd acted out of simple, neighborly concern. But nothing about him was simple, he had no neighborly concern, and women were too much trouble.

Women always wanted to know about *feelings.* He didn't want any goddamn feelings. Women wanted *commitments.* How did the song go?—Freedom means you got nothing more to lose. Yeah. He wanted nothing more to lose.

This barefoot girl with her lively face, her brown eyes and mane of dark hair spooked him. She seemed seductively full of life when he was empty of it. She'd even made him smile.

But, he thought bitterly, he'd also smiled when he'd grabbed Peavey. He should hate violence. Was there still that much anger in him, that much resentment? *Hadn't he learned anything?*

2

THE NEXT MORNING, nature gave Rita a pleasant surprise. The mimosa tree in her yard had bloomed late this year, and now it had visitors she hadn't expected.

A great flock of black swallowtail butterflies fluttered and nuzzled in the pink blossoms. The butterflies were beautiful and beyond counting.

She'd come outside to watch the aerial ballet. She leaned against the mimosa's trunk and lost herself in staring at the dizzying dance of the swallowtails.

Her contentment lasted fully five minutes, until her red-haired neighbor, Joe Johanssen, staggered out his door and to the edge of his porch.

Oh, no, Rita thought, her euphoria vanishing. She knew Joe, who was in his late thirties, often drank on weekends and drank hard. But she'd never seen him this plastered—or drunk this early in the day.

He stood, swaying, at the porch's edge. He glowered blearily at George Peavey's house. Then he tried to take a step, lurched instead, and tumbled with a clatter down his front steps. He crashed to the ground headfirst.

For a moment, Joe lay ominously still. Then he moaned and tried to rise. He lifted his head, and his brow was scarlet with blood.

He collapsed to earth again with another moan, more piteous than the first.

Oh, God! This time he's done it—he's really hurt himself.

She ran to his side and knelt, putting her hand on his shoulder. She sucked in her breath. She didn't want to see his cut forehead, but she had no choice.

"Joe?" she said questioningly, trying to turn him over. He struck weakly at her hands and groaned for her to go away.

Then, as if by a miracle, A. Smith materialized and knelt beside her. Since yesterday, she had forced herself not to think of Smith, but she was glad for any help—even from him. She gave him a glance of reluctant gratitude, but he didn't look at her. He frowned down at Joe.

"Turn over," A. Smith growled. "Let me see." Roughly he rolled Joe onto his back. Joe's face was masked with blood and blackened by dirt.

"I'll get some towels," Rita said. "My God, we've got to get him to a doctor. Is he . . . all right?"

"It's just a scalp wound," Smith said in disgust. "They always bleed like crazy. Get the towel, we need a compress."

Rita sprang up, ran back to her house. She returned with a sloshing dishpan of water and ice cubes, and all the clean towels she had.

Together she and Smith cleaned Joe's face. Smith half supported, half hauled Joe to Smith's white pickup truck. Rita stayed beside Joe, pressing a wet towel against the cut.

Smith lifted Joe and almost shoved him into the passenger seat. He turned and looked down at Rita, as if seeing her for the first time. "Are you coming?" he asked brusquely. "You don't have to."

"We have to keep pressure on the wound. He looks like he's going to pass out. Will he?"

"Who knows?" Smith said without sympathy.

She squared her shoulders and climbed in beside Joe. As Smith gunned the truck's motor into life, Joe grunted in protest, sighed, then sank into unconsciousness. His head slumped onto Rita's shoulder. She pressed the towel against his scalp more desperately.

"Oh my God," she said. "What if he's bleeding to death? What if he's in a coma?"

"He's just drunk," Smith said in contempt. "Don't let him bleed on my upholstery."

Don't you have any feelings at all? she wanted to snap. But she couldn't spare the energy. It took all her concentration to hold Joe semi-upright and to keep her hands from shaking as she pressed the towel more tightly against his forehead.

AT THE EMERGENCY WARD, a pair of men in green hospital fatigues transferred Joe to a gurney and wheeled him away, while a nurse held a fresh compress to his wound.

Rita, dazed, gave what information she could to the woman filling out the admissions form. Rita knew Joe's name, address, and that he worked at the post office. He was separated from his wife; she had left him six months ago, but Rita didn't know where she was.

Neither did she know Joe's exact age, his medical history, his doctor, his insurance status, or if he had relatives nearby.

The admissions woman eyed Rita balefully, as if insulted by such ignorance. "And just what is your relation to the patient?" she asked, scrutinizing Rita's bare feet and blood-speckled T-shirt.

"Neighbor," Rita mumbled, shaking her head. "Just neighbors."

"Humph," said the woman and dismissed them.

Rita turned away wearily. From the moment Joe had crashed down the stairs, she'd operated on adrenaline, and now it deserted her. It deserted, in fact, at a dizzying rate, and all she wanted was to sit down.

A bank of chairs was arrayed against the opposite wall, and numbly she moved toward them—or tried. Her mind felt stuffed with cotton, and her knees seemed so weak they might be melting.

It occurred to her, dimly, that it would be perfectly logical to sink to the floor and sit there. With a wavering little sigh, she closed her eyes and decided to do so.

Suddenly A. Smith's arms were around her, supporting her. His chest felt solid beneath her cold cheek, his arms reassuringly strong.

Light-headed, she was surprised to feel his hand upon her hair, stroking it as he might a length of silk. "Come on," he said. "Sit. The blood's leaving your head."

"Don't say 'blood,'" she begged. "Don't say 'head.'"

"Ha," he said in her ear. "Squeamish—I knew it."

She shut her eyes more tightly and kept her face pressed against his chest. "I've *never* done this before. But I've never seen so much blood. My mother always wanted me to be a nurse—ha."

"Shh," he breathed, caressing her hair again. "Just get your breath, calm down. You did great. It's all right."

But something, Rita realized dimly, was starting to *happen*. His touch, meant at first merely to comfort, grew increasingly sensual. It gave her a sweet, shivery feeling in the pit of her stomach—but it shouldn't.

This is ridiculous. In the emergency ward? This is insane.

She pushed away from his embrace a bit too quickly, and looked, perhaps a bit too wildly, into his eyes. Their expression showed he felt every bit as wary and dubious as she did.

Still dizzied, she shook her head and looked away. His hand, tangled in her tumbled hair, went motionless. Then he drew it away.

"Feel okay?" he asked gruffly.

She nodded, staring into a corner of the room without seeing it.

"Good." She heard him crack his knuckles. "Come on," he said. "I'll buy you a cup of coffee. We'll wait to hear if we can take home What's-his-name."

She did not protest. She went with him, trying to act normal, unconcerned. But she sensed something had changed between them—something profound.

THEY SAT FACING EACH other at a white-topped table in the hospital's small lounge. She could tell that he was retreating behind his mask again.

"So why," he asked, his voice so casual he sounded bored, "were you staring up into that tree? Having visions, like Joan of Arc?"

Rita didn't want him to laugh at her, but neither would she lie. "I was watching butterflies."

"Butteflies," he echoed tonelessly.

"Yes," she said, feeling defensive. "The mimosa isn't usually in bloom when the swallowtails hatch. There were a lot of them, and I wanted to watch."

"Why?"

"Because they're beautiful," she said, wondering how he could not know such a thing.

"I see." His smile was small and sarcastic.

"Forget about me staring into trees," she said, taking the offensive. "Where'd *you* come from? When Joe fell? You just . . . materialized."

"I'd just come out. I saw him bounce down the steps."

She lifted her chin. "You're very cool in a crisis. How come? Did you earn the first-aid badge in Boy Scouts or something?"

"I'm no Boy Scout," he said. "Believe it."

"Then, what *are* you?" she asked.

His steady gaze was unreadable. "Just a guy named Smith."

"*What* Smith? Your name can't just be A. What is it?

"A.—that's enough," he replied.

"Why be so evasive?" she demanded irritably. "What do you think—I'll steal your soul if I know your name? You've *got* to have more than an initial."

He shook his head. His smile twitched out of existence, then back in. "An initial's fine."

"Well, A. Smith, what do people *call* you? I mean, your mother couldn't just say, 'Now, stop that, A.—don't put peanut butter on the dog.' You must have had a nickname or something."

He flicked her a cool glance. "I did. Now I don't. I go by Smith."

"But it's so . . . impersonal," she objected.

"So am I."

When you touched me, it seemed plenty personal, she thought, but didn't say it. If A. Smith wanted to play hard-to-get, he should find another partner. She didn't play games. She was a straightforward person—to a maddening degree, Sterling had maintained.

She changed the subject. "I hope they release Joe and let us take him home. That he's not hurt badly."

"He's not hurt much," Smith said. "A couple of stitches. Maybe they'll keep him overnight for observation. Trust me."

She squared her jaw in exasperation. "*Why* should I trust you? What do you know about it?"

"I've seen guys take hits in the head before."

Rita's patience was worn thin. "Yes? Like where? In the boxing ring? Reform school? Or do you belong to a club where people hit each other on the head?"

His lip curled slightly. "I used to play basketball. College basketball—okay?"

Well, well, Rita thought. *Imagine that: a major revelation. He used to play basketball. If, of course, he's telling the truth.*

"You're not very big for a basketball player," she said skeptically.

"It wasn't a very big college," he answered. "I played guard. I had to be fast, not tall."

"You can dribble, so you became an expert on head wounds. I see. It makes perfect sense."

He leaned across the table. He lifted his forelock of gold hair and held it back. He pointed to a long scar with stitch marks just below the hairline. "See that?"

"Yes. So?"

"*This* was a head wound."

"Who gave it to you? Somebody trying to pry information out of you?"

"No. A forward named Malcolm Washington. He was six foot nine, he weighed two hundred and forty pounds, and he told me to stay out of his face."

"And?" Rita asked, unimpressed. She crossed her arms.

"I stayed in his face. The next thing I knew, I was flat on the court counting bluebirds whirling 'round my head. A concussion and twenty-five stitches. It's about twenty more stitches than your friend'll need. You want to see more scars? I got one under my chin. A couple of others, we'll have to part my hair to see, but if that's what it takes—"

"Okay, okay," she said, shrugging. "So you've been hit in the head. You've got every reason to be proud. Well, I hope they don't keep Joe overnight. I'll have to drive in tomorrow to get him. He's got no way home."

A. Smith leaned closer. His smile, his whole smirky manner disappeared. "No. I'll do it."

She sat back, not sure she liked what he was saying. Her expression must have told him as much.

"Look," he said. His voice was atypically earnest. "I don't want to scare you. But this—Joe? I've seen him watching you, too. Maybe he's harmless, but he's obviously got this drinking problem, and that means he's unpredictable. You don't want to encourage him."

"Oh, for heaven's sake," she said in disgust. "So *what!* He watches me—a little. He'd watch anything female. I can handle Joe. I've been doing it for over six months, ever since his wife left."

Something flickered in Smith's eyes—anger or determination, she couldn't tell. "He's a loose cannon. You should—"

"I can take care of myself. I'm a big girl. What are you trying to do? Make me paranoid? According to you, the whole world is watching."

"Look," he said from between his teeth, "you seem to live in your own daffy little world. Did it ever occur to you that you're the only woman out there? And there are four—count 'em—*four* guys who watch you? That maybe you should be careful?"

His observation took her aback. She'd known that Joe, in his cups, cast wistful glances in her direction, but she'd ignored them and kept a polite distance from him.

As for Sig Hobbler, her other neighbor, he seemed harmless enough. He struck her as a leftover from the sixties, a graying hippie. He lived in a run-down house, kept a ragtag pack of mongrels and worked in town at a health-food store. Evenings he sat on his deck playing Grateful Dead albums and smoking hand-rolled cigarettes that she knew did not contain tobacco. During his stoned meditations, he, too, sometimes gazed in her direction. But Sig was so shy with women that he hardly ever spoke to her.

Peavey, however, was the one who'd thrown a monkey wrench into the works. She hadn't expected him to notice her—he'd struck her as too ill-tempered to have a sex drive. But since their scene yesterday, Peavey made her uneasy. There was something irrational and volatile about him.

Besides that, here was the enigmatic A. Smith, with his own supply of monkey wrenches. And he was right. She was alone out there with four men.

"I—I wasn't always the only woman," she said defensively. "I wouldn't be now if the Spectors weren't in Minnesota. They're only gone for the summer. Betsy Spector's usually around."

"But she's not now," Smith said.

"Last year, a young couple rented your place. Her name was Corinna. She—"

"She's not there now."

"And Joe's wife was there until last year," Rita argued. "It's not like I've always been the only woman. And the Spectors come back in September."

He drained the last of his coffee and set down the cup. "I just mean you should be careful. You don't want to play Florence Nightingale to this Johanssen. He'll take it wrong. What's his problem, anyway? You said his wife left him. Is that why he drinks?"

She made a helpless gesture. "It gets—circular. She left him because he drank. He drank because he was afraid she'd leave him."

"What set him off this morning?" Smith asked. "He usually doesn't get this bad. Or does he?"

"No," she said. "He works at the post office, and as far as I know, he's perfectly dependable. He never drinks on the job. But he does at night. Weekends are hard on him. He starts early sometimes."

Smith looked thoughtful. "But not this early—or this hard?"

She shook her head sadly. "No. Something must have upset him—badly. Maybe the divorce. He's desperate to sell his house. And she's pressuring him to drop the price, to take any offer. It's getting messy."

"That's enough," Smith said. "I don't need his life story. I don't want it. What about the other one? The one with all the dogs. What's his name—Hobbler?"

She nodded. "Sig Hobbler. He keeps to himself. He doesn't bother anybody—unless they bother him first."

Smith raised a questioning brow.

"Last Fourth of July," she said, "some college kids, out in a boat. They decided to put ashore in the cove. I don't know why—I think they had the wrong place. They were pretty wasted."

She paused, frowning pensively at the recollection.

"Yes?" he said.

"A couple of Joe's dogs came down to the bank, barking at them. The boys started throwing firecrackers at them. Sig came charging out of his house with a shotgun—"

Smith's body tensed. "A shotgun?"

"Oh, he was stoned and a little paranoid, probably," Rita said quickly. "He shot over their heads—he didn't mean to hurt anybody."

"Stoned and shooting," he said, his expression grim. "And this guy doesn't make you nervous?"

She shrugged in exasperation. "I *know* he shouldn't have shot. The sheriff came and talked to him. But no complaints were filed. If you leave Sig alone, he'll leave you alone. He's usually quiet as a mouse."

"Well, well." Smith nodded ironically. "Quite a little group you've got. One drunk, one pothead with a temper and a shotgun, and Peavey—an old crank ready to fight the world."

She looked into her cold coffee, then up into his eyes. "But nobody's ever hurt me—or tried to. Except for yesterday, and that shouldn't count. It was really very minor—"

"Margarita," he said from between his teeth, "listen to me."

"Rita," she said curtly. "I go by Rita."

"Rita, then," he said, a twist to his mouth. "*Listen*. It's been a long, hot summer. Ever since Peavey got here, tension's been building. You've got some lonely men out there, frustrated men."

"How can you tell they're lonely?" she challenged. "Or frustrated? Can you read minds?"

"My God," he said, "it hangs over the place like a cloud. All those guys . . . Look at them—losers, every one. The failure's so thick you can smell it. Failure and loneliness."

"You can't say that. We *like* being alone. That's why we live out there."

"No. *You* like being alone. The others don't have a choice. You've got a drunk, a guy marooned in the sixties and an antisocial twerp whose own mother probably couldn't love him. And you—you wake up things in them."

"Don't say that," she said. "It's not true. I'm not some siren singing my song. I have brothers. They'd look at any woman it didn't mean anything. Why would these people *watch* me?"

"Why were you watching the butterflies?"

She shook her head. "That's different. What could they see in me? I don't try to—"

"What do they see?" he interrupted with surprising intensity. "Maybe everything they don't have, but wish they did—everything they dream of. Maybe everything they've lost or never had. Or maybe it's just sex."

"I'm *not* sexy," she argued, angry. "Look at me—am I trying to be sexy?" She gestured at her tumbled hair, her baggy, spattered shirt.

He clenched his teeth more tightly. "Don't you *know*? You've got this . . . presence. A—a vitality. Like you're connected to life, to creation—and they're not. But you make them wish they were. You make them think they could be."

She tossed her head in annoyance. "I see. I'm alive, and that'll do. The sex goddess of the failure set. Well, they'll probably fail to act on it, so why don't you just quit talking about it?"

"You don't understand."

"Is that how you see yourself?" she demanded. "As a fail-ure, too? Or are you the one superior male out there?"

His face went almost frighteningly stony. "I'm a man. That's all."

"Oh? And how do you characterize yourself? Dangerous loner? Solitary observer? Drifter?"

His expression stayed harsh. "Drifter'll do. I'm here for the summer, that's all. I'm fixing up the place for Patterson." He hesitated, then regarded her with narrowed eyes. "You know Patterson?"

She clasped both hands around her cup. "All I know is that he's a lawyer. How do *you* know him?"

For a moment she thought he was going to give her a straight answer. His mouth twitched as if he were going to speak in spite of his better judgment. But all he said was, "I know him, that's all."

She sighed and turned her face away. If he loved his bloody privacy that much, let him keep it. One moment he would look at her with hunger, the next with coldness. It was like being whipped around by an emotional roller coaster, and she was sick of it.

"I'm going for a walk," she muttered. "I want some fresh air. I hate hospitals."

"Whatever you want," he said, unsmiling. "Just don't go far. I don't want to chase after you when it's time to go."

"Good. I don't want to be chased, so we'll both be happy, won't we?" she said with false politeness. "I won't go off the grounds."

She ran her hand over her tousled hair and turned to go, but a tall young doctor appeared in the doorway. On his la-pel was a name tag reading, Edmund Sweeney, MD.

"Mr. and Mrs. O'Casey, is it?" he asked. "You brought in the Johanssen man?"

Both Smith and Rita stared at the man in astonishment. "We're not married," she said shortly.

"I'm Smith," Smith said just as curtly. "She's Miss O'Casey. We're his neighbors."

Sweeney's face was shadowed from tiredness, as if he had been on duty too long. But he eyed them with wry interest.

"I see," he said dryly. "Johanssen's condition is stable. The gash only took five stitches, but he's got a slight concussion and we'd like to keep him under observation overnight."

Smith cast Rita a superior glance that said *I told you so*. She pretended she didn't see it and held her chin high.

"So I can pick him up tomorrow?" she asked.

"*I'll* pick him up," Smith contradicted.

Sweeney gave them another measuring look. "Whoever. Just phone first. Unfortunately, there's another problem."

Rita's stomach tightened. She shot Smith a defiant look to tell him she'd *known* Joe could be seriously hurt. He ignored her.

The doctor put one fist on his hip. "The problem's his drinking. He does this often?"

Rita didn't quite know how to answer. Smith, his face impassive, said, "He does his share."

The doctor frowned. "He did *more* than his share this morning. Some neighborhood argument, I take it?"

Rita had no idea and again said nothing.

"It could have been," Smith muttered. "I don't know."

"He keeps babbling about somebody named Peavey—did this Peavey set him off? Were there blows? Did Peavey hit him?"

Rita's eyes widened in uneasy surprise. Was it Peavey who had reduced Joe to his sorry state?

"He fell," Smith said without emotion. "Just like we told Admissions. Yeah, we've got a Peavey out there. Yeah, he might have set him off. He's a real assho—"

"He's contentious," Rita interrupted. "Very...contentious."

"I see," the doctor said. "Apparently there's a quarrel over a property line."

"Yeah," Smith said. "They've had words."

"Well, they seem to have had more this morning," Sweeney said. "Johanssen claims Peavey is out to *destroy* him. Which is probably the liquor talking. I just want to make sure we've got an accident here, not an assault."

"Destroy him?" Rita repeated in horror. "But—"

Smith shook his head. "Johanssen was alone. Peavey wasn't anywhere near."

"As I say," the doctor said with a sigh, "probably just the liquor talking. Well, Johanssen needs help, that's obvious. Does he have anyone?"

Rita shook her head. "Not that I know. He's alone."

The doctor massaged the bridge of his nose and looked more tired than before. "You live at the lake? That Blue Heron Cove settlement?"

"Yeah," Smith answered, and Rita nodded.

"Is there anybody out there that can—kind of stay between Johanssen and this Peavey until things cool off?"

"No," Smith said immediately. "Johanssen'll have to deal with it. Nobody's going to step in."

"*I* can step in," Rita offered, lifting her chin higher. "I mean, if clashing with Peavey's going to lead to *this*—"

Smith put up his hand, a signal for her to stop. Disgust mingled with impatience in his expression. "Don't get caught up in this, Rita. It's nothing but trouble. You can't—"

"I can't stand by and let him ruin himself just because Peavey—"

"You're not your brother's keeper. Don't try—"

"Don't give me orders," she retorted. "I'm just trying to be neighborly and—"

"Stay *out* of it," Smith ordered. "I mean it."

"*You* stay out of it. I remember when Joe moved in out there. He and my grandfather used to—"

"You're going to be sorry if—"

She cut him off. "I'd be sorrier if I stood by and did nothing."

"That's exactly what you should do, if you've got one grain of sense," he countered.

Sweeney threw up his hands in defeat. "Work it out," he said. "I've said what I had to say. Call tomorrow."

"I *will*," Rita said emphatically.

"*I* will," Smith said with even more conviction.

Sweeney shook his head, turned and left them. They hardly noticed. They were too intent on glaring at each other. Both were breathing hard. Rita was too angry to speak, and perhaps Smith was, too, for he said nothing, only glowered as stubbornly as she.

Then, slowly, his glower died. His eyes, more troubled than angry, searched her face, and she felt her own expression softening.

"I don't want you to get hurt." His voice was quiet, almost gentle. "That's all."

"There's—there's nothing to worry about," she replied, wanting to believe her words were true.

"I see things from a man's perspective, that's all. And...I'm concerned. Maybe I show it wrong. Maybe I say it wrong."

His eyes held hers, and something unsaid, perhaps unsayable, passed between them.

He raised one hand, palm up, in a gesture of conciliation. "Let's not fight—okay?" he said softly. "Let's just go home."

Then, to her astonishment, he stretched his hand toward her, silently asking for hers. Her lips parted slightly, and she found she couldn't take her gaze from his.

No, no, no, she told herself. *He doesn't want to get involved and neither do I. I won't begin anything that's doomed from the start.*

Yet she found herself, almost against her will, putting her hand in his. Only for a moment.

Then they drew swiftly away from each other as if they had both touched fire. They did not look at each other again.

3

ARCHER WAS STILL HAUNTED by her touch even when they got into the truck. His fingers tingled as if fire ran beneath his skin.

He vowed not to touch her again. He set his jaw, kept his eyes on the road and pretended to concentrate on driving.

He sensed her watching him warily from the corner of her eye. The silence between them seemed to have a smothering weight. In defense, he flicked on the cassette player.

Dwight Yoakam's silken moan pierced the silence. But Yoakam was singing "Try Not to Look So Pretty," which made Archer want to switch the damn thing off—it was too appropriate. If she didn't look so pretty, maybe he wouldn't act like such a fool.

He let the tune play out, then wished he hadn't. He'd forgotten that the next song, "Wild Ride," was even worse because it was so grindingly, achingly sexual.

He clenched his teeth tighter and steadied himself. He knew, rationally, that Rita had told the truth: She didn't *try* to look sexy.

She wore no makeup, and although she had swept her dark hair up into a high-riding ponytail, it was coming loose, strands brushing her cheeks, her ears, the nape of her neck. Her earrings glinted in the morning light—her only ornament; those big, round, crazy earrings.

Her hands lay clasped tensely in her lap. Her nails were short and unpolished. She had a Band-Aid strip circling the base of her left thumb.

When he'd touched her hand, he'd been surprised by its delicacy and strength—and the roughness of her fingertips. They had an unexpected texture, like fine sandpaper, and he supposed it was from cutting and grinding glass. He hadn't given a damn. Instead he'd wondered what those slender, raspy fingers would feel like stroking his naked body.

Stop it, he told himself fiercely. *Stop being a fool! Stop thinking about what can't be and focus on the problem at hand.*

Rita's nature was too open and her impulses too soft-hearted—for her own good. She'd play caretaker to that lush, Johanssen, which could get her into God knew what kind of trouble. Worse, she'd try to be peacemaker between Johanssen and Peavey—a situation she shouldn't touch with a ten-foot silver pole.

Accursed are the peacemakers, Archer thought cynically. *For they shall inherit everybody else's garbage—and then some.*

All right, he thought grumpily. It was within reasonable limits to tell her to butt out of Johanssen's business.

He hadn't wanted to fight with her, so he'd offered his hand in friendship—a platonic gesture that she'd happened to accept. He'd have done the same thing after a well-meaning disagreement with his little sister—if he had a sister.

Wrong. He'd reached to her because he'd been wanting to since the first time he'd seen her. He'd done it because he hadn't been able to resist any longer. And it had been as platonic as the *Kama Sutra*.

Maybe he just needed a woman. Well, that could be taken care of; he was a free man. What he didn't need was a relationship.

He didn't know if he could even *have* a relationship. The part of him that trusted people had been pretty well blown to hell. The part of him that could care—he didn't even know if that part of him still existed.

Yet he'd wanted to reach out. Not to anybody, but to her.

What he'd told her was true. Whether or not she realized it, something in her stirred men's fantasies. He wasn't so different from the other three men at the lake—younger, that was all.

But there was something hollowed out, ruined, incomplete about all four of them. She alone seemed vital, fully alive, complete in herself. It was too easy to imagine a sensual rebirth in touching her, having her.

Like a damned schoolboy, he'd held her hand for a moment and let it mean too much, when it should have meant nothing. He wondered, in the name of all that was holy, why she had let him. If she knew the truth about him, would she have shrunk from him?

But she didn't know the truth. For some reason, for a moment only, she'd clung to his hand as tightly as he'd clung to hers, and he'd sensed the same thought running scared through both their minds: *What fresh hell is this?*

His fingers tightened on the steering wheel. She didn't want this attraction any more than he did—he could tell.

Now, as they rode together, still not speaking, he sensed she was as uneasy as he was. Dwight Yoakam sang that lonesome roads were the only kind to travel, and Archer knew it was true. So, he suspected, did the woman.

But he also wondered what it would be like for them to be naked, their bodies locked together, shielded from the world by her bedroom walls and the silken curtain of her hair.

SHE DIDN'T SPEAK to him because she couldn't think of anything to say that made sense.

You're dangerous. I want you. I don't want you. Tell me about yourself. Don't tell me about yourself—I don't want to know.

Ever since she'd left Sterling, she'd struggled to be emotionally self-sufficient. She kept in touch with her family and with old friends, but that was it.

Now here was this handsome man with something haunted in his eyes, who was by turns flirtatious, aloof, combative, gentle.

And she had to deal with an unpleasant fact: He was the first man in three years who'd awakened a sexual urge in her.

The lure of the forbidden, she thought bleakly. Maybe some perverse side of her was being drawn to the dark side of the Force. Well, she was not careless or driven, and she refused to be self-destructive. She could resist the lure.

Yet, she sensed something more than simple sexual tension between them. When he had looked at her in the hospital coffee room, when he'd offered her his hand, something stranger—and rarer—than sex had seemed to tremble in the air.

It was almost as if they might care for each other. But that, of course, was impossible. Neither of them *wanted* to care—she knew that by instinct. She was still recovering from Sterling. And A. Smith had too many secrets. She didn't want another man with secrets.

She was relieved when he turned the truck down the rutted side road that led to the cove. But she was also immediately unsettled—the road had changed during their brief absence.

This morning it had been simply a twisting, dusty, southern road, lined with trees and scrub. Now, every fifty yards, the trees had sprouted signs, all of them unfriendly: Keep Out, Private Property, No Trespassing, No Hunting, No Dumping, Trespassers Will Be Prosecuted, Private Road, No Fishing, Private, Keep Out, Keep Out, Keep Out.

Rita was appalled. "Oh, Lord—look at this—the whole woods is a billboard. Why would anybody do this?"

A. Smith threw her a sardonic look. "It's your friend, Peavey, no doubt. Being a ray of sunshine, as usual."

Rita tossed her head. "He's *not* my friend. He can't do this—can he? This isn't a private road. The county maintains it. He can't say No Fishing—the public has a fifty-foot right-of-way to the shore."

Smith shrugged. "So he's not friendly. What did you expect? A welcome mat?"

She glared resentfully at the nearest sign. It was the sort sold in hardware stores. "I'd like to tear every one of them down," she said and meant it. "We've never shut people out."

"Tear them down, and you'll have Peavey threatening mayhem. He'll say these signs are his personal property, and you destroyed them."

Rita sighed. Smith was right. Peavey would rant. She had volunteered to try to make peace between Peavey and Johanssen, and she didn't want to anger the older man.

But the signs would cause trouble, she was sure. Bart and Betsy Spector wouldn't like them; Sig Hobbler would hate anything artificial marring his beloved woods, and Joe Johanssen might get drunk and tear them down for the simple pleasure of it.

Archer seemed to read her thoughts. "Stay out of it." He stared at the road, not at her, and his voice was quiet, without emotion.

I can't stay out of it, she wanted to counter. But she said nothing, only shook her head and stared sadly out the window. Until the last few weeks she'd loved this stretch of road. It had been the way back to home and peace. But home no longer seemed peaceful or safe.

When they reached the slope where the houses clustered, she saw Peavey with a pair of workmen. Parked in Peavey's dirt driveway was a red truck that had Allsop's Fencing painted on the door of the cab.

Peavey was gesticulating at a strip of ground where Joe Johanssen had a small, weedy vegetable garden. With his forefinger, Peavey described a line that would cut the garden exactly in half.

He glowered at Smith's truck as it rolled past him and stopped beside Rita's cabin. Smith's jaw was set at a grimmer angle than before. The afternoon sunlight fell through the windshield, glinting on his gold hair.

He narrowed his eyes against the brightness, but kept staring straight ahead, even though the truck was stationary.

"Did you see that?" Rita asked excitedly. "He's putting up a fence—a spite fence. And he's going to put it right through Joe's garden. That must be what set Joe off. No wonder he got upset."

"Stop staring," Archer said in the same flat tone. "And stay out of it."

Rita, never one to leap to obey, kept staring. "But he's going to take in a good five feet of Joe's land, all along that south side. He'll take in that beautiful pine tree of Joe's—it's the oldest tree out here. And the wisteria—the wisteria's the prettiest thing on Joe's lot."

"Rita, don't get in the middle of this—you'll regret it."

"Oh, go sulk in your house and ignore everything," she retorted, reaching for the door handle. "What he's doing isn't *right*. That's the bottom line."

She jumped from the truck and headed toward Peavey and the two workmen. *Don't stalk,* she cautioned to herself. *And don't frown. Don't sound angry. Honey catches more flies than vinegar.*

So she tried to keep a spring in her step and the approximation of a smile on her face. Peavey's expression was mixed. His mouth had a malicious twist, but his eyes swept over her with a sort of hunger that seemed both hot and cold at once.

She did her best to remain unfazed. "Hi," she said, smiling brightly. "Whatcha doin'?"

Peavey scowled. "What's it look like?"

"Well," Rita said, trying to seem cheerful and reasonable, "it looks like you're putting up a fence. But part of it's going on Joe's land."

Peavey's eyes flashed with such hostility she was taken aback. "I'm putting a fence on *my* land. I've talked to the abstract company. For years this land has been surveyed wrong. If Johanssen wants to argue, I'll take him to court."

Rita took a deep breath and willed herself to be calm. "Mr. Peavey, ever since I can remember, this strip of property has belonged to the other lot."

"What you remember is a long history of error."

"Now, I don't want to seem to interfere—"

"Then don't. Go away. I don't need you flouncing around distracting my workers."

She bit back a sharp answer. She forced her smile to stay in place. "I don't want to seem to interfere, but Joe's in the hospital right now, and I don't think that this is…a nice thing to do when someone's…unwell."

"He's not 'unwell,'" Peavey countered in disgust. "He was drunk and fell down his own steps. Served him right."

So, Rita thought, her temper rising, *you saw it happen, and you didn't do a thing. You'd have let him lie in the dirt and bleed.*

Her smile faded, but she tried to keep her voice sweet. "It's true Joe has a weakness. But he's best when things are calm. If you purposely upset him, you have to expect—"

"I didn't purposely upset anybody," Peavey practically spat. His glasses had slid down his sharp nose and he jabbed them back into place. "I can't help it if he's a drunk. I can't reason with a drunk. I refuse to try."

"He's not drunk," Rita countered. "Not all the time. He's always been a good neighbor. And he's trying to sell his house. The last thing he needs is a property dispute—nobody's going to buy a house with a disputed boundary."

"That's not my problem," Peavey said. "I have to think of my own interests. This is my property, and I have to protect it."

"Protect it from *what?*" she demanded.

"From those damnable dogs, for one thing!" Peavey cried. One of Sig Hobbler's mongrels had slunk to the edge of Peavey's yard and stood eyeing the workmen.

Peavey picked up a rock and flung it at the dog, hitting its ribs. The dog yipped and fled.

"Mr. Peavey," Rita said, outraged, "that's mean."

Peavey was so angry he almost sputtered. "Those animals get on my property. They all look diseased, and they defecate on my lawn—I won't have it. They bark and howl, and I'll shoot them if Hobbler doesn't make them shut up."

Rita put her hands on her hips. "Those dogs don't hurt anybody here. And they're good watchdogs. I happen to *like* those dogs. If you lay one finger on them, Sig'll shoot *you.* And if he doesn't, *I* will."

Peavey's head snapped back as if he'd been struck. "Are you threatening me, young woman? Are you threatening me?"

"No," she said, stamping her foot. "I'm telling you that we try to be friendly out here, but you—"

"Some 'friendly' bunch," Peavey raged. "You threaten to kill me. Yesterday you tried to choke me to death with your poison. Off my property—you sassy piece of baggage!"

He turned to the workmen. "Ignore her," he said imperiously. "She's always parading around here trying to get noticed. In my day, we had a word for women like her."

"Oh!" Rita cried. "Oh! You've got nerve, you—"

"Look at you," he said with a contemptuous glance. "Strutting around, showing off your legs. Going barefoot, like you just got naked out of the bathtub or something. Tossing your hair and wearing no brassiere so you bounce and shake and tease."

Rita doubled up her right fist. "You dirty-minded old geezer," she said, voice shaking. "I do so wear a brassiere. You ought to wear a gag, you filthy old—"

"Off my property, you tease, you flirt, you floozy. You men—get to work. Ignore her. Damn! That dog's *back?* I'll show him. I'll knock his head off."

He stooped for another rock. Rita snatched at his hand, but he dodged her. "Hit that dog," she warned, "and I'll brain you with a rock yourself."

Peavey scuttled backward like a crab, shaking his finger at her. "Off my property—off! Off!"

"Consider her off," said A. Smith's voice. Rita was astonished to find herself hoisted up into Smith's arms. He'd caught her up so quickly, held her so fast that it was like being snatched by a supernatural force.

She kicked and flailed, trying to free herself. All she wanted was to get at Peavey. "Put me down," she cried. "I'll bean him with a brick! I will!"

Smith jerked her more tightly against his chest. "Shut your pretty mouth," he said in her ear, "and keep it shut."

He wheeled and bore her away from Peavey and the two workmen. She kicked harder and tried to push free.

"Put me down," she ordered, so giddy with rage she was half faint. She felt his muscles harden as he wrestled her more firmly into submission.

She heard Peavey's voice behind her, shrill and cold. "I'll have the law on you! Threatening a poor old man . . ."

"Oh!" Rita huffed impotently. "I'll—I'll—"

"You'll shut *up*," A. Smith ordered. He'd reached her door, which was open with the screen door standing slightly ajar.

He raised his knee and knocked the door open, carrying her inside. The screen banged shut behind them.

"Put me down," she demanded again, ready to hit him if necessary. She wanted to go back and nail Peavey's hide to the barn door where it belonged.

Smith set her squarely on her feet with an unceremonious thump. But he didn't release her. He held her by her upper arms to keep her from bolting. Her fists were clenched.

"That disgusting old . . . goat," she said, tossing her hair. "I ought to call the sheriff on him. He's got no legal right to put up that fence. I'll put the law on him."

She tried to move toward the phone on her cluttered kitchen counter. Smith gritted his teeth and gave her a shake—small, but hard enough to surprise her into silence. She stared at him in shock, as if just realizing where she was and what she was saying.

He gripped her more tightly and brought his face close to hers. "Stay *out* of it. Do you understand what you just did? You made it worse."

She stared into his green-blue eyes. Cold anger, tightly contained, sparked in them. Her own anger, naked and not in the least contained, suddenly humiliated her. She struggled to justify it.

"That man's impossible."

"You *knew* that," he told her, bending nearer. "But you were going to be Miss Fix-it. You were going to be the peacemaker."

He gave a short, unpleasant laugh. "Nice work, peacemaker. You started off grinning like a Cheshire cat and ended up threatening assault. A born negotiator. With people like you around, Vietnam wouldn't have been a mere nine-year military flop. *You* could have turned it into a full-scale nuclear holocaust."

Her cheeks burned, and tears blurred her vision. They were tears partly of anger, partly of shame. Her emotions tumbled over each other, impossible to sort.

"I didn't mean to get mad," she said, fiercely blinking back the tears. "It's just—it's just— Did you see him throw that rock at the dog?"

"I saw."

"I just sort of—sort of snapped. And then did you hear what he *said*? About me?"

"I heard."

"It was a terrible thing to say," she declared, almost beseeching him to agree.

"Yes. It was."

"I couldn't help it. I just . . . lost it. He made me so mad, I just lost it. I've never done that before. Ever. What was I supposed to do? Just walk away?"

"Yes. You were."

She hung her head, unable to meet his eyes. She stared down at the rag rug. "Oh, God, I was *awful*," she said miserably. "I—am—so—ashamed. You can let go of me. I'm not going to do anything. I'm . . . sorry."

"It's all right," he said, gathering her into his arms. His breath was warm against her ear and tingled. "Just stay away from him, all right?"

She should have been astonished that instead of thrusting her away, he embraced her, but she wasn't. She should have resisted the arms that wound around her, the lips so near her cheek, but didn't.

She found herself clinging to him, laying her cheek against his chest. The morning had emotionally exhausted her, and rage had drained her, leaving her weak. For a moment she, usually so independent, wanted nothing more than to lean on someone.

Besides, she was so mortified, it was easier to keep her face hidden. And if he held her in his arms, it meant he didn't totally despise her. At the moment she despised herself. Never in her life had she given in to such an outburst.

She squeezed her eyes shut, trying to blind herself to the memory. Her hair had come loose and he stroked it comfortingly, smoothing its unruliness.

"Listen to me—please," he said in her ear. "He's not rational. You meet somebody like that, you get out of his way, stay out. Understand?"

She nodded, but she didn't understand. A few weeks ago, Peavey had appeared, and since then, peace seemed to have disappeared completely.

How could one ill-tempered, aging man throw everything into such chaos?

"He's trouble," A. Smith said, his breath hotter against her ear. "When you find trouble like that, you walk away. It's the only safe thing to do. Trust me."

She hugged him tighter because it felt right. "I was such a gigantically stupid, asinine fool," she said. Her forehead had started to ache, and she rubbed it tiredly against his chest.

His muscles tautened, and his hand, tangled in her hair, went still. She could feel his heartbeat, and it sped, grew harder.

Rita went motionless, with her eyes still shut, her forehead resting against his chest. *Step away from him*, she told herself.

But she didn't. All her being gathered itself into a motionless suspense, waiting. She held her breath. The room seemed to fill with expectant silence. Her heartbeat, still racing from Peavey's words, thudded painfully in her chest.

Slowly his face inched closer to hers, and he kissed her ear. It was a surprisingly gentle kiss, and surprisingly long. She felt as if she'd been waiting for it all her life.

She exhaled raggedly. He did, too, his lips still against her ear. His hand moved to her face so slowly that the movement seemed reluctant. His fingers framed her chin, lifting her face to his, and his mouth descended to take hers. Her ear tingled so hard that it rang, dizzying her.

"No," she breathed, but didn't resist him.

His lips touched hers, tentatively at first, then with more force. It was a muted kiss, tense with restraint. It communicated what she knew they both felt. *I want this. I don't want this. I shouldn't do this. I have to do this.*

She should turn her face away, tell him to go. She couldn't. But she feared that if she showed even a flicker of response, it would set them both off like wildfire.

He drew back slightly. "I'm taking advantage of you," he said in almost a whisper.

So take advantage of me, said her most primitive self.

He's right. I'm not myself. This shouldn't be happening, said her logical self.

She, too, withdrew. Her arms had been around his waist. She pulled them away as if she'd been grasping fire. She put them behind her back and locked them together.

But he didn't release her. One arm stayed around her, holding her near. His other hand stroked her hair, then settled on the side of her throat. He looked at her mouth, then into her eyes. She knew what he was thinking: *Tell me not to stop.*

"We've got to stop," she said, her voice tight.

He shook his head. "I wasn't going to do this."

"Yes," she said, looking away in confusion. "No. I wasn't, either."

He started to lower his mouth to hers again. "But I kept thinking about it."

She summoned all her willpower and pulled away, turning her back to him. She stared at the sun catchers in the window, breaking the light into rainbow colors. "I thought about it, too. It's not a good idea."

He stepped nearer, put his hand on her shoulder as if he would turn her to face him again.

"No," she said, keeping her eyes on the sun catchers—what was normal, what was everyday reality. "We don't even know each other. This is crazy."

She tried to push his hand away, but he caught hers and held it. "My name is John Archer Smith," he said, lacing his fingers through hers. "I go by Archer. I'm thirty years old. I'm from St. Louis. I've never been married."

Again she wanted to break away from him, but could not bring herself to do it. At least she wasn't looking at him, and that helped her keep her resolve. "I'm twenty-six. I was married for two years."

"Why'd he let you get away? Was he crazy?"

She swallowed. "I like to think so. Is your name really John Smith?"

"John Archer Smith."

"And what do you do in St. Louis, John Archer Smith?"

He was silent a moment. His thumb played over her knuckles. "I was . . . a basketball coach," he said. "At a junior college."

She tried not to think of his touch. "Why use the past tense?"

Another pause. "I don't do that anymore."

"Why?"

"I do something else."

"What?"

Their linked hands rested on her shoulder, and she felt the tension mounting in his. "I'm scoping it out," he replied.

"Which means?"

His grip grew tighter. "I think . . . I might stick around here for a while. Buy a house, fix it up, sell it. Keep doing it. Maybe. Maybe somewhere else."

She took a deep breath. "You mean be a . . . builder?"

"A builder, yes."

"And that's what you're doing this summer for Patterson?"

"Yes. And looking at houses. Town or country. It doesn't matter."

She nodded as if she understood, but in truth she was confused. "How do you know Patterson?"

"I just know him."

Oh, God, he's doing it again. What's wrong with him? Why does he do this? She swallowed again. "Why'd you quit coaching?

"Why?" she insisted. "Why'd you come here, of all places? And why are you so . . . secretive?"

He was silent a moment. "I don't talk about it."

She sighed in exasperation and jerked her hand free. She stepped out of range of his reach and turned to face him. His look was shuttered. Worry lines etched his forehead.

She made a helpless gesture. "You don't seem to want to get involved."

"No. I don't."

"And yet, you—you act like you do. I don't have time for games. I don't play games."

He nodded as if resigned. "I didn't think you did."

"Now me," she said, pointing her thumb at her chest, "I don't want to get involved, either. I was married two years to this upwardly-mobile neatnik who drove me nuts. Lonely is bliss, thank you."

"Is it?"

It was until you came along, she was tempted to say. "Yes," she said with conviction. "And I'm not about to start a—a relationship that isn't. Isn't a relationship, I mean."

His face grew hard. "Too bad."

"No," she said. "Only sensible."

His upper lip twisted sarcastically. "Fine. If you're going to be sensible about this, be sensible about everything. And stay away from Peavey."

The mention of Peavey made her flush, which she hated. "Don't worry. I've learned my lesson."

"Have you?"

"Yes," she said in exasperation. "And I'll be frank. What happened just now? Between you and me? It never would have happened if I hadn't been an emotional basket case. First Joe and all that blood, then that nasty old crank—"

"Forget it. Think of it as a thank-you for carrying you off before you got in more trouble."

Damn! she thought. He'd thrown her off-balance yet again. "I suppose I should thank you," she said. "I just wish you hadn't picked me up . . . like I was a—a child or something."

"It was that or drag you. I saw the fire in your eye. Hell, I should get a thank-you note from Peavey for saving his skin. But I doubt it'll happen."

She crossed her arms, still embarrassed by the memory. "I told you—I learned my lesson."

"Good. Then let me pick up Johanssen tomorrow. He and Peavey are going to feud, and it's going to be ugly. Stay away from both of them and keep your nose clean."

She started to protest, but realized he was right. "Fine," she said, crossing her arms more tightly. "I'll stay away from everybody. God! I'll be glad when Bart and Betsy get home."

"Right," he said. "So . . . thanks for an interesting morning. Particularly the latter part."

She sighed with disgust. "Forget it all. Especially the latter part. *I* plan to."

One corner of his mouth turned up in a bitter smile. "Too bad we couldn't be . . . more casual about it, you and I. We're missing something. It's pretty obvious."

"I'm missing *nothing*," she said.

"You're lying and you know it." His smile quirked even more bitterly. "Know why?"

"No," she said. "And I don't lie. I had it put into the divorce settlement. My ex-husband got all the lies. He was so good with them."

"Oh, hell." He looked her up and down. "Look at us. It's happening again. Right now. I'd better get out of here."

"What's happening?" she demanded in exasperation. "*Nothing's* happening."

His gaze, seeming amused and troubled at once, rested on hers. "Every time we're together, sparks fly," he said. "You know it. I know it."

4

HIS WORDS ANGERED her because they were true. There was a chemistry between them that both attracted and frightened her.

"I think you'd better leave," she said from between clenched teeth.

"That's what I said. And I am. I'm outta here."

He headed toward the screen door and pushed it open. He paused and gave her one last glance. He was right. Sparks still flew between them. They also danced, tingling, through her blood, in her stomach and her thighs.

Then he turned and left, letting the door shut softly behind him. She raked her fingers through her hair and tried to think straight.

The world was going mad, and she'd gone maddest of all. After the disillusioning mess with Sterling, she'd vowed never to become one of those women who plunge from a disastrous marriage into an equally disastrous affair.

She'd planned on keeping away from men and putting herself back together as a person. Happy and whole and true to herself—that's what she'd wanted to be. And she'd thought she'd been doing a pretty damn good job of it. Sex, at this point, meant only bad memories and complications for which she wasn't ready.

She liked her life plan, considered it flawless, and Archer Smith didn't fit into it—and yet, she thought with a pang of unexpected yearning, it had felt satisfying to be in his arms; and his lips had fit hers with a dizzying perfection....

But she didn't have time to brood on this dilemma, for she glanced out the window and saw a sight that chilled her. A sheriff's-department car was parked beside George Peavey's house, and now a middle-aged deputy was walking with slow, purposeful tread toward her house.

Oh, *no*, Rita thought, heart plummeting. Peavey had actually done it—the wretch, the rat. He had called the police on her. Could her life be more absurd?

The deputy banged at the screen door. "Miss O'Casey?" His voice had that bored, authoritative tone that seemed reserved for law officers. "Margarita O'Casey?"

Rita sighed and stalked to the door. She probably *looked* like a potential murderess. Her shirt was spattered with blood, her hair had come loose, and she knew her cheeks were flushed a hectic pink—thanks to Archer.

Damn Archer Smith, she thought bleakly as she opened the door. Damn all men, including this one in his tan uniform and Smokey the Bear hat.

"Yes?" she said shortly, looking up at the big deputy.

He stared at her sternly. "I'm Officer Fleshmann of the sheriff's department. I'm afraid a complaint's been phoned in against you."

"Oh, come in," Rita said in disgust. "I know what it's about. It's that Peavey person, isn't it?"

"That's correct, ma'am."

She showed him inside and saw his narrowed eyes taking in her eccentric, somewhat untidy house. She offered him a seat on the couch, but he refused. Perhaps he preferred to stay standing to maintain a psychological advantage over her.

Rita didn't care. She sat down on the sofa, picked up one of her grandmother's pillows and hugged it. She looked Officer Fleshmann straight in the eye.

"There's no problem," she said evenly. "Peavey and I had words. He's building a fence where he's got no business building one."

Fleshmann hitched up his belt, adjusting it to better accommodate his sizable stomach. "This fence on your land?"

"No," she admitted. "But the neighbor whose land it's on is in the hospital, and—"

"If it ain't your land," Fleshmann said flatly, "it ain't your problem."

Rita tossed her head rebelliously. "He also threw a rock at another neighbor's dog—he hit it *hard*. When he tried a second time, I told him to stop."

"Was it your dog?"

"Well . . . no," Rita muttered. "But isn't there an ordinance against cruelty to animals?"

"Was the dog on his property?"

She felt stymied, helpless. "Well . . . yes. But that's no reason to—to stone it."

Fleshmann sighed as if he were dealing with someone simple-minded. "If it ain't your dog, it ain't your problem. My advice is to stay out of it."

Everybody's advice is to stay out of it, Rita thought darkly. *Maybe I should just dig a deep hole and live like a mole from now on. Maybe I should go in a cave and hide.*

"Now," Fleshmann said with another weary sigh, "this Peavey claims you threatened to shoot him. The men putting up the fence agree that you said it."

"How could I shoot him?" she challenged. "I don't even own a gun."

"Margarita, three people say you made a statement to the effect that you would."

Rita threw down the pillow and spread her hands in an annoyed gesture. "I spoke . . . in anger. I didn't mean it. It was an expression—that's all."

Fleshmann shrugged. "I deduced that was the case."

Then why are you bothering me? she wanted to scream, but she stayed quiet, forced herself to behave.

"Now, Margarita," Fleshmann said, shifting his belt again. "I'm gonna give you some good advice. I don't believe you're gonna shoot off a gun. But don't shoot off your mouth, either. That old boy up there is mighty crabby. I can tell—I got experience with this type of individual."

"Yes, fine," Rita agreed, eager to be done with this humiliating experience. "I *intend* to stay away from him."

"Good." Fleshmann reached into his pocket and pulled out a notebook. He wrote something in it.

He was probably writing her a summons or a fine, she thought glumly. But he didn't tear the page out, he simply closed the book and stared at her, his face emotionless.

"Margarita," he said solemnly. "I'm lettin' you off with a warning. But don't go makin' threats at that old boy again. He's a troublemaker, no two ways about it."

Rita rose to see him to the door. "But what are we supposed to *do?*" she asked. "He's making our lives miserable. He seems set on fighting with everyone, and he's vindictive and petty—"

"I'll tell you what you do," Fleshmann replied, squinting wisely. "*Nothing*—that's what. That's the problem livin' out like this. One bad apple can move in and spoil the lot. And it looks like you folks got yourself one real bad apple. Yes sirree. One real rotten apple."

He shook his head as if in reluctant admiration, and left. Rita went back to the couch and put her elbows on her knees, and her face in her hands. She struggled to sort out her emotions. She couldn't.

And worst of all, her lips still burned and tingled from the touch of Archer Smith's mouth. *No, no, no,* she thought. But they burned and tingled anyway.

IGNORING PEAVEY WAS more easily said than done. When Sig Hobbler got home that evening from the health-food store, there was an argument too loud for Rita to ignore.

Sig was normally a quiet man, but he loved the lake, the woods and his animals, and he could be militant about them. His outbursts weren't frequent, but they could be vehement.

Last fall he'd practically come to blows with a pair of men for deer hunting too near the houses of the cove. And there was a persistent rumor that he'd once run a driver off the road and that he'd struck the man for purposely running over a dog on the highway.

Rita had heard him when he drove his truck into his ramshackle yard, and a few moments later, she heard his gravelly voice clashing in argument with Peavey's.

"What kind of—abomination to God and nature is *that?*" Sig shouted, and he sounded so angry that Rita winced. Drawn to the window as if hypnotized, she peeked out.

Peavey stood inside his new fence—a new, shiny, hideous, chain-link fence. He wore baggy slacks and a white button-down shirt gray from too many washings.

Sig was taller and lankier than Peavey. He was also wilder looking, although by nature he was by far quieter. Sig's ancient jeans were faded, his tie-dyed shirt had seen better days, and he kept his long, graying hair bound with an old red bandanna, Apache-style.

"This is a fence," snapped Peavey, setting his hand possessively on one of its posts.

"Yeah?" Sig said in disgust. "Well, it looks like hell."

He was right, Rita thought bleakly. The fence *did* look like hell. Except for Peavey's half acre, the land rolled naturally and unconfined down to the shore. Nobody had wanted to spoil the cove's essential wildness.

Now the fence, angular and unfriendly, severed Peavey's property from the rest, as if his house was a fortress grimly cut apart from theirs.

"This fence is fine," Peavey snapped. "If anything around here looks like hell, it's that mess you call a yard. It looks like a trash heap. It *is* a trash heap."

"My yard's none of your goddamn business," Sig retorted.

"It's unsightly, it affects my property value, and it's probably got rats. I ought to call the health department on you. I *will*. A lawyer, too."

"I don't got rats," Sig retorted, clearly insulted. "My dogs keep vermin out of here."

"Your dogs *are* vermin," Peavey sneered. "They all look inbred and like they have rickets and God knows what else. I won't have them on my property, fouling and digging and fornicating in the front yard. You ought to chain them. They're a nuisance, and somebody's going to shoot them."

Sig took a step backward, as if trying to control himself, but his fists were clenched. "You talking about shooting my dogs?" he cried. "You talking about shooting my dogs?"

"I'm not talking to you at all," Peavey said with contempt, and turned away. "I moved out here for peace and quiet. I paid for it, and I intend to have it."

Sig stared after him, his lips working angrily, but no words came out. His face had grown red and the veins in his neck bulged.

Peavey stalked into his house, slamming the door. Sig stared after him, his mouth still working impotently. Then he wheeled and strode across his own cluttered yard to his falling-down toolshed. When he emerged, his face was still red, the veins in his neck still stood out and a wild light flashed in his eyes. He carried a pair of wire cutters.

Wire cutters? Rita thought in panic. *He can't cut that fence—there'll be full-scale war.*

She didn't think twice. She ran out the door as fast as she could and caught Sig's elbow. "Sig—don't!" she begged.

She pulled on his arm hard enough to halt him. He stared down at her in surprise, but the wildness and anger still shone in his eyes. And she had been right—foam did fleck his lips.

She put her other hand on the wire cutters, shaking her head. "Sig...listen. I know you're angry—I feel the same way. But today I objected, and he called the police on me. If you touch that fence, he'll do the same thing to you—only they won't let you off with a warning. He'll throw you in jail or sue you."

Sig looked at her as if he couldn't comprehend what she said. She gripped his arm more tightly. "The deputy warned me, Sig. He warned us all. Did you know that Joe Johanssen's in the hospital? Yes. It's because he tangled with Peavey over that fence. Sig . . . *please*, don't get involved. He's turning this whole cove upside down."

"Joe's in the hospital?" Sig repeated, as if dazed by disbelief. "The police came for *you?*"

"Come on," Rita said, drawing him toward his house. "Let me talk to you a minute. I can explain. But please, put down those wire cutters—enough's happened. *Promise* me you won't do anything to that fence."

She pleaded, she wheedled, she reasoned, she cajoled. And she finally got him safely inside his own house and talked him into letting her keep the wire cutters in her custody—at least for a while.

He offered her a drink. She didn't accept it. She had never been inside Sig's house before, and it made her nervous. The inside was as ramshackle and unkempt as the outside. It was as Archer had said—there was an aura of loneliness and failure about it. He had many pictures of half-naked women taped to his walls.

He lit up one of his handmade cigarettes. He didn't ask her permission, and she decided it was best not to object. He had made enough concessions to her, and maybe smoking would calm him.

She had always known he was quiet. But she'd never before realized how difficult he was to talk to. He had trouble understanding things, and she found herself explaining about Joe Johanssen and the fence several times before the story sank in.

Then she was forced to repeat the tale of her own clash with Peavey and how the deputy had come. She purposely left out that Peavey had struck one of the dogs—she didn't want to set Sig off again.

The longer she talked to him, the more she realized that some part of his mind seemed absent, on vacation. It was not as if his IQ was low, but more as if somewhere, somehow in his life, something had happened to his process of reasoning, and he didn't think like other people.

The realization unsettled her. He was old enough to have gone to Vietnam. Did he suffer some post-stress syndrome? Or had he overindulged in the psychedelic sixties and suffered some chemical short circuit?

All she knew for certain was that he was the wrong man to clash with Peavey. So she worked as hard as she could to convince him that the fence was not his problem, and that the best thing he could do was stay out of Peavey's way.

"And if you're worried about the dogs," she said at last, "maybe you *should* chain them for a while. There's no sense provoking him. The important thing is that they're safe. That's what we want—for the dogs to be safe."

She smiled and stood to go. He stood, too, and followed her to the door. "I can't chain them," he said softly, as if he'd just realized what she'd said. "It'd break their hearts."

"But the important thing," she repeated, "is that they're safe, right?"

He stood looking down at her, sadness in his gaze. "You want them to be safe, too?" he asked.

"Of course," she said, and put her hand on the doorknob to let herself out.

She turned her back to him and was startled to feel his fingers on her hair. Such apprehension surged through her that she went motionless for an instant.

But that was all he did—barely brush his fingertips against her hair, so softly it was hardly a touch at all.

"You're a special woman," he breathed. "I'll look out for you, too. I'll look out for us all."

I've got to get out of here, she told herself. "I can take care of myself, Sig," she said politely, but firmly. Quickly she stepped away from his touch and let herself out the door. She walked as quickly as she could to her own house.

Oh, good grief! Archer had been right about Sig, too. Sig had proved to be much stranger than she'd believed—much, much stranger.

But what else could she have done? Let Sig cut the fence? Let a whole new chapter of battles start?

She'd sincerely tried to do the right thing, but perhaps she'd been wrong. She glanced furtively down toward Archer's house. Evening was drawing near, and he was out on his listing dock, working on its lights.

She didn't look at him long enough to see if he was gazing back. He'd think she was crazy for interfering with Sig, and maybe she was. She hardly knew any longer.

But she had the distinct, eerie feeling that eyes were following her across the shadowy grass. Sig Hobbler, still watching from his house? Or maybe it was Peavey. He could stand in one of his darkened windows, spying, and she couldn't tell—not for sure.

She was relieved to reach home and lock the door behind her. She checked her blinds to make sure they were tightly shut. She sighed and forced herself back to her worktable. She had bevels to solder to the edge of her glass panel; she had a career and a life that didn't center on George Peavey or any other man at the cove.

But she had not been inside the safety of her home ten minutes before her phone rang. Startled, she picked it up and said hello.

No one answered. She said hello again, wondering if something was wrong with the connection.

Then she heard it—breathing. A man's breathing. It was growing faster, harder, like panting.

She slammed the phone down, feeling angry and threatened. On an impulse, she opened a slat in the blind and stared down at the lake. Archer was still alone on his dock, adjusting its lights.

Almost immediately the phone rang again. Still watching Archer on the dock, she hesitated, then picked up the receiver and said hello again.

All she could hear was the man's breathing—even faster now, and more ragged. He made a nasty little moan.

She crashed the receiver back down so hard that the shock ran up her arm. She sat, her knuckles pressed against her lips. She hadn't been able to recognize the caller, had no clue. All she knew was that it wasn't Archer. It might have been Sig. It might have been Peavey. It might have been anybody.

The phone rang six more times that night. She stopped answering it, and at last unplugged it. But she had the violated feeling of being under sexual siege, and it sickened and angered her.

She woke early the next morning, hoping she could turn the phone back on—she had, after all, a business to run. She prayed the calls had been a fluke—someone having a night of jollies at her expense; someone who perhaps didn't even know her, and had seen her name and phone number on a card in a craft store, perhaps.

But when she went outside to refill her hummingbird feeder, a new surprise jolted her. A gallon jar of wildflowers sat beside her door. The flowers were Queen Anne's lace, goldenrod and purple blossoms she could not name.

She stared at them a moment, then looked about rather wildly. Who had left this strange bouquet? She looked first at Sig Hobbler's house, then Peavey's. Both were silent; no one in sight.

She bit her lip. Sig had said he'd take care of her, he'd touched her hair in that peculiar way. Had he now left her flowers?

Certainly Peavey wouldn't put them there—would he? But maybe it was his idea of a joke; the flowers were, after all, little more than weeds. She doubted the bouquet had been left by Archer. He'd said he would stay away, and a surreptitious gift of wildflowers hardly seemed his style.

She bit her lip harder. To accept the flowers, to take them inside, might seem too accepting, as if she welcomed this strange attention and might welcome more.

She decided to neither accept nor reject the offered bouquet—exactly. She had a small redwood picnic table in her backyard.

She set the jar on the center of the table, stepped back as if mildly admiring it, then went back to her task at the hummingbird feeder.

The sky was a flawless blue, the lake particularly peaceful, and once again the pink blooms of the mimosa tree were aflutter with hummingbirds and butterflies. But today she didn't linger outside. Today she was glad to go back in. She felt safer there, hidden from any spying eyes.

She struggled to keep her mind occupied with her work. At about ten o'clock, she heard Archer's truck leaving, then the cove was quiet again. At eleven, the truck returned and stopped at Joe Johanssen's house.

She moved softly to her side window and peeked out. Archer sat in the driver's seat, staring at the lake. He didn't look toward her house. Joe Johanssen was hobbling through his yard and up his steps.

As soon as Joe reached his porch, Archer tossed him a glance, put his truck in gear and drove down to his own place. Joe gave him a vague wave. Then he just stood by his door, as if uncertain what to do next. He had a large piece of white tape on his forehead. He stared at Peavey's fence with a benumbed, unhappy expression.

Then he went inside. In a few moments, he reappeared on his porch, a bottle of beer in his hand, and sat in his rocker. He kept staring at Peavey's fence as if devising evil plans against it.

He was already drinking again, Rita thought in dismay. Hadn't he learned his lesson? What if he got snockered, and this time *he* went after Peavey's fence with wire cutters?

Oh, she thought wearily, they were just going to have to settle it among themselves—she would have no further part in it. She went back to her worktable.

When she glanced up from her soldering, she could see the lake through her picture window. And at the lake, she could see Archer, working on Patterson's dock.

He'd stripped off his shirt and hung it on one of the guy wires. He was tearing up rotted boards, and a neat stack of new ones stood ready to replace them. His torso, she noted with reluctant sexual awareness, was broad-shouldered and hard muscled. He was brown from the summer sun, and his dark gold hair gleamed as it tossed in the breeze.

I will not look at him that way, she vowed silently. *I will not look at him as if he was—desirable.* But she found that she kept stealing glimpses at him anyway.

Shortly after noon, she heard another vehicle leaving the cove. When she glanced out the window, she was relieved to see that it was Peavey's white compact car going up the dusty road. He'd kept a low profile all morning, which was good. Now he was gone, which was even better.

But Joe Johanssen still sat on his porch, glowering impotently at the fence and drinking beer. One of Sig Hobbler's mongrels came sniffing in Joe's yard, inspected the lopsided

For Sale sign, lifted a leg, and urinated on it. Joe glowered at the dog, too.

She saw Sig Hobbler come from inside his house. He'd turned up his music, which was, as usual, the Grateful Dead, and they were singing "Brown-Eyed Woman." He sat down on the stairs and fondled the ears of one of his dogs. He lit one of his homemade cigarettes.

Then he rose again, went back inside the house and turned the music up a notch higher. This time when he returned, he carried his shotgun. Rita drew in her breath.

Sig leaned the shotgun against the frame of his front door. Then he sat on a backless chair and began to play solitaire on an old cable spool he used as a table. He smoked his cigarette. Sometimes he glanced at Peavey's empty house. Sometimes he glanced at the gun.

Rita knew what message Sig was sending: Anybody who touches one of my dogs deals with *me*. And I have a gun.

Oh, God, she thought. *A gun now.* She couldn't watch any longer. She left the window and went back to her worktable. She tried to concentrate on her glass—and not look in the direction of Archer Smith, bare-chested on his dock.

At three o'clock, she was deep enough in her project to be startled when a knock shook her door. She opened it with trepidation. Joe Johanssen stood there. *Oh, Lord,* she thought with dismay. *He's drunk. What's he want?*

He shifted his feet, ran a hand over his thinning red hair. "I—I brought you some tomatoes from my garden," he said. "Just picked 'em."

She opened the screen door and accepted a battered sack, partly filled with tomatoes. "Thanks," she said, and started to close the door again. But he placed his hand on the doorframe, leaning against it. She was forced to leave the door open.

Joe stared down at the cement. His ruddy face was redder than usual. "And I came to thank you," he muttered. "For yesterday. For . . . helping me."

"It's all right, Joe," she said, trying to sound chipper and uninvolved. "Think nothing of it."

He raised his face, meeting her eyes. His were pale blue and bloodshot. "I have to think of it. It's the first kind thing a woman's done for me—without being paid—since I can't remember when. You're an understanding woman, Rita."

She didn't like this turn in the conversation. "Think nothing of it," she repeated and made another motion to close the door.

But this time he caught the door, held it open. He looked into her face beseechingly. "Rita, can I come in? I've gotta talk to somebody, and you're the only one."

She kept her expression firm. "I don't think it's a good idea. Now, if you'll excuse me . . ."

But he held the door open, would not let her close it. "Rita . . . my ex-wife's all over me—she never stops nagging. She wants her share of the money from our place. And she wants it *now*. Did you see what Peavey did? Did you *see*?"

"The fence? Yes—but it won't do any good getting upset. Peavey likes getting people upset. You'll just have to work it out through a lawyer."

"I can't *afford* a lawyer," Joe almost wailed. "I've got to sell my place . . . but how? Peavey's trying to tie me up in a lawsuit, Sig's place looks like an open garbage can. He lets those goddamn dogs run all over the place. Now he's sitting out on his porch with a *shotgun*, for God's sake—like the crazed hermit from hell who wants to kill people. How'm I gonna sell my house when those two—"

"Joe," she tried again, "don't start a fight with Sig, too. I know you're concerned, but you've been drinking, and this is no time—"

"Rita . . . with the Spectors gone, you're the only sane person here I can talk to. I mean, that Smith guy, he's really a cold SOB. He doesn't want to get involved."

"Joe, I don't mean to sound cruel, but *I* don't want to get involved. Now, go home—please."

She pushed harder at the door, but he covered her hand with his own. "You're not cruel. And my home's not a home any longer. Rita, did I ever tell you that I dream about you?

Even before the divorce. I'd be sleeping beside her, but I'd be dreaming about you—"

"No!" she protested. "No. Now close this door."

"Let me come in. Let me talk to you, just a little while. I got so many feelings in me, it's like I'm going to explode—"

Suddenly Sig Hobbler appeared behind Joe. Sig's eyes were both dreamy and cold at once. "He botherin' you?" he said in his soft, gravelly voice. He hadn't shaven, and the gray stubble made his face look gaunter than usual.

Slowly, almost casually, he settled one hand on Joe Johanssen's shoulder. Rita had never noticed how large and powerful Sig's hands were.

Joe looked at the taller man with resentment. "What are you doing? What are you touching me for?"

Sig looked only at Rita. "I asked, is he botherin' you?" he repeated in his eerily calm voice.

"You stay out of this," Joe warned, his cheek muscles tensing. "This is between Rita and me."

"I think you should leave her alone," Sig said in nearly a whisper and nodded, as if to himself.

"I think you should mind your own business," Joe said angrily. "If you got time on your hands, clean up your junky yard. Train your dogs not to—"

Sig's hand tightened convulsively on Joe's shoulder. His eyes went dreamier and colder. "My dogs?" he asked. "You talkin' about my dogs?"

It was at this point that Peavey returned. He parked his car and got out. He opened the hatchback and took out what seemed a new purchase—a chain saw.

Rita alone seemed to notice. She stared at the chain saw with a feeling of sickness. What was he going to do now? The idea of Peavey with a chain saw alarmed her.

"My dogs," Sig repeated, as if in wonder. He bent his face closer to Joe's. "What were you sayin' about my dogs?"

"Nothing," Joe answered quickly, suddenly looking more frightened than angry. "Nothing at all. Never mind. This is between Rita and me."

Sig appeared to think about this. "That's for Rita to decide, ain't it?" He looked at Rita, a kind of sad adoration in his eyes. "You want him to go away, Rita?"

Peavey stood watching, his body tensed, an excited, almost gloating expression on his face. His gaze was fixed on her, and he seemed to be saying, *Are you happy now? Is this how you like it? It is, isn't it? Happy, aren't you?*

Rita could stand it no longer. "I'm leaving," she said furiously. "And I don't want anybody here when I get back. I mean it. I just want—to be alone."

"Well, well," Peavey said with a sarcastic smirk. "If it isn't Greta Garbo."

Rita shot him a quelling look, turned and marched into the house. She grabbed her purse and car keys and stalked to the porch. She shut her heavy door behind her and wrenched the screen door from Joe's grasp. She slammed it shut so hard that the sound rang out like a shot.

She strode to her car, got in and slammed that door just as hard. She stuck the key into the ignition and stepped on the starter.

Nothing happened. Red dashboard lights flickered, then died. The car growled but refused to start. Angrily, she tried again, but the engine wouldn't turn over.

The men stared at her. Sig looked puzzled and concerned. Joe's face was flushed, and conflicting emotions crossed it. Peavey kept his demonic smirk.

Rita got out of the car, ready to weep with frustration. She feared all three men would end up fighting on her very doorstep, and short of walking the twenty miles to town, she could think of only one avenue of escape.

She threw the strap of her purse over her shoulder and walked quickly down to the shore, where Archer knelt on the dock, hammering in a new board.

She was too upset to speak. She marched up the metal walkway of his dock, not waiting to be invited.

He looked at her in surprise, a hank of blond hair falling over his eyes. He squinted against the sunlight, and derision rose in his gaze.

"Well. Look at you, barefoot, but carrying your purse. Is this your idea of formal? To what do I owe this pleasure?"

She moved to the corner of the dock farthest from him and sat down with a thump, crossing her legs and flinging her purse into her lap. "They're all crazy, and my car won't start," she said, her voice shaking.

"Who's crazy?"

"*All* of them. And somebody kept phoning me last night and—and *breathing* at me, and this morning somebody left flowers on my doorstep, and Sig's got his gun out because of his dogs, and Joe Johanssen said he—*dreamed* about me, and Peavey's got a *chain saw* now. And now Joe and Sig are fighting—and I tried to get away, but my car won't start, and— Oh, *forget* it."

She didn't want him to see how close she was to tears, so she put her elbows on her knees, lowered her head and hid her eyes behind her fists. She was breathing hard, big, sobbing racks of breath that hurt. Her heart hammered.

For a long moment he let her sit that way, alone, her face hidden, trying to control her emotions. Then he came to her and knelt beside her. He put his arm around her.

"It's all right," he said, his voice low in her ear.

She leaned her head against his hot, bare shoulder. And for an impossible moment, it did seem all right, there in the strong crook of his arm.

5

ARCHER COILED HIS ARM around her and held her closer, his heart beating crazily.

He tried to sound calm, rational, brotherly as he urged the story from her. He felt none of those things.

She'd come to him—as he'd always secretly wanted. Now he held her in broad daylight, for all the world to see.

For the other men to see. Maybe he was no better than they were, and this whole mess was some primitive sexual war, with her as the prize. For the moment he had won; she was his.

Her hair fluttered against his jaw, and he fought against his desire to kiss her cheek, her ear, her earring, her lips.

He pretended his embrace was merely to give her comfort. But it was more. It fed the fire she woke in him. Was that all he wanted from her? Sex? Was that all any of them wanted?

Or did he imagine she offered more—some promise of a richer life, a life with greater meaning? And was that all such a promise was—imagination, delusion?

He closed his eyes, letting his forehead rest against hers. The afternoon sun burned his skin while a darker heat burned inside him.

"Why'd you come to me?" he breathed, nuzzling her velvety cheek.

Her hands were on his biceps, holding on to him with a tremulousness that made him shaky himself.

"This seemed like the only place left," she said. "I had to get away from them."

"You're using me, then?" He let his lips brush against her earring, only touch it, that was all.

"Maybe. Maybe I am. I don't know."

"They can see us," he said, letting his cheekbone rub the soft curve of hers. "If they want to, they can see all of this."

"I know," she said. She sounded half ashamed, half rebellious.

"Is that what you want?" He let his jaw rest against her temple. He could feel the thrust of her pulse leaping there.

"I don't know. I don't know."

"What if I kissed you? What then?"

Her hands slid up to his shoulders, gripped him more tensely. "I don't know."

He put one hand to her face. "They might leave you alone—" he said raggedly "—if they thought you were mine."

"They might," she said. But she shook her head, as if she wasn't sure.

"Is that what you want?" he asked. He forced himself to draw back slightly. He framed her chin with his thumb and forefinger. He made her look into his face. Her eyes were richly brown, and full of too many emotions to read.

"Is that what you want?" he repeated softly. "To make it seem like you're mine?"

"I don't know," she said.

"That's what it'd be? Seems—not real?"

"I don't know," she said, trying to look away. Something in her tone wrenched his heart, because he couldn't, for the life of him, tell if she was pretending or not.

"Don't look away from me," he said.

She blinked hard, then forced her gaze to meet his again. She looked innocent, she looked knowing, she looked brave, she looked fearful. She searched his face, and he searched hers. The breeze riffled their hair, mingling his forelock with her dark waves.

He stroked her chin with his thumb. "Kiss me," he said in a low voice.

His heart pounded once, twice, three times—so hard he felt it throb through his body and deep in his groin, making him hard.

With aching slowness, she lifted her lips to his. She kissed him with a mixture of shyness and boldness that made him want to take her, right there on the dock. And when he kissed her back, he knew his touch told her that, hotly and with eloquence.

SHE DREW BACK, SHAKEN, because she wasn't quite sure how things had come to this. *He's like the others—he wants me,* she thought with apprehension. *But he's different, because I want him back.*

She let her hands fall from his shoulders. She looked away, out at the placid blue lake. "Maybe this isn't such a good idea," she said, distraught by what she had done, what she had let him do.

He didn't let her pull away completely. He kept his hands on her upper arms. "This is a hell of a time to change your mind."

She flushed and didn't meet his gaze. He'd spoken with biting irony, and he had the right. She'd let him take her in his arms, they'd kissed with passion that seemed all too real and the other three men could have seen. She supposed they *had* seen, all of them, and that she had wanted them to.

She pushed her hand through her hair. *My God,* she thought in fresh dismay. *What have I done now?* "It just . . . may not have been the most felicitous decision," she said.

"The 'most felicitous decision,'" he mocked. "That's a helluva way to put it."

"How *am* I supposed to put it?" she asked, sincerely perplexed.

"A damned good question," he said. "How should we put it?"

She shook her head. "I don't know. . . . That you're pretending to be my. . .protector. Until they come to their senses."

"Your 'protector.' Another interesting way to put it. Well, they'll think I'm your lover, so get used to it."

"I've never needed a protector before in my life," she countered. "I've always taken care of myself. I had two big brothers who thought life's greatest pleasure was beating up on me. I could handle *them.*"

He looked her up and down. He laughed. "What the boys up the hill have in mind for you isn't exactly brotherly."

"Nothing like this has ever happened before," she said. She wished he'd let go of her, and just as perversely, she hoped he would not.

He looked her up and down again, smiling crookedly. "You never put thoughts into men's heads? I doubt that."

"No," she said with passion. "I *didn't*. I was this skinny kid, too tall, with flyaway hair. I had braces on my teeth. I wore big glasses. I didn't like clothes and dolls and dances. I liked climbing trees and drawing pictures."

He looked skeptical. "And then—like magic—the plain caterpillar turned into a gorgeous moth? Come on, Rita, that's too trite."

"I'm *not* gorgeous," she said earnestly. "All through high school and most of college I was a geek, a nerd . . . a nerdess. And I just turned into a plain moth. What's happening to me shouldn't happen to a plain old moth."

He sighed, smiled and let go of her. He sat back, leaning one hand against the dock. "You're really something. You can't believe that. Can you?"

She glanced at him resentfully. She wished he didn't have such a perfect chest. It looked as if it had been cast in bronze. "I'm the only woman out here," she said defensively. "You said so yourself."

He smiled more crookedly. "So the braces came off your teeth. That I understand. What happened to the 'big glasses'? You don't wear contacts. I can tell."

She crossed her legs and hugged her knees. "I had contacts, but they made me squint one eye like Popeye. My ex-husband gave me radial keratotomy for a wedding present."

Archer laughed, damn him. "What a romantic."

"My husband was into appearances. He didn't like appearing to be married to Popeye. Some women get diamonds. Some women get convertibles. I got eye surgery."

"So," he said with a dubious smile, "what's that leave? The flyaway hair?"

"It's still flying away."

"I like it."

"He didn't. I wore it in a chignon. God, before I met him, I couldn't even pronounce *chignon*. When I wore it down, he said I looked like the guy who was the hairdresser in *The Crying Game*."

"He sounds like a charmer. So how did he cure you of being skinny? Force-feed you? Like a gourmet's goose?"

She felt her face go rigid with old sorrow and resentment. "Biology, that's all. I was always underweight. Then I had a miscarriage. Afterwards...I wasn't...as skinny."

His smile died. "I'm sorry," he said.

She shook her head sadly. "Don't be. Oh, I cried and cried then, but it would have been wrong to have a child with Sterling as the father. What's meant to be is meant to be."

He raised an eyebrow. "So Sterling wasn't a sterling character?"

She hugged her knees more tightly, fighting her way back through the bitter memories. "No. Sterling wasn't sterling."

He rubbed his shoulder, and she couldn't help remembering what it had felt like to lean her face against that hard, bare flesh.

"So why'd you marry him?" he asked.

She pushed her hand through her hair again. "Because I was this...nerdess. He was the first attractive man who ever paid attention to me. We were art students together. I was all rough edges, and he was all smooth, and I was in awe of him. I was...dazzled."

Archer sat up straighter, crossed his arms over his bent knee. He rested his chin on one wrist and stared at her. His eyes were greener than the lake behind him, bluer than the hills beyond. "So why," he asked with deliberation, "did he fall for you, if you were such a...nerdess?"

"He said I was a diamond in the rough. He said I was waiting to be awakened."

"Yeah?"

"Yeah," she countered rebelliously. "And I'm still in the rough, and I'm still not wakened. He may have put me to sleep permanently."

"I don't think so." He said it in such a tone, and with such a look, it made her shiver in spite of the day's heat.

"Well, I wasn't woman enough for *him*," she said. If Archer had the mistaken idea she was a simmering sexpot, she must put the record straight. "He had affairs right and left. I was too naive to figure it out—for a whole year. Then he said just because I married him didn't mean I *owned* him. He was artistic, he said. He needed all these 'experiences.'"

Archer's face had sobered. The wind stirred his streaked hair, and she was conscious once again of the fine worry lines around his eyes. "I suppose he said you were free to play around, too. Did you?"

She drew herself straighter, insulted. "Why? To sink to his level?"

He narrowed his eyes. "To find somebody. Who could make you happy."

She felt the line of her mouth freeze into cynicism. "Why? Love didn't make me happy the first time. I decided I was responsible for my own happiness. A woman doesn't have to—to have a man to be whole, to be alive."

"But someday," he said, his eyes still narrowed, "you might fall in love . . . someday."

Her heart took a hard, unexpected swoop. "Someday. I might."

"But not now."

She looked away. "No. Not now."

"Good," he said, but he didn't sound particularly happy.

A motorboat sped by in the distance, and she watched the white plume of its wake. "You're the same way," she said. "You don't want to get involved with anybody, either."

"Right."

"So why are you getting involved with this . . . helping me?"

He was silent a moment. She stole a glance at him. He sat up straight again, massaged the back of his neck with one hand. "I don't know. I didn't intend to."

"But you did."

"You came to me this time. Not the other way around."

She bowed her head and nodded. "I wasn't thinking straight. I had to get away. If the Spectors were here, everything would be different. None of this would have happened if *they* were here."

"You would have gone to them. Not me."

A pair of crows called harshly from the shore. She turned her face to watch them. "Yes. Them. Not you."

"So tell me one thing," he said, his voice level. "*Why'd* you come to me? Why was I even an option? Why should I be?"

Her back stiffened. He had asked the one question she could both answer and not answer. She thought a moment and decided to tell him the truth.

"Because," she said, still watching the shore. "For some reason I don't understand, I trust you. Should I?"

Again he was silent. The crows jeered. Waves from the boat's wake lapped at the shore.

"Trust me?" he said at last. "Maybe. We'll see, I guess."

She swallowed hard. Perhaps she had reached the heart of her paradox. From the first time she had seen this man she had both trusted and not trusted him.

She sensed a lonely integrity in him that set him apart from others. And yet there was his secrecy, his haunted air.

"What do we do next?" she asked, swallowing again.

"We act like we like each other," he said. "You just sit there, talk while I work. Then I'll go look at your car, see what we can do. Can you handle that? Pretending to like me?"

She raised her chin a fraction of an inch higher. "I can handle it. Can you handle doing it back to me?"

"I suppose. But I'll tell you something—up front."

"Yes?" she said, then waited for his answer.

"You'll kiss me again. And maybe more."

"And maybe not," she said more flippantly than she felt. But she didn't really argue. He was right, and they both knew it. The sparks were still flying. The sparks were setting a fire.

HE WORKED ON THE DOCK. She sat, her hand shading her eyes, watching him. They talked. The conversation was trivial, meaningless. The conversation was weighted with meaning.

He wouldn't talk about the recent past. So they talked about the distant past. She told him that the happiest moment of her childhood was slamming a dictionary shut, very hard, on her brother Rick's nose.

She told him that her best friend had been a large woolly dog named Egor, and that sometimes she cried into Egor's fur because she was skinny and ugly. Egor had lived to be seventeen, and after he'd died, she'd been too bereft to ever get another dog.

She talked easily, artlessly, and Archer could only look at her and wonder. Was she as genuine as she seemed, as unselfconscious? And if she was, what kind of goddam fool had Sterling been?

He was careful about what he told her, yet he knew he was revealing himself. It seemed inevitable. He let it happen. But he knew there were things he couldn't tell her, never wanted her to know.

So instead he told her about his own cavalcade of childhood dogs, and how it had ended for him when he was sixteen. He'd had a part-wolf, part-German-shepherd crossbreed named Sass, who got hit by a car. Her back broken, she'd had to be put to sleep. It had nearly killed him. Like Rita, he hadn't been able to face the idea of another dog.

He'd been an only child. His family was English-Irish and Catholic. His favorite cousin, Gerry, could imitate the voices of cartoon characters, and had once broken him up into a laughing fit so badly in religion class that they both did a month's detention. Gerry had died at nineteen, shot to death working at a gas station.

He shouldn't have told her about Gerry, he supposed; that was too personal, too close to home. So he'd changed the subject to something else, something dumb; but even dumb things seemed to mean something.

I don't want this to happen, he kept thinking. *I can't let this happen.*

But they talked anyway. They were both conscious of Joe Johanssen, back on his porch, beer in hand, his chin on his chest, sinking into a deeper stupor. They were both aware of

Sig Hobbler on his deck, smoking and playing solitaire, and from time to time looking furtively in their direction.

Archer quit working when the sun started to sink behind the hills across the lake. He shrugged back into his blue work shirt and buttoned it halfway up. He wanted to ask her out to supper, but thought he probably shouldn't.

He walked her back to her house. Because he knew both Joe Johanssen and Sig were watching in their secretive way, he took her hand. He made the motion possessive.

He was surprised and intrigued again by the roughness of her fingertips. She must have sensed his notice, because she apologized and said it was from working with glass, especially grinding glass. She had really unpresentable hands, she said.

He said nothing. He didn't mind her hands; he liked them. They were delicately boned, neatly muscled, tingling with life.

When he and she walked past Johanssen's and Hobbler's houses, he held her hand more tightly, more possessively. He tried to make each man meet his eye. Johanssen wouldn't or couldn't. Hobbler did for an enigmatic moment, then gazed off at the horizon.

Archer knew how to bear himself so that he conveyed a certain message, and the message was, *Don't cross me. I am dangerous—more dangerous than you are, more dangerous than you can imagine.* He carried himself that way now, for Rita's sake.

When they reached her house, they saw Peavey. He had a brick A-frame house with a little balcony, and he sat on his balcony at a table, writing furiously in a book.

When Archer tried to make eye contact with Peavey he succeeded better than he'd wished. Peavey didn't look away. He stared back with a gaze so unwavering it bordered on madness. It blazed with hate and jealousy.

Then, without warning, Peavey's eyes flicked to Rita. His look was full of such cold, reptilian hunger that Archer was jolted. But as suddenly as Peavey had turned his attention to

Rita, he turned it away again. He bent over his book, writing fiercely.

"He gives me the creeps," Rita breathed.

"He'd give Godzilla the creeps," Archer replied. She smiled, but he could tell that she was spooked.

Together, they examined her car, decided the problem was the battery. Archer brought up his truck and attached cables to give the battery a charge. It took it, and Rita seemed relieved.

"We'll try it again in an hour or so," Archer told her. "To make sure we've got it right."

And until then? he wondered, looking into her brown eyes. *What do we do until then?*

She must have felt the same, for she seemed atypically self-conscious. "I could make you supper," she said at last. "I'm a lousy cook, but . . ." Her voice trailed off.

He took her hand again—her beautiful, rough little hand. "You put yourself down a lot, you know?"

He was surprised she didn't draw away. She looked at him and smiled. It made his heart tumble like a skier off-balance, rolling downhill. "I *am* a lousy cook," she said.

He drew her a fraction of an inch closer. "I'm not. I'm almost decent. I could cook you supper—if you've got anything to cook. I don't. I'm Mr. Microwave."

"I'm *Mrs.* Microwave," she said. She smiled again. His heart fell all the way downhill again.

"Then let's go eat at the ice-cream stand," he said. "They do a burger good and greasy. And fries curly, the way God meant 'em to be. Or is that kind of food politically incorrect to you?"

"I strive to be as politically incorrect as possible."

"Good," he said and squeezed her hand. And for a moment he even forgot about Peavey, behind them in the failing light, bent over his table, scribbling, scribbling; scribbling vehemently.

THE ICE-CREAM PLACE was a humble cinder-block building located at the juncture of the county road and the highway.

It stood alone, with woods on either side and stretching behind, but it was always crowded.

Teenagers from the farms used it as a center, the farmers themselves came to socialize and the lake's fishermen were drawn to it by the lure of hot coffee, juicy hamburgers, cold desserts.

Rita and Archer sat in a tiny booth with a Formica-topped table, and ate and talked. How strange he was, she thought. So nice, so genuine, really, when he opened up; but he barely spoke of anything after his time in college. It was as if he had erased the last eight or nine years of his life.

He harbored some secret and guarded it jealously. The fact disturbed her, yet she found herself, oddly, respecting his privacy. A man like Archer, she sensed, would not be cryptic merely to seem interesting. If he was withdrawn, he must have good reason.

The more they talked—even when the talk seemed inconsequential—the more her instincts told her to trust him. And the more she liked him. He had an offbeat sense of humor, an almost boyish modesty.

"So," she asked, "were you a basketball *star* in college?"

"Once a guy grabbed me by my shorts, then fell. I almost became a basketball moon."

"No." She laughed. "I mean it. You were probably very good, weren't you? Come on, I want to know."

"I was . . . okay. I'm only six feet tall. The big guys didn't see me half the time. I was the invisible troll. I stole the ball. It was my specialty."

"Basketball players have such little bitty uniforms," she said, eating her last French fry. "Was it embarrassing? I always wondered if it was embarrassing in front of all those people."

"The first couple of times. But when you play, that's all you think of—the game. You don't care how you look. You could be painted green and wear an aardvark on your head."

She smiled. He had a funny way of talking out of the corner of his mouth, and a very nice mouth it was. At the moment, it had a grain of salt at its corner, and she resisted the urge to reach out and brush it off. She was disappointed when he sensed it and licked it away.

"Okay," she said, toying with the straw in her cola. "Lots of times basketball players have nicknames. Like in Arkansas, we've had Super Sid, Rocket Crockett, The Big O— Did you have a nickname?"

"Ouch," he said and looked away, obviously embarrassed. "Don't ask."

"I'm nosy," she said, still bending her straw. "You know that. I'm asking."

He looked at the ceiling as if asking pardon from heaven. "All right. I had this shot—see? This long curve from left of key—a kind of hook."

"Yes?"

He looked at the ceiling again. "Okay. It *arched.* I was St. Louis Arch."

She looked at him, trying not to laugh. "St. Louis Arch. You mean like that big thing that stands by the river? The thing that looks like a croquet wicket?"

"Don't badmouth our croquet wicket," he said. "It's St. Louis's answer to the Eiffel Tower."

"I didn't know the Eiffel Tower asked a question. Why'd St. Louis have to answer?"

"Oh, come on," he said earnestly. "You're an artist. Which is better looking? The Eiffel tower or the arch?"

She bit her straw and thought. "That's not a fair question. It's like comparing apples and oranges."

He pushed away his empty cola cup and gave her a wry look. "That's not a fair answer. I hate it when people say, 'It's like comparing apples and oranges.' Come on—which is better looking? Be honest, dammit."

She nibbled at her straw more pensively. "Well...the arch. The Eiffel tower looks like an oil derrick. But it has this incredible advantage—"

"Of being in Paris," he finished for her. "And the arch has this incredible disadvantage—"

"Of being in Missouri," she concluded, nodding. "Okay, it's like somebody put a Roman aqueduct in Omaha, but—"

"But what's wrong with Omaha? If Omaha was in France—"

"It wouldn't be Omaha. If it was, France would kick it out. The French are very. . .French."

He gave her a rueful stare. "And Omaha?" he asked.

"Isn't," she said with finality.

"This is a pointless conversation," he said.

"Exactly the point I was about to make," she said. But she thought, *It isn't pointless, we're amusing each other. We like each other. We can operate on the same wavelength. We click. It works.*

His face had gone sober, back to its usual shuttered expression. "I should take you home," he said. "We should see if your battery kept the charge."

She nodded. Home. Her suddenly threatened home. She didn't want to return. Or rather, she only wanted to return if she could go back with him. But what would happen when they got home? What was happening now, at this very moment, when they were silent together in a funny little icecream restaurant in the middle of nowhere?

They drove back, making small talk that was not just small talk. Somehow, Rita knew, it was freighted with more than it said. She and Archer were on an inevitable course that both of them feared and both of them wanted. She knew it. They both knew it.

The car, when they got back, hadn't kept its charge. Archer sighed harshly and said the battery might need water. He'd check. Did she have a flashlight?

She, too, sighed, and said she did; it was inside. Together they went into her cabin. The cove seemed deserted tonight, it seemed safe. None of the other men was visible, was about. It was as if she and Archer were alone.

She opened a cluttered drawer in her kitchen to look for her flashlight—she'd thought it was there. But she couldn't find it, and was frustrated by her lack of organization.

She pulled open another drawer and rifled through it. Archer stepped close behind her. She sensed his nearness so strongly it was like being drugged.

He didn't touch her. He didn't have to. She knew the flashlight, the battery, the car, none of it mattered.

They were going to make love.

6

SHE TURNED AND LOOKED at him, her heart beating hard.

"Oh, my God," he said, closing his eyes momentarily. "This is so awkward. Listen." He met her eyes again, his forehead creased.

He didn't touch her, but he took a deep breath. "I'm . . . healthy. I had a doctor's exam just before I moved here. I . . . never take stupid chances. I would never hurt you. Ever."

Oh, heavens, she thought in confusion. *It's come to this, has it?* She shook her head and looked away. "I—I'm healthy, too," she said, her voice choked. "I kept checking. After Sterling . . . I was afraid. It made me so furious, having to be afraid. . . ."

"Sterling," he said, his voice tight, "must have been a world-class jerk. He hurt you pretty bad, didn't he?"

Her eyes filled with tears. Still she didn't look at him. "It's scary to want to feel again."

"Yeah," he said. "Yeah."

He jammed his hands in the back pockets of his jeans and shifted his weight. "There are things I'm not telling you. Things I can't tell you."

She stared at the sun catchers in the dark window. They seemed lifeless, impotent without light streaming through them. "Something bad happened to you, didn't it? Something really bad."

"Yes."

Her mouth gave a nervous twitch. "I—I don't like secrets."

"Yeah," he said. "Well."

They were silent. The air throbbed between them.

"Listen," he said, his voice intense. "I never did anything illegal. I swear it. But I was . . . accused. I was in trouble. But I was cleared, so I'm not—I never—I didn't—"

He didn't finish. She looked at him. His expression was troubled, almost anguished.

She took a deep breath. "You were a coach," she said, trying to guess the truth about him.

"Yes." His eyes searched hers again. *I want you,* they said. *This isn't easy,* they said.

She laced her fingers together nervously. "It could have been something like—like being accused of fixing games. Like people thought you had. But you hadn't."

He blinked. He nodded, and his stance was tense. "Yeah. Something . . . like that."

"It's why you quit coaching?"

"Yes."

"It's why you left St. Louis?"

"Yes."

"It's something you're . . . still sorting out?"

"Yes."

She laced her fingers more tightly together. "And you don't want to . . . really get involved with anybody. Not until you've got it sorted out."

"No."

She shrugged helplessly. She had a foolish wall clock, shaped like a cat whose eyes darted back and forth with each tick, whose tail wagged in time. Tick-tock went the clock. Tick-tock. *What he's saying,* she thought unhappily, *is that we have no future. We only have now.*

Tick-tock, said the clock.

He reached out, putting his hand on her shoulder. His touch went through her, sweeping over her system, and she felt as if she were being washed in lightning.

"Oh," she breathed, and closed her eyes a moment.

He gripped her shoulder more tightly. "Do I frighten you?"

"Yes," she said, her eyes still closed. "No. Yes. No."

"Yeah," he said softly. "Me, too."

She opened her eyes and saw him bending to her. Her lips parted and she found herself lifting her face, almost hesitantly, to his.

"I can't make you any promises," he whispered, his lips hovering over hers.

Her heart contracted with a yearning so deep it hurt. "I didn't ask for any," she said.

"Oh, God," he said. "Oh, God." He kissed her.

The kiss was restrained, almost shy at first. But then he gasped, or she gasped—she wasn't sure which. Then his arms were around her, pulling her powerfully against him, and his mouth bore down on hers with fierce possessiveness.

He had mobile, questing lips, eager to take pleasure and to give it. Their touch told her complicated, wonderful things.

Does this please you?

I want you.

Does this please you more?

I want you.

Can I please you more, still? I will.

I want you. I want to make you want me.

Rita wound her arms around his neck. His tongue teased and tasted hers. His hands roamed slowly up and down her body. She rose on tiptoe to press herself more closely against him. Every place he touched her seemed the right place. Every move his lips, his tongue made against hers, seemed more than right; it seemed so perfect it might break her heart.

He lifted her, sitting her on the countertop, then stepped forward so that his body was insinuated between her legs. She shuddered and instinctively she wrapped her legs around him, kissing him more deeply.

"Oh, Rita," he said against her mouth. He reached beneath her shapeless T-shirt and unsnapped her bra. He took her breasts in his hands, and she ached with pleasure. She hugged him more tightly.

She could feel his erection, hot and lively, pressing against her. He kissed the nape of her neck, and she sighed and buried her face in the warm curve of his throat.

"Don't move," he whispered, and lifted her again. She nodded, kissing his neck, his jaw. She wrapped her legs more tightly around him. He carried her to the bedroom, sat on the bed with her in his lap. He stripped off her T-shirt, drew away her bra.

His mouth and hands explored her breasts intimately. "Unbutton my shirt," he whispered.

Her fingers shaking, she did so. He shrugged out of the shirt, pressed his naked chest against hers. His flesh felt hard, muscular, aggressive. Hers was softer, more curving, yielding. They seemed made to fit each other.

So this is how it's supposed to be, she thought in wonder. *So this is how it's supposed to feel.*

He undid her cutoffs, touched her until she trembled because it felt so right. It felt right when he guided her hand to unzip his jeans, to close her fingers around the hard warmth of his erection.

They laughed together softly—at the awkwardness of getting out of the rest of their clothes, at his fumbling through his pocket for his wallet, then the foil packet.

When he entered her, she wound her legs around him again, hugged him tightly. They rocked and swayed together, trying to join their bodies as inextricably as possible. And as it happened, as fulfillment swept over her body in wave after dizzying wave, she thought, *This is right, this is wonderful, this is right.*

She wanted to say, "I love you." But she said nothing. And neither did he. Only their bodies spoke.

Afterward, she lay beside him, one hand on his bare chest and the other on his shoulder. They held each other gently, but with a sort of strange desperation, as if afraid to let go. Yet conversation wasn't awkward; it seemed as natural as the sex.

"How come you were prepared for this?" she asked, her voice shaky. "When you were so determined to stay aloof, not to get involved?"

She lay with her head on the pillow, her hair fanning out. He took a strand, running it through his fingers as if it were silk. "You know when I bought the condoms?" he asked. "Can't you guess?"

She shook her head. The room was dark and his face was shadowy. She touched it, liking to feel the strong plane of his cheekbone. "How could I know such a thing? I'm too young and innocent."

He exhaled raggedly. "The first morning I was here, I walked out of Patterson's house and looked up the hill. I saw you. You were filling your bird feeder. You wore a yellow T-shirt and your hair was loose. It was blowing in the breeze. You saw me and smiled."

"I remember," she said, stroking his face. "I waved. You didn't wave back. You didn't smile. You turned away."

"I turned inside out," he said. "And the next time I was in town, I found myself buying them. Surprised the hell out of me."

"Thought you were going to get lucky?" she whispered. "Conceited thing, aren't you?"

"I don't know what I thought. Except of you. I thought of you."

She took his face between her hands. "This was something we weren't going to do."

He kissed her. "It was something we had to do. You know it. I know it."

"I was afraid. I was afraid it would be like it was with Sterling."

He kissed her again. "It wasn't good with him?"

"No." She kissed him back. "It was always fast and . . . too hard and . . . like he was selfish. You're not selfish."

"It was all right?" he asked. "The first time, sometimes it's . . . You're finding your way."

She ran her hand over his hair. It felt smooth and thick beneath her fingers. "I think we found our way fine."

"Good. Good." He pressed his lips between her breasts. She sighed with pleasure.

"Sex is like basketball," he murmured against her skin.

She laughed and ran her fingers through his hair. "Why? Because you have to score?"

"No. To be really good at it, you have to practice. And practice. And practice."

He raised himself on his elbow, then bent and kissed her on the lips. He began to make love to her all over again. "I was always a great one," he said, "for practice."

HE WOKE HER SHORTLY before dawn. "I'm leaving. I don't want the others to see me coming out of your house in the morning. They've got enough ideas in their heads. I'll call you about ten."

"Archer?" she murmured sleepily, not wanting him to go.

"What?" He touched her hair.

"What will we do tomorrow?"

"I'll check your car. We'll work. We'll do what we have to do. If you want to take a break, come sit on the dock and talk to me. I'll take you to supper. I'll make love to you again."

"Archer?"

"Yes?"

"Are we . . . friends now?"

He kissed her throat. "I guess you could call it that."

HE HAD NOT BEEN GONE half an hour before her phone rang. She glanced sleepily at the digital clock—half past four, it said. The morning sky was still dark.

The phone kept ringing, shrill and persistent. Groggily, without thinking, she rose. She made her way into the darkened living room.

But when she lifted the receiver all she heard was the sound of a man breathing, breathing so heavily he almost panted.

Alarmed into wakefulness, she slammed down the phone. Her heart lunged in her chest, pounding. Why now? she asked herself in alarm. Why was someone calling now? Did he know Archer had spent most of the night? That she was alone again? Was someone really watching?

Almost immediately the phone rang again. She snatched it up. "Stop it!" she said, clutching the receiver tightly. "Just stop it!"

But only ragged breathing answered her, more labored now. Then there was a moan. Then a strangled word, repeated three times. "Slut. Slut. Slut."

She banged the receiver back into the cradle, hot tears of anger and frustration rising. She yanked the phone cord out of its plug so savagely that the phone crashed to the floor with a phantom ring of protest. She let it lie there, like a vanquished enemy.

She went from window to window, looking at the other houses—Sig's, Joe's, Peavey's. All were quiet, all were dark. *Who?* she thought. *Which one? Is it one of you?*

She went back to bed, but couldn't sleep. She rose at dawn, vowing to lose herself in work until Archer called.

But when she opened her door, she found another gallon jar of wildflowers sitting on her step. But this time a dead bird had been thrust among the crowded blossoms. It was a grackle, with one black wing spread out stiffly. It looked as if its neck was broken.

Her hand flew to her mouth. "Oh, God," she said, feeling sick. She didn't want to touch the thing, but forced herself. She flung the dead bird far away, loathing the feel of it. She pushed the jar of flowers out of sight, to the farthest corner of her porch. She would not pick them up. She would leave them to wither, ignored, in the sun.

Stunned, she realized that this whole time she had been hearing the buzz of men's voices. Angry voices, arguing.

She looked across her yard. George Peavey was exchanging heated words with both Joe Johanssen and Sig Hobbler. She sucked in her breath when she saw what the argument must be about.

Peavey's new chain-link fence was rent by a large, jagged rip. Someone, during the night, had cut a section open.

Peavey turned and saw Rita standing on her porch. His arm shot straight out as he pointed at her. "You!" he accused. "Was it you?"

She stared at him, aghast. "Me? Of course not."

"You—or that brute you sleep with?" Peavey flung out. "He dislikes me. He's bullied me. I wouldn't put anything past the two of you—anything."

So, Rita thought, he *did* know she'd been with Archer last night. He *had* been watching. And now he had announced it to the world.

She wrestled down her anger. "Neither of us would do anything to you," she told Peavey in contempt. "I won't sink to fighting with you."

Her eyes flashed and she turned to face Joe Johanssen and Sig. Joe's broad face was red with anger. Sig, gaunt and pale, looked both angry and strangely stricken.

"You, too," she told them, her voice trembling. "You shouldn't lower yourselves to his level. Can't you see that's what he *wants?* We used to live out here in—in harmony, in peace. He's ruining it. Don't fight with him. You're just hurting yourselves. You're hurting all of us. *Ignore* him."

Peavey was inside his ruined fence, but he took a step nearer to her, gripping a fence pole. "Don't you say vicious things about me. I'll take you to court—for slander. You can't say things like that."

Rita tossed her hair and refused to dignify him with a reply. "I mean it," she told Joe and Sig. "If either one of you fights with him again, I'll—I'll be ashamed of you."

She turned on her heel and marched inside. Her heart banging, she locked the door behind her. She'd seldom locked her door in broad daylight before—but before this, she'd felt safe.

She didn't want to go to her window, to spy on the men, but she found herself there anyway, as if drawn by an irresistible force. She parted the slats of the blind and peered out. Miraculously, her words seemed to have had some effect on Joe and Sig.

Both men looked disgusted but in fierce control of themselves. It was Monday, and Joe, thank God, seemed sober. Both he and Sig should soon be on their way to work. Maybe for once, sanity would reign. Maybe.

Sig was the first to turn away from Peavey. With his head ducked down, he stormed back toward his house. Joe Johanssen called something out angrily after him. Sig ignored him.

Peavey, his fingers laced through the openings in the chain link, shook the fence like a creature trying to escape a cage. He cried out something that made Sig pause. But Sig didn't turn. He ducked his head a fraction of an inch lower and walked up his steps and into his house.

Joe's face had flushed more deeply, and he spat only a few words at Peavey. He wheeled away and headed for his own house. Peavey glared after him, gave the fence one last rebellious shake, then stalked inside his A-frame.

Rita, relieved, gave a long, shaky sigh. She went to her worktable and stared down at the glass she had cut yesterday. But work seemed a distant concern with her heart still drumming from the morning's charged encounter. That—and now she was having an affair with Archer. And all the other men knew it.

An *affair*: the word filled her with both wonder and reservation. Not that she regretted being with Archer. No, that had been wonderful. The memory pulsed in her mind like a small ball of pure light, warming her throughout.

And it wasn't that she was ashamed of what had happened. Nothing they'd done seemed shameful. With him, each touch, each action, flowed as naturally as rivers flowing homeward to sea.

No. Something else troubled her: She'd come to *care* a frightening amount for Archer. She'd been struck by the forbidden impulse to say, "I love you," to him.

She was foolish to think of loving him—he'd made it clear he wouldn't love her back; that he was incapable of love—not at this point in his life, maybe not ever. And he had secrets that he intended to keep.

So, she supposed unhappily, she was having a fling—the sort of thing Sterling had always done so heedlessly. But it didn't feel like a fling. It felt like a healing, a learning-to-be-whole-again.

Oh, Archer, she thought, staring unseeingly at the pieces of glass. *Why couldn't we have met before we both needed to be healed? When we were both still whole? What might we have had if we'd found each other then? Would it have been love? Could it have been?*

ARCHER PHONED AT TEN, as he'd promised. She sounded a bit embarrassed on the phone, a bit hesitant. He supposed he sounded the same way himself.

The morning-after syndrome, he thought ruefully. Now that we've slept together, been physically as intimate as people can be, what do we *say* to each other? Is there *anything* to say?

Hell, he thought, driving up the slope to her little house. He'd got himself into this. He'd warned himself against it. What if they couldn't even talk now? Or if suddenly she wanted—God forbid—commitments or something? Well, he'd warned himself. It was his own damn fault.

But as soon as she swung the door open and he saw her, doubt fled from his mind like smoke in the wind. His heart collided against his ribs, a dizzying little jolt hit him in the stomach and heated his loins.

She looked wary, unsure of herself for a second. But then their eyes met, and she smiled. God—what a smile! he thought. It lit up her face, it lit up the house, it lit up the world.

"Hello," she said and held the screen door open. He stepped inside. She shut the door again and looked up at him. She smiled again.

He found he was smiling back. She wore jeans today. Maybe she was hiding her beautiful legs from Peavey and the others. Good, he thought, she ought to keep them hidden. He remembered the feel of them tightening around his body, and felt that inner jolt of heat again.

He could see in her eyes that she remembered, too. She wore a big yellow T-shirt, far too large for her; but he was used to that, he liked it. The color was good on her, complemented her dark hair, her deep brown eyes.

She'd pulled her hair back casually, fastening it with a rubber band. Lipstick was all the makeup that she wore. Her only other ornament was her pair of hoop earrings.

"Hello," he said quietly and bent to kiss her.

She went into his arms as easily and naturally as if they'd been doing this for years. He kissed her, then held her tightly. He knew, suddenly, that there wasn't going to be any problem making conversation.

"You all right?" he asked gruffly. "Not full of regrets?"

She snuggled more closely against his chest. "I had a few. Didn't you?"

He kissed her temple. "A few. Then I saw you, and they went away."

"Yes." She wrapped her arms around his waist. "It was the same for me."

For a moment they simply held each other. *My God,* he thought, rubbing his cheek against her hair. *Maybe this could work. Maybe I could tell her everything. Maybe she'd understand. If anybody could understand, it might be her....*

But the thought sobered him, made him go cold and bitter. How could he make her understand, when he didn't understand it himself? How could she forgive him for what he was? He hadn't forgiven himself yet.

She must have sensed his sudden conflict. She drew back and looked at him. "Archer," she said, "you told me you couldn't make any promises. I told you I didn't ask for any. I won't. But you said we were friends now. So as far as I'm concerned, we're just friends . . . who go to bed."

He took her face between his hands. "I think I'd better look at your car. Or I—or we—it'll happen again."

She smiled and stepped away from him lightly. She was, of course, barefoot. "I'm new at this. I'm not ready for...too much, too soon. Maybe I can only be so shameless."

He nodded, although his body was flooded with desire. He looked away from her. "Maybe that's wise."

"Do you want coffee?" she asked.

"Do you make good coffee?"

"Incredibly lousy coffee in the microwave," she said, honest as usual.

He smiled. He felt sadness tugging at the smile and wondered what it would have been like to have met her three years ago—before everything had gone so wrong. But that was impossible. Three years ago she had been married, and he had almost been married. What good did it do to think of what could never be?

"I'll pass on your incredibly lousy coffee. Let's go look at your car. Did you ever find your flashlight?"

She nodded, and he thought she blushed. They'd started out last night looking for the flashlight, but ended up making love. She was remembering, too, he knew.

"Then come on," he said. "Let's get out into the open."

It was easier outside. Inside her place he always felt as if the walls were pushing them together, magnetizing them. And then the house seemed too small to contain all the sexual energy it awoke.

He opened the hood of her Mercury Lynx and took the flashlight from her. He unscrewed a battery cap and shone the beam inside. "I think it needs water," he said. "We'll try that."

"I didn't even know a battery needed water," she said, leaning next to him. "I thought it just needed electricity."

The morning wind tousled her hair, and she smelled like soap and water and shampoo. Her clean scent clashed with the oil and gas-sharp odor of the car.

They talked while he poured water into the battery, then fastened the cables between it and the truck and began to recharge it again.

She told him about the morning's newest clash, but how Joe and Sig had finally walked away from Peavey. He frowned when she recounted to him what Peavey had said about her. He frowned harder still when she told him about the phone calls, the flowers, the dead bird.

The car started—at last. But Archer was worried. What if the stalled car hadn't been an accident? Water could be removed from a battery. Maybe somebody had *wanted* to keep

Rita at home, with no way to escape. He was worried. He would keep a close watch on her, he promised himself.

"Maybe you should start unplugging your phone at night." She nodded glumly. "I suppose."

The crows were jeering in the trees again, loud and raucous. "Do you think it's Peavey?" Archer asked.

Her expression was uncertain. "I can't tell. But I think so. I really do. It never happened before he came."

He slammed down the hood of her car, wiped his hands on the thighs of his jeans. "Is there any way you can find out more about the guy? Where he's from, if he's made trouble like this before? If he's dangerous?"

He didn't like the worry he saw deepening in her dark eyes. "I suppose," she said. "I could try the realtor. I know her. She was a friend of my grandparents. . . . Maybe I should call the phone company, too, and complain. It couldn't hurt."

He nodded. "Right. Look, I need to get back to work. How about supper tonight? At six. You want to dress up for a change and go to a real restaurant?"

She was silent a moment, thinking. Then she shook her head. The glance she gave him was almost mischievous. "Naw. I know a place in town where you can get the most wonderful chili. It's called Mickie's. We could go there."

He was about to tease her, ask if she ever dressed up, but a loud, snarling whine rent the air. It drowned out even the screaming crows. Startled, Archer and Rita looked toward Peavey's yard.

Peavey stood, hunched, at the south side of his fence, and he had just turned on his chain saw. He faced the large wisteria bush as if taking aim at it.

"Oh, *no*," Rita said, her face a mask of dismay. "He's going to cut down Joe's wisteria bush—the one he claims is in his yard. Joe'll *kill*."

"Oh, jeez," Archer said from between his teeth. "Can't he wait until the law decides who owns the damn thing? He's begging for trouble. He's crazy."

She put her hand on his arm. "Archer, I know you keep saying not to get involved, but shouldn't he be stopped? Joe's going to raise hell, he truly will. He'll come home and get mad and then get drunk. Then who knows what—?"

She was right, dammit. And there was such pleading in her tone that he knew he had no choice except to try. He squared his jaw and set off for Peavey's yard.

Peavey didn't seem used to the chain saw, and it bucked and jumped in his hands. He struck wildly at the top of the big shrub—as if he was scalping it.

Archer had to yell to make himself heard over the machine's roar. When Peavey saw him, he got that cold, snaky gleam in his eyes, but he turned off the saw. Archer was not unsettled by the look, but it bothered him. He had seen another such look somewhere—years ago. He wished he could remember where.

"Yes?" Peavey hissed. "What? What? Did you come to confess about my fence?"

"I didn't touch your fence," Archer replied. "That's not what I came to talk about."

Peavey jerked his head in the direction of Sig's and Joe Johanssen's houses. "*They* both claim they didn't do it. Maybe they didn't. Maybe it was you."

Archer put his fist on his hip. "Why would I? It's nowhere near my property."

"You . . ." Peavey sneered. "*That's* your property, there." He jerked his head in Rita's direction. "You don't like me close to *that*."

Archer narrowed his eyes. He knew he could look dangerous when he tried, and he did so now. "I wouldn't talk like that if I were you."

Peavey's gaze wavered but didn't drop. "Why? Because you're young and healthy? And I'm not? You think I'm less than human, don't you? You laugh about me behind my back, the two of you. And you resent me—you don't want me near her. Well, what would I want with her? A woman like *that*."

Archer tried to press back his anger. "I don't resent you. And nobody's laughing, because nothing's funny. The person making the most trouble for you is *you*. Now, there's a dispute about where that fence goes, and you know—because you started it. Which means that there's a dispute about who owns that—that wisteria thing there."

"Mind your own business," Peavey practically spat.

"I'd like nothing better. But Johanssen thinks—"

Peavey stepped to the fence, his back stiff with anger. "I said to mind your own business. I'm asking only for peace and quiet," he said with vehemence. "That's why I moved here—for peace and quiet."

"Trust me," Archer said sarcastically, "there'll be a lot more peace and quiet if you don't cut that thing down."

Peavey pointed at the wisteria, his finger shaking with emotion. "It's an overgrown, aggressive vine. It'll *eat* my fence. Besides, it has flowers. I'm allergic."

Archer clamped his mouth shut to keep from swearing.

"I'll cut it all down if I please," Peavey said, gesturing at his yard. "Every single thing that grows on my property. All the nasty things that rain down pollen and leaf dust and smells that make me sick."

Archer's patience snapped. He should have known better than to try to reason with the older man. "Why did you move to the country if you can't stand pollen and trees?"

"For peace and quiet!" Peavey almost screamed. "You think there aren't trees and flowers in the city? And too many people? I wanted away from it. For years I've struggled to get away from it. Well, now I'm here, and you won't ruin it for me—none of you."

"You're ruining it for yourself. Now, I—"

"Peace and quiet!" Peavey shouted. "Peace and quiet! And no people! Leave me alone—all of you!"

Peavey turned on the chain saw again. For a crazy instant Archer thought the man might come through the fence with it and go for *him*.

But instead Peavey turned and attacked the wisteria more wildly than before. But this time, he aimed the blade at the vine's thick trunk. It took him several passes, but at last the saw's teeth gnawed through, the trunk cracked and the vine's ruined bushlike head fell, severed, to the earth.

Next, Peavey turned his fury on a mimosa sapling and hacked it down, too. Then he stalked to the big pine that stood on the disputed property. He made a series of slashing cuts at it, so undisciplined that Archer was surprised the chain saw blade didn't break.

Great gouges flew out of the pine's bark, and the scents of sawdust and resin filled the air. But either the tree was too big a job for Peavey, or his own rage had exhausted him, and at last, defeated, he switched the saw off.

His baggy white shirt was wet with sweat, and he was almost panting. He stood staring at the tree as if it were his personal enemy and must be fought to the death. The tree did, indeed, seem almost mortally wounded. It was lacerated and half butchered.

Archer felt sick to his stomach. He turned away, knowing there was nothing more to say to the man.

He walked back to Rita and put his arm around her shoulders. She looked up at him expectantly, concern in her eyes. "Come sit on the dock with me again," he said, casting a wary look over his shoulder at Peavey. "I don't think you should be up here alone with him, the mood he's in."

Rita shook her head. "I won't be chased from my own house. I have work to do. I'll . . . just keep the door locked."

"Then let's make it supper at five instead of six. Let's not be here when Joe gets back. It's going to be ugly. I can *feel* it."

She nodded solemnly. "We'll—we'll stay out of it," she vowed. "Just like you've said all along."

"Yeah," he said, his eyes going hard. "We'll stay out of it."

7

RITA FOUND IT DIFFICULT to concentrate on work. Today the copper foil refused to obey her fingers. It twisted, crinkled and creased, resisting all her efforts to make it fit the edges of the glass smoothly.

She needed a new bottle of flux and scolded herself for running so close to empty. She spot-soldered the pieces together, but her touch wasn't as sure as it should have been.

She brushed a strand of hair from her forehead and looked out the window. She could see Archer, shirtless, working on the dock, and each time she stole a glimpse it sent a strong, pleasant tingle through her.

She forced herself to look away. He might be gone by autumn. She had to remember that.

In the meantime, if she couldn't keep her mind on stained glass, she should work on another set of problems—Peavey and her unpleasant phone calls.

She called the phone company first and was finally referred to a tired-sounding woman in customer relations. The woman's name was Mrs. Dogberry.

"I'm sorry," Mrs. Dogberry said. "We can't do anything. If he makes a threat, that's something else. Then we can bring the police into it, tap your phone. But if he's just...breathing, there's nothing we can do."

"But," Rita protested, "he called me a name, too. Doesn't that count? I mean, this is harassment, darn it."

"He called you just one name?" Mrs. Dogberry asked.

"Well . . . yes. But it's still harassment."

"Ma'am," Mrs. Dogberry said with a sigh, "be glad he called you only *one* name. You wouldn't believe what some of these characters say. You're lucky."

"Lucky," Rita echoed with unamused irony.

"Here's what you do," Mrs. Dogberry said in her spent way. "Don't listen to him. Don't speak to him. Don't even tell him to stop. Do exactly what you've been doing. Hang up. Unplug the phone."

"But," Rita protested, "I—I think I know who's been calling. Isn't there *anything* you can do?"

"Only if a threat is made," Mrs. Dogberry replied mechanically. "That's company policy. I'm sorry." She paused a moment, then added, "I shouldn't say this, but what you can do is buy a whistle. A *loud* one. Next time he calls, blow his eardrum out."

"A whistle?" Rita said. "That's all you can tell me?"

"It's better than nothing," Mrs. Dogberry said.

Rita hung up, disillusioned about the powerlessness of the phone company. She opened the telephone book and looked up the real-estate office that had handled Peavey's property.

She punched the number and asked to talk to Katy McInty, who had listed the house. Katy was a brisk, energetic woman of about fifty.

"Peavey?" Katy said. "I honestly can't tell you much. I didn't handle the sale. Harry Macon did, and he's on vacation. Won't be back for a week."

Rita took a deep breath. She knew she was asking her grandparents' old friend to gossip, but she didn't care; she was desperate. "Did Harry say anything about him? That Peavey was difficult—or acted strange? Because, really, Katy, this guy is driving everybody nuts. It may... come to blows or something."

"Just what *sort* of trouble's brewing out there?" Katy asked, frankly curious.

Rita explained as succinctly as she could. Katy listened, then was silent for a full fifteen seconds. At last she spoke. "Harry... didn't like him. He said the man was temperamental . . . erratic."

"Yes? Go on," Rita encouraged.

Katy paused again. "Okay, that house had been on the market over two years. It had been empty all that time. To be honest, it was falling into disrepair."

"I know," Rita said. "Somebody inherited it, right? So it had an absentee owner?"

"Yes. A retired woman had owned it. She moved to Mississippi to live with her son's family."

"Yes," Rita said, "I heard that."

"Mrs. Fetters put too high a price on it," Katy said. "She died, and her son didn't want to fool with the place. His attitude was 'Get rid of it—I want the money.' He dropped the price to rock bottom. I thought it was *too* low."

"And then Peavey came along?"

"Right," Katy said, sounding piqued at the memory. "Like he had it timed. He insisted on lakefront property, but he wasn't willing to pay much. He also insisted he wanted it to be by itself."

Rita frowned and toyed with a piece of glass shaped like a teardrop. "But it's not by itself."

"Right. He complained that it was too close to the other houses. But it was all he could afford. He made an offer on it—the first offer—the only offer—in two years."

"And it was accepted."

"It was even lower than the asking price, but Johnny Fetters took it. Maybe because it was cash. Johnny could have the money in his pocket in a flash."

"So, Katy, exactly how was Peavey difficult?"

Katy sighed. "All right. I suppose it's all right to tell you. Harry said the guy was a complainer. Not now and then, but constantly. Harry showed him thirty-two different pieces of property. Nothing would do. Not even the one he bought satisfied him. Like I said, he thought the rest of you were too close. He gave the impression that he wanted to be alone— very alone. That maybe he *should* be alone, that he didn't deal well with people."

Rita gritted her teeth. "Where's he from? What did he do? How does he support himself?"

"Honey," Katy said patiently, "I have no idea. No bank had to check him out. He had the cash—sixty thousand dollars. Harry had the impression that he'd inherited it."

Rita picked up the glass teardrop, weighed it in her hand. "He must have come from *somewhere*. He didn't pop up out of the ground like a toadstool—or maybe he did."

"I can't remember," Katy said. "Let me check around the office. Somebody may know. If I find out anything, I'll call you back. If you haven't heard from me by the first of the week, call again. Harry should be back by then."

Rita shrugged helplessly. Katy hadn't told her much. But it was better than nothing. She thanked her and started to say goodbye.

"Wait," Katy said suddenly. "I do remember one thing Harry said about him. It was . . . weird."

"Weird?" Rita echoed, a flutter of apprehension in her stomach. "What?"

Katy paused. "Well . . . I don't want to alarm you."

"What do you mean, alarm me? I'm already alarmed."

"Now, now," Katy said, trying to soothe her. "I mean, don't take it *too* seriously. It probably means nothing."

"Katy—*please*."

"All right," Katy said, but she sounded reluctant. "Just don't read too much into it. Harry's from Texas. He went to the University of Texas. Well, you know Texans. Harry's got the university sticker on his bumper and the decal on his windshield, he's got the U.T. ring. There's this U.T. longhorn statue on his desk—he's even got this tie with little tiny longhorns on it."

Rita squeezed the glass teardrop impatiently. "Yes, yes. And?"

"I mean," Katy said wryly, "you can't be around Harry for half an hour without knowing he went to U.T. And his son goes to U.T. now. So most people talk to him about football. Not Peavey. Peavey wanted to know about—Whitman."

Rita frowned, puzzled. The name seemed familiar, but she couldn't place it. "Whitman?"

Another pause. Katy seemed to be forcing her voice to stay rueful, not truly serious. "Charles Whitman, honey. You know—that student that climbed that big tower on campus and started shooting people with a rifle. *That* Whitman."

Rita's insides twisted and turned cold. "Charles Whitman *murdered* people. He shot a bunch before they got him down from there."

"Yes." Katy's voice had lost its falsely cheerful tone. "Peavey wanted to know all about it. If Harry was actually *at* U.T. that day when Whitman climbed the tower."

Rita glanced out the window to look for Archer's reassuring figure. But he was gone. The dock was empty.

"Now the weird thing is," Katy went on, "that Harry really was there. He was having lunch when he heard the news on the radio. He had a good friend who was actually pinned down by gunfire and hid behind a bush the whole time."

"My God." Numbly, Rita stared at the empty dock as if she could make Archer appear by sheer willpower.

"Harry said it was the first time Peavey seemed interested in anything except himself. He kept prodding Harry for more. And at the end, Peavey said, 'How do you suppose he felt up there? Killing all those people?'"

"He—he said *that?*"

"Yes. And Harry said he asked it in a really creepy way. When Harry didn't answer, Peavey said, 'He must have hated everyone. Really hated them—every last one.' Something to that effect."

Something to that effect.

"Harry said he said it with a sort of satisfaction. And that he smiled. To himself, sort of. Harry said it was the only time he'd ever seen him smile."

Rita shook her head helplessly. "The only time he ever smiled was about a mass murderer? And you people sold him a house right behind *mine?*"

Katy's voice suddenly went defensive. "I told you not to read anything into it. It probably means nothing. And you know *we're* not responsible for who buys these houses. The seller accepts an offer—or he doesn't. We're only the middle people."

"I—I know, Katy."

"Besides," Katy said, almost righteously, "federal law says we can't discriminate. If we turned away everybody who had a peculiar streak, we'd be out of business. He's unpleasant, and he's odd, but there's no law against that."

"I'm sorry," Rita said. "I didn't mean to say it's your fault. It's just he's making a lot of people miserable."

Katy, whose emotions were quickly touched, seemed placated. "Look, sweetie, that's one of the hazards of living in these informal subdivisions. There're no zoning laws. No ordinances. If the guy next door to you decides to raise pigs, he can raise 'em. And you're stuck with it."

"Well," Rita said glumly, "at least he isn't raising pigs—yet."

"Just try to stay out of it," Katy advised her. "And if I hear anything, I'll let you know."

Rita thanked her again and hung up. Once more she looked for Archer, but still he was nowhere in sight. Usually she loved the shoreline best when it was deserted, but today it made her uneasy.

A sudden awareness of warmth and stickiness in her hand startled her. She looked at her hand. She had squeezed the glass teardrop too hard. Its point had pierced the web of flesh between her thumb and forefinger, and now blood smeared her palm, filling up her lifeline.

She gasped and went to wash it. She tried not to think that Peavey had smiled when he thought about a mass murderer. But she knew the story would haunt her.

SHE AND ARCHER LEFT the cove precisely at five, before either Sig or Joe Johanssen would return from work.

They went into town to Mickie's. The interior was dim but friendly, with checkered tablecloths and the scent of spicy food in the air. The walls were decorated with sports memorabilia.

Archer and Rita sat at a corner table beneath an Arkansas Razorbacks basketball poster. Rita saw him glance at it, regret or nostalgia in his eyes.

She understood. She looked first at the poster, with a picture of a player driving down the court, then at Archer. "You miss it? A lot?"

He shook his head and seemed to force the emotion out of his expression. "No. But it's easier not to talk about it."

"Sorry," she said.

He flicked her a rueful one-cornered smile. "Hey, we've got bigger things to worry about."

She played nervously with her earring. "Archer, I really don't like what Katy told me. About Peavey smiling about Whitman shooting people from that tower."

He covered her hand with his, squeezed it. "She's right—don't read too much into it. A lot of people have a morbid curiosity about stuff like that."

She twined her fingers through his and squeezed back. "I know. But it makes me nervous. Does he have fantasies of shooting people?"

He smiled again. "Your imagination's working overtime. He's not the type. Mass murderers? Those guys are always 'quiet loners' who mind their own business. Their neighbors always say, 'Him? He never bothered anybody. Kept to himself a lot. Seemed like a nice guy.'"

She smiled back. "You're right. And nobody would ever accuse Peavey of keeping to himself."

Her smile faded. "But I'm worried," she said. "I wonder if I should have warned Joe. He's going to come home and see that wisteria cut down, and God only knows what he'll do."

Archer picked up her hand, held it between both of his. "Look," he said, "you've *got* to stay out of it. What if you did call? Two things would happen. One, he'd just start getting mad sooner. He'd probably stop for a couple of beers on the way home, just to get his courage up. Then he'd hit the cove both mad *and* drunk."

She dropped her gaze. "I suppose you're right."

"Trust me. Two, if Peavey ever found out you told—and Joe doesn't exactly keep secrets—he'd get even. I don't want him getting even with you."

He brought her hand to his lips and kissed her knuckles. She was so surprised, she raised her eyes, met his again. "I want you safe," he said. The intensity in his stare sent a vibration of desire trembling through her.

But then a large, hearty waitress descended on them, joking and laughing. Archer lowered Rita's hand back to the table. But he kept holding it; he didn't let go.

They ordered Mexican beers with twists of lime, nachos and chili, the specialty of the house. The waitress cracked a few more jokes, then ended by elbowing Archer in the shoulder. "You sure keep a good hold on her." She laughed. "Whatsa matter? Afraid she'll get away?"

Archer looked embarrassed and said nothing. "I'm a dangerous character," Rita said. "He's got to keep me under control."

The waitress laughed louder and ambled off to the kitchen. Archer cast an aggrieved glance after her. Then he looked at his hand locked around hers.

"She's right," he said. "I shouldn't do this." He drew his hand away.

Rita felt a sense of loss and an inexplicable hurt. "I didn't mind. I . . . liked it."

"Yeah," he said, gazing up at the basketball poster. "I did, too."

She sensed complex emotions warring inside him. Something had gone terribly wrong in his life, and he was still struggling to come to terms with it. She also sensed it would be a mistake to push him to speak of it—he wasn't ready. She wondered if he would ever be ready.

She tried to steer the conversation back to the cove. "What'll happen, do you think? When Joe sees what Peavey did to the wisteria? And that tree—oh, that poor tree. It makes me sick to think of it."

He shook his head. His expression wasn't optimistic. "Anything might happen. You don't know Joe well?"

She shook her head. "No. I knew his wife better."

"What do you think? Did he cut Peavey's fence open? Peavey said he'd denied it. Would he do it, then lie? Is he capable?"

"I just don't know," she said, then sighed. "I suspect he could."

"What about Sig Hobbler? He seems the kind of guy who holds a grudge. Would he cut the fence? Which one did it?"

Somebody had dropped a coin in the jukebox. Dwight Yoakam started singing, "I'll Be Gone." Rita fought against flinching. The song reminded her too poignantly of her relationship with Archer. It was about a man making love to a woman, but telling her that in the morning he had to move on.

She ducked her head and tried not to think about him leaving. "I don't know who cut the fence," she said. "I suppose it could have been either. Sig gave me his wire cutters—but he could have another pair. With all that junk, he could have two of everything."

He nodded. "What about the flowers? Who's leaving them?"

She picked a paper napkin from the holder and began to shred it aimlessly. "I think it's probably Sig. I don't know why—just instinct."

"I think you're right. But what about the dead bird? Who do you think did that?"

She tore the larger pieces into smaller ones. "I don't know. Peavey...doesn't like me. Whenever he looks at me, I feel like he wants to . . . punish me. But Joe . . . Well, I pretty much rejected Joe. I suppose I hurt his feelings. Maybe he was angry. But then, Sig . . ." Her voice trailed off sadly.

He folded his arms, leaned them on the table and bent his head nearer hers. "What about Sig?"

She clenched her teeth and kept shredding the paper. "I suppose Sig could have seen us on the dock—when we kissed. I suppose he knows you . . . stayed with me last night. Maybe he doesn't . . . approve."

"I don't think any of them *approve*. I just hoped it'd make them keep their distance from you. Maybe I've made it worse."

Another song jangled and wailed from the jukebox. Garth Brooks bemoaned the plight of a woman whose lover deserted her to follow the adventures of rodeo.

Rita swept the fragments of her torn napkin into the ashtray. "No. You didn't make it worse. Peavey hasn't touched me again. And I don't think Joe'll come around anymore. A few phone calls, a dead bird—that's not so bad. I can deal with it."

She glanced up at him and was taken aback once more by the intensity of his gaze. She found herself looking into his eyes, trying to read the complicated message she saw there. She wondered what he read in hers.

"I—" he began, then hesitated. "I like you. It's more than just the sex. I wanted you to know that."

"Oh," she said and looked away. She fought the compulsion to shred another napkin.

She took a deep breath. "I like you, too."

He was silent a moment. "But I suppose we shouldn't like each other...too much. I may be gone, come fall. And I may not be exactly... what you think I am. I wouldn't want to disappoint you."

She had a strange, dizzying feeling in the pit of her stomach. "I see," she said, but didn't; not really. "And you're probably never going to tell me about it. Whatever bad thing it was that happened to you."

Again he took a long time to answer. "No," he said at last. "I probably won't. I'd rather not. Let's just take things the way they are."

She shrugged as if it didn't matter. She looked up at the basketball poster again. He, almost pointedly, did not. She swallowed.

She imagined that she had guessed too closely to the truth yesterday. He had been a coach, and people gambled on college basketball—all the time and with big money.

Sometimes coaches got bribed or bribed players. The flimsiest evidence of wrongdoing could lose a coach his job. If actually accused and brought to trial, a man could be ruined by the scandal—even if he was innocent.

"See," he said, his face grim. "It wasn't just that there was trouble. A lot went wrong at the same time. I lost my father. Then my mother. And...there was...this woman, too. She couldn't take it. I . . . lost her, too."

"A...woman?" she said and wondered if he was still in love with her.

"Hell," he said impatiently, "I can't talk about it. If I could talk about it with anybody, I'd do it with—"

But then the big, relentlessly jolly waitress reappeared and set their beers and frosted mugs before them. "Bet you thought I got lost, huh? Well, no rest for the weary, I always say. Run here, run there, runaround Sue, that's me."

She jabbed Archer's shoulder with her elbow again. "Ha. I see you finally set her free. So you *can* let go of her if you hafta, huh?"

Archer, unamused, glanced up at her. "Yeah," he said out of the side of his mouth. "I can let go of her."

A new tune issued from the jukebox. Glen Campbell sang "Gentle on My Mind," the song of a man who has left his woman far behind.

Rita set her jaw and tuned out the waitress's chatter. *Why, she thought bitterly, does every damn country-western song in the world have to be about a man leaving?*

BY THE TIME THEY REACHED the road to the cove, their relationship had undergone another of its strange transformations. Rita was both amazed and bewildered by how well they could get along at times.

Their conversation stayed rigorously trained on neutral subjects—favorite movies, books, albums. But between them, somehow, even neutral subjects lost neutrality, became personal to the point of intimacy.

They found they had eerily similar tastes. They both had the same favorite actor, Harrison Ford; favorite movie, *Star*

Wars; favorite rock group, U2; favorite female singer, Tina Turner; favorite song, "Layla," by Eric Clapton.

They gave each other wary looks when they discovered that they both thought *Ishtar* was one of the funniest films ever made.

"Get serious," Archer said. "Nobody else in the world thought it was funny."

"It was a *stitch*," Rita insisted. "Remember when Dustin Hoffman was out on the ledge, and even then he couldn't stop making up terrible music. He made up this awful song about being on a ledge?"

"Oh, God," Archer groaned. "And when they were crawling through the desert—with buzzards following them—and they *still* made up bad songs . . ."

Rita laughed. "*Awful* songs. Remember 'Software'?"

Archer sang a few bars.

"Don't," Rita begged, laughing. "Stop!"

But by then he'd launched into "Hot Fudge Love," until he, too, was laughing too hard to go on.

Suddenly he pulled the truck over to the side of the road.

"What are you doing?" she asked, almost helpless with giggling.

"I can't drive," he said, wiping his eyes. "I laughed till I cried. I couldn't see."

Rita tried to curl up into a knot of pained glee, but couldn't because of her seat belt. She began to sing "Telling the Truth Can Be Dangerous Business."

"Don't," he ordered. "You'll kill me. I'll die. Quit. Stop."

Then he was out of his seat belt and unbuckling hers, and she was in his arms. They laughed and hugged each other tightly. And then, slowly, the laughter died away. They simply held each other.

"Good God," he said, in her ear. "I don't know how long it's been since I laughed like that."

She hid her face against his shoulder, exhausted from merriment. "Me, either."

He kissed her cheek.

Oh, she thought helplessly, *it's happening again. He's making me go weak. He's setting me on fire. He touches me and sparks fly. They fill my whole body.*

He pulled her closer, kissed her mouth hungrily, then laid his cheek against hers. His voice was low and fierce. "Rita, let's not go back to the cove. Let's go someplace else. Where there isn't any trouble. Where there isn't anything in the world—except you and me."

"We can't," she said, holding him close. "No. We can't let them drive us away."

"Please." He kissed the edge of her jaw.

"No, no," she begged. "We can't hide from this. We have to face it, sooner or later."

"Later. Tonight, let's—"

She drew back from him reluctantly. "We're almost home, Archer. I don't want to go anywhere else. We couldn't pull into a motel like this—with not even a toothbrush. It'd seem . . . sordid. I'd be embarrassed. I guess I've been hussy enough I shouldn't mind, but . . ."

He leaned to her, framed her chin with his hand. "You're not a hussy. You're anything but. I—"

She shook her head. "No. I've got a home. I want to be there. Not at some…motel." Her voice dropped sadly when she said "motel." She didn't even know why the idea depressed her. Maybe it emphasized that all they were having was an affair, that it wasn't permanent; and she was, at heart, a permanent sort of person.

He paused. Then he bent to her, kissed her lips. "You're right, Rita," he said softly. "I'll take you home."

He put the truck in gear, and they jolted the bumpy last quarter mile to the cove. They almost reestablished their equilibrium. Archer was teasing her about the "Half an Hour" song from *Ishtar,* making her giggle again.

But then the truck's headlights caught the little cluster of houses in its beams, and Rita shrank back against her seat.

A knot of people stood in the center of the road, between Peavey's house and Joe Johanssen's. Parked at the road's edge was a car from the sheriff's department. Its blue light spun, casting a sinister, surreal flicker over the landscape.

There had been trouble, all right. Enough for the police to have come.

8

THE CAR FROM THE sheriff's department blocked the narrow road. Archer had to stop the truck.

His stomach contracted, and he got a bitter, coppery taste in his mouth. All he wanted was to turn around somehow and flee.

Don't run. It won't look good if you run.

And Rita—he had to think of Rita because in a crisis she never, dammit, thought of herself.

He would have sat in the truck, as motionless and emotionless as a statue. That was his gut impulse. *Don't draw attention to yourself. Don't get involved.*

But Rita was already opening the door, getting out of the truck.

"Don't—" he started to say.

It was too late, she was gone. She'd joined the knot of people in the roadway, her face pale and distraught in the glow from the headlights. He had no choice but to follow her, keep her safe.

He got out, put his arm around her, drew her close.

The deputy was a tall man who looked absurdly young, like a gangly boy wearing a lawman's costume. "Now, now, now," he was saying to Joe Johanssen.

Joe was obviously drunk, and he seemed near tears. "He—he—" he pointed at George Peavey "—he cut down the floors—the flowers—the vine. He killed my *tree*."

"It's *my* bush, it's *my* tree," George Peavey snarled. "It's my property. It's my yard. It's mine. *Mine*."

"And—and—" stammered Joe, gesturing wildly at Sig Hobbler "—his goddamn dog *bit* me. I—I'm making a citizen's protest—my legal right—and his goddamn—goddamn dog *bit* me."

Archer saw that Joe's right hand was wrapped, haphazardly, with a blood-soaked handkerchief.

Sig Hobbler, hollow-cheeked in the shifting light, held his biggest dog by the collar.

"Buster ain't a mean dog," Sig said. "You scared him, is what—yellin' and carryin' on . . ."

"You were pounding on my door," Peavey accused Joe. "Like a crazy man! You were drunk and abusive. The dog knew it—the dog knew it!"

Joe's voice was tearful. "I knocked your door 'cause I wanted to know what rike—what right you got to cut down my vine and kill my tree."

"You were drunk," Peavey raged. "You deserved to be bitten. You were drunk and threatening."

"I didn't threaten anybody," Joe retorted. "I didn't threaten nothing. I never said anything but, 'You come out here and talk to me—talk.'"

"You threatened me!" Peavey cried.

The young officer held up his hands for everyone to be quiet. He looked at Sig Hobbler, struggling to keep the excited dog in place. "Did he threaten him?" he asked. "Did you hear?"

"I heard it," Sig said. "No. He didn't threaten nothing. He yelled, 'Come out,' is all."

"And then," Joe almost sobbed, "your damn dog bit me—and all I did is say, 'Come out.'" He turned to Peavey. "If you'd come out, I wouldn't got bite—got bit. It's your fault, you coward."

"That stinking dog wouldn't have been on my property," Peavey retorted, "if *you* hadn't cut a hole in my fence."

"I didn't cut a hole in your frigging fence," Joe raged. "*He* musta done it." He pointed at Sig.

Sig's voice was cold and deadly calm. "I didn't cut on no fence. You done it yourself. It's your own self you can blame that Buster bit you."

"I *didn't* cut the fence!" Joe almost screamed.

"Somebody cut my fence," Peavey said with venom. "Arrest somebody—*now*."

"All I can do," said the young officer, shaking his head, "is write out your complaint. It doesn't appear clear who cut your fence."

"They all might have done it!" Peavey cried. "Them, too." He pointed at Archer and Rita. "They sleep together. She's no better than a slut. She's propositioned me. She's threatened me. He's a thug, *her* thug."

"I *never* propositioned him," Rita declared, outraged. Archer pulled her closer to him, squeezing her shoulder to signal her to be quiet. She tensed against him, but she clamped her mouth shut, as if determined that Peavey wouldn't make her speak again.

"All these people are against me," Peavey told the officer. "They conspire against me. I came out here to live in peace and quiet. They've made my life a living hell. Arrest them all!"

The young deputy put up his hands again. His face was so smooth that Archer wondered if the kid even shaved yet. He was obviously out of his league in this free-for-all.

"Now, look—" the deputy said.

"I was making a citizen's protest," Joe argued. "All I was doin' was makin' a legal protest."

"Now, *look*," the deputy said with a disgusted shake of his head. "I don't *know* who owned the vine, the—the tree. Sounds like a court's gonna have to decide."

"I called you out here to arrest somebody," Peavey spat. "Arrest somebody—or I'll have your badge. What's your name? What's the number of your badge?"

Archer saw the young man swallow, struggling to control his temper. He pointed at Joe. "This man says all he did was knock on your door and yell for you to come out."

"He beat on my door," stormed Peavey. "He almost knocked it down. He screamed he was going to kill me. I called the police for protection. Protect me—arrest him."

"I didn't make any threats," Joe protested.

"He didn't make no threats," Sig Hobbler said. "Down, Buster."

"Arrest them both!" ordered Peavey. "Arrest them all—especially *her*."

He glared at Rita, and once again Archer saw something in the man's eyes that was both familiar and elusive. Archer was afraid of little, but he took an instinctive step backward, as if from a poisonous snake. He made Rita step back with him, and kept his arm firmly around her.

The deputy sighed with exasperation. "What I got is conflicting testimony. I don't see any harm's been done—except to your fence. And all I can do is report that. The main thing is for everybody just to calm down—"

"Arrest somebody!" Peavey insisted. "Arrest everybody!"

"All right—" the young officer cast a baleful look at Buster "—I'm taking this dog into custody."

"It was trespassing on my property," Peavey said angrily.

"It bit me, the goddamn mutt," Joe said. "I prob'ly got rabbits—rabies, now."

"Buster ain't no mean dog," Sig said with his same deadly calm. "He don't like trouble, is all."

"I'm taking him in," the deputy said with a grim nod. "Put him in the back of the car," he told Sig.

He swung open the back door of the patrol car, and Sig led the dog to it. "Buster's a *good* dog," he said. "You'll see."

He urged the dog inside. The animal was overexcited, but it obeyed. The deputy slammed the door behind it. Then he turned and pointed at Peavey.

"Now, I'm giving everybody warning. That includes you, mister."

"Don't talk down to me," Peavey retorted. "I called you here on this case."

The deputy put his hands on his hips. "The only case this is, is a case of nuttiness. What I'm telling you people is to all go back home and stay there and stop carrying on like a bunch of—kindergartners. I'm reporting the fence, I'm taking the dog, I'm warning you all to quit this carrying on—and that's *that*."

He made a slicing motion in the air with his hand, as if cutting off further discussion.

Joe mumbled something sullenly.

"I want that dog back," Sig demanded, a sinister note in his voice. "You ain't keepin' my dog."

"He'll have to be checked by a vet," the deputy said matter-of-factly. "Call the department tomorrow."

"This man," Peavey said, stabbing a finger in Joe's direction, "was publicly drunk and disorderly."

"I said to get back in your house, Mr. Peavey," the deputy said, and he sounded as if he meant business. "Or I'll arrest *you*."

"He's drunk and disorderly!" Peavey insisted, outraged. "Everybody knows he's a drunk." He whirled suddenly to face Archer. "You!" he cried at Archer. "This morning, you told me he was a drunken troublemaker—you said it yourself."

Archer raised his chin in disdain and refused to reply. Peavey had lied and would twist anything that was said.

Joe stared blearily at Archer. "You called me a drunk? What right you got to talk about me?"

Archer felt Rita flinch against him. "I'm not getting into this argument, Johanssen," he said quietly. "We can talk later."

The deputy jerked his chin up impatiently. "I got one guy here who's makin' sense. The rest of you—get the hell back in your houses or I'll run you in. You can get the hell out of each other's faces—or spend the night in the hoosegow. Take your choice."

Joe Johanssen was the first to turn away, muttering to himself. He made his way, swaying slightly, to his stairs.

"You can't—" Peavey began to protest.

But the young deputy's patience had clearly snapped. "In your house, or I'll haul you in for disobeying a direct order from the sheriff's department."

Peavey swore under his breath, but he wheeled and stamped back onto his own lawn, up his stairs and into his house. He slammed his door.

"You," the deputy said, turning to Sig. "What are you waiting for? What you staring at?"

Archer realized with a jolt that Sig was staring at Rita. Even in the unsteady light, Archer could see the man's pale gray eyes fastened on her. Instinctively, his hand tightened on her shoulder.

"I said," the deputy spoke grimly, "get in your house and stay there. I get another call out here tonight, I'll run you all in."

Sig's head snapped back slightly. The officer's words seemed to register. He turned his gaze from Rita and looked the deputy up and down. Wordlessly, he turned and left.

"Buncha losers," the deputy grumbled. "They all need a chill pill."

Archer wanted only for the officer to get in his car and leave. He said nothing.

But Rita, blast it, piped up. "Things have been bad out here, and they keep getting worse."

"Yeah," the deputy said sarcastically. "Well, take my advice and keep your distance."

Joe's dog, Buster, began to bark and howl inside the car. "Oh, *hell*," said the deputy. Buster howled more loudly.

"I try to keep my distance," Rita told him. "But they're not keeping theirs. Somebody keeps calling up and not saying anything—or calling me names. Somebody keeps leaving flowers on my porch. Today a dead bird was in them."

"Lady," he said wearily, "I can't do a thing about that kind of call. And it's not illegal for somebody to leave you flowers. Or a dead bird. I can't help you."

"But—" Rita tried to protest.

"I can't help you," he repeated curtly.

Buster began to thrash about in the back seat, yowling and looking for a path of escape. "Shut up!" the deputy ordered angrily. He swore, banging his open hand on the car roof. "Gonna have a carful of fleas now," he muttered.

He climbed into his vehicle, slammed the door and pulled around Archer's truck. He cut the blue light spinning atop his car, then disappeared up the road in a cloud of dust.

Archer felt Rita's shoulders droop slightly. "He was no help at all," she said in dismay.

Archer's lip curled in disdain. He had a nasty, empty sensation in the pit of his stomach. "They never are."

Cops, he thought bleakly. Just the sight of one—even after all this time—set him on edge.

Rita gave him a questioning glance. "Archer? What's wrong?"

"Nothing," he lied.

HER LITTLE HOUSE SEEMED like a sanctuary to her, cramped and littered as it was. The old couch looked comforting, the crocheted pillows homey and soft. Even the foolish-looking cat clock with its darting eyes and wagging tail was a welcome sight.

But her worktable was cluttered, she hadn't sorted her magazines for weeks, and the tiny kitchen, as usual, seemed crowded with too many objects.

"I'm sorry," she apologized to Archer. "I should have cleaned up. It's just that everything's been so . . . crazy lately. Oh, I am a slob. I'm hopeless."

"Hey," he said, turning to her and touching the tip of her nose with his forefinger. "Don't talk like that. You don't have enough room, that's all. I could build you some shelves, even add a room."

She looked up into his green-blue eyes. They were unreadable yet kind. Oh, she thought helplessly, he was so full of paradoxes. What had somebody once said? "A riddle wrapped in a mystery wrapped in an enigma"—or something like that. That was Archer.

She could tell that for some reason the deputy's presence had bothered him. She could tell, too, by some mysterious insight, that she shouldn't ask him about this—at least, not now.

He had been in trouble, he'd admitted that. He'd sworn he hadn't done anything illegal, and she believed him. He'd said other things had happened during the bad period; he'd lost both parents—and a woman he'd cared for.

She realized she was staring at him, losing herself in his eyes and what they did and did not say. She looked away.

"Peavey's too weird for words," she said, trying to force conversation into something manageable. "How could he say I *propositioned* him? What a lie. Lord, it makes me furious."

"Wishful thinking," Archer said, and put his fingers beneath her chin. He turned her face so that she had to meet his eyes again.

His touch was so gentle, his gaze so kind—yet mysterious—the day had been so fraught with emotion that she had the sudden irrational impulse to cry.

He seemed to understand. He took her face between his hands. "Don't worry. Nobody'd ever believe you propositioned him. A girl like you? A girl as special as you? Never."

"Oh, Archer," she murmured, "I'm in the middle of something I don't understand at all." *I don't understand Peavey. I don't understand what's happened to the cove. I don't understand you and me.*

"He won't hurt you. I swear I won't let him hurt you," he said.

"What about you?" she asked, tears brimming in her eyes. "He could hurt you as easily as me."

"No," he breathed, tilting her face nearer his. "He won't. Haven't you noticed?"

She shook her head. "Noticed what?"

"He doesn't want to mess with me," Archer muttered. "I don't think he wants to mess with Sig Hobbler, either. He's clashed with every one of us. Who'd he call the police on? Not me. And I'm the only one who's ever actually touched him."

"What do you mean?" she asked, her heart starting to beat hard. "He called the police on me and on Joe—what's that mean?"

Archer bent nearer. His thumbs caressed her cheekbones. "He's not scared of you two. Joe's a drunk and you're a woman."

"A woman? That's sexist. He isn't afraid to torment me because I'm a *woman?*"

His fingers stroked the corners of her mouth. "You expected him to be enlightened? Liberated?"

She sighed. "No. But why's he afraid of you and Sig?"

His hands on her face went tensely still. "Because he should be afraid."

"What's he see . . . in the two of you?"

"I don't know. What's there, I guess."

She put her hands on his shoulders. "You think Sig could be dangerous?"

He nodded somberly. "Yeah. And don't ask me how I know. I just know it, all right? So does Peavey."

She gripped his shoulders more tightly. He seemed the one reassuringly solid, strong thing in a shifting, quicksand world. She felt tears biting her eyes again. "What about you? Should Peavey be afraid of you?"

His thumbs touched the corners of her lips again. He stared down at her, his expression troubled. "Yes," he said quietly. "He should."

She closed her eyes, then opened them again. She slid her hands behind his neck and locked them there, hanging on to him tightly. "Archer?"

His features were taut. "Yes?"

She drew in her breath slowly and painfully. She looked into his eyes—eyes that sent such conflicting messages. "Should . . . *I* be frightened of you?"

He shook his head as if he didn't know the answer. But then he nodded. "Probably," he said.

I should be frightened, she thought. *Even he says it.*

But when he bent to take her lips, she rose to meet his kiss, and she wasn't frightened. She felt as if she was coming home, to the place that was safe, right, and where she belonged.

ARCHER WANTED TO TOUCH her all over, to kiss her up and down. He wanted to have her immediately, yet he wanted to do everything as slowly as possible, to savor her like a fine wine.

"Archer . . . ?" she said hesitantly against his lips.

"Yes?" His breath came to him painfully.

"Those men—they make me feel dirty all over."

He held her more tightly, more desperately. Maybe she really didn't want to make love—not after what Peavey had said. He would try to understand. He'd follow her wishes, even if it killed him. It probably would kill him. "I know," he said, and kissed the silky spot where her throat joined her shoulder. "I know. Me, too. I'm sorry, love. Sorry."

Love, he thought with a sinking feeling. It wasn't a word he should use. But it had slipped out, he had said it.

Her lips moved against his ear. "Can I . . . ask you something?" she said, in the same tentative way.

Her warm breath tickled and maddened him. He slid his hands under her T-shirt, spread them over the soft curves of her breasts. "Yes?" he said raggedly.

"If I said let's get in the shower, would you still respect me in the morning?"

Oh, God, Archer thought, his head spinning. The woman was a genius. The woman was a gift from heaven. "Rita," he murmured against her throat, "I would respect you like *crazy*. I might respect you to *death*."

She gave a guilty laugh he found delicious. She drew away from him, took both his hands from her breasts and locked her fingers through his. She looked up at him shyly. She was a strange mixture of boldness and shyness, and it excited him.

He smiled at her a bit drunkenly. That was how he felt—drunk on her, flying wild and high on desire. And she had given him an erection that felt like it should belong to a stallion.

She glanced at his jeans, then to his eyes again and smiled, too, still shy. Wordlessly she backed into the bathroom, her hands linked with his.

It was a tiny bathroom, and she'd spilled bath powder on the edge of the sink. The flowery smell of it tickled his nostrils. He pushed back the sliding door of the shower, not wanting to take his gaze from hers. He turned on the faucet, adjusted the heat.

His hand was wet when he withdrew it, and she took it in her own. She looked so lovely at that moment that his fingers tightened around hers convulsively, and his groin pounded.

"Let me—let me undo your hair," he said in a husky voice. She turned her back. With unsteady fingers he undid the rubber band that held back her wealth of dark hair, freeing it to tumble over her shoulders and down her back.

He caught his breath. "Now," he whispered, "let me undress you."

She turned to face him, her eyes now solemn. She looked at him with such trust that it pinched his heart, as if it were caught by tongs.

Rita, Rita, he thought, *don't trust me so much. I don't deserve it. Letting you do it is wrong.*

But he wanted her too much to dwell on what was right or wrong. He reached beneath her T-shirt, unsnapped her bra. She blinked when she heard the tiny click it made.

He swallowed and started to draw off her oversize shirt. She helped him. It fell softly to the floor. He pushed down her bra straps, and slipped the bra away. It fell atop her shirt.

He stared in hungry wonder at her breasts. They were full and round, pale from being covered by her swimsuit. He could see the light bands the suit's straps had made.

He remembered seeing her in that suit. It was maddeningly modest—a one-piece job—and to make it worse, she usually wore her cutoffs over it, even in the water. He supposed she'd been trying to expose as little flesh as possible because of all the men at the cove.

He had wondered, back then, about her breasts, imagining they were beautiful. They were, with soft brown nipples. He stepped nearer to her, shaping his hands to fit her breasts. He lowered his mouth to hers and kissed her until he was breathless from it.

Then he bent, kissing her breasts, making love to them until she gave a long, shaky sigh. She was a quiet lover. He liked that. She made few sighs or moans, and meant those she made.

He rose, one hand caressing her breasts, the other on her face. She lifted her hand to his shirt and began, with trembling fingers, to undo his buttons.

He had to help her. "You made me shaky all over," she said softly.

"You're doing a pretty good job on me, too," he replied, pulling off his shirt. He reached to unsnap her jeans. "Oh, God," he said from between his teeth, "whose idea was it to invent clothes? Let's become nudists."

She slipped out of her jeans. "Archer," she said, shaking her head so that her long hair swung. "I'm embarrassed. I've got a—a kind of a tummy. It's too big."

She was crazy, he thought with affection and desire. He liked her shape exactly as it was. "It's a lovely tum," he said, stroking its slight curve. "I like women who are shaped like women."

Somehow, they shucked off the rest of their clothes, and when they were both naked, he took her by the hand and drew her under the warm spray of the shower, coaxing her naked body against his.

The water cascaded around them, making their skin silky wet. Their hands glided and flowed over each other. Her drenched hair hung down in streaming ebony waves. Her dark lashes were starred with water, her lips were deliciously wet.

She put her arms around his neck, sighing with pleasure. "You know," she said, "I've never really done this before. I've just read about it. It's . . . nice, isn't it?"

He groaned, but managed to smile. "You really never have? Then you don't know the half of it yet."

She blinked against the water. "I don't?"

"No," he replied, feeling delightfully horny, happy, sensual and wicked. "You don't. Allow me to introduce you to our new friend—Mr. Soap."

He reached for the bar and sudsed his hand, then reached to stroke her where it would give her most pleasure.

"Oh," Rita said, shutting her eyes and quivering. "Hello, Mr. Soap."

"Hello, indeed," whispered Archer and put the bar in her hand.

9

RITA LAY CURLED AGAINST Archer, her back to his chest. He had one arm draped across her, holding her near, and she could feel the warmth and rhythm of his steady breathing against her bare shoulder.

She sighed happily and nestled closer to him. They had dallied in the shower until they were both half-delirious with craving. Then they'd dried each other, still kissing and fondling, and, wrapped together in one towel, kissed and caressed their way into the bedroom.

He was a playful, considerate lover. Her body still throbbed and hummed from his touch; a pleasant heat still warmed her most feminine parts.

He had brought her to a tremulous climax, a sweet bodystorm of pleasure. After his own, he'd held her in his arms a long time, his face buried against her damp hair. He'd even mumbled tender nonsense in her ear, calling her his gypsy girl.

His. She supposed she both was and wasn't *his.* She remembered all those country-western songs about leaving, going away, being gone, gone in the morning. She snuggled still closer to him. He was here now. She would try not to think of tomorrow.

But tomorrow had a way of intruding on her thoughts, and she wondered why he had said perhaps she should be afraid of him. She was so close to loving him that it hurt not to. Was he trying to keep her from even sharper hurt?

Or was he telling her his secrets were deeper and more dangerous than he'd hinted they were? He could carry himself like a dangerous man. He had a peculiar aura of potential violence about him sometimes—peculiar because it struck her as acquired, not innate.

Yet, his arm lay so protectively around her, she couldn't fear him. He seemed fundamentally a *decent* man—good, smart, courageous, sensible. He could be funny, and he could be sensitive. When he made love to her, that was precisely what he did—*made love*. She couldn't call it *screwing* or *banging* or any of those other vulgar terms that Sterling used. No—Sterling screwed and banged. Archer made love.

He had said that he'd been accused of something like game fixing. It had ruined his career as a coach; that's why he was bitter and didn't like to talk about it. He hadn't done anything really wrong. He couldn't have. She had a blind, instinctive faith in him.

I trusted Sterling once, too, she reflected with a sudden frisson of apprehension. *I thought I knew him, too.*

Archer sighed in his sleep and drew her closer. Wearily, she shut her eyes and tried not to think, just to drink in his nearness, his strength, his warmth.

At last she slept.

THEY WERE AWAKENED shortly after dawn by the howling of a dog—shrill, ceaseless and mournful.

"What?" Rita said groggily, raising herself up on one elbow. She opened a slat in the blinds and peered out. It was foggy, and the dog's wailing was ghostly, like a banshee's.

"What the hell?" Archer sat up yawning. He put a hand on Rita's bare shoulder.

He, too, peered out the window, then frowned and swore under his breath. "It's light. I should have been gone hours ago. At least, it's foggy. God, it's like pea soup out there. Nobody'll see—"

The dog keened more wildly than before. Rita looked at Archer. "Something's wrong," she said. "I know which dog that is—it's Trilly. She's never carried on like that before. Something's *wrong*."

She threw off the sheet, snatched up the bath towel, wrapped it around herself, Indian-blanket-style, and went to her chest of drawers.

The dog howled an even eerier plaint, high and unearthly.

"What are you doing?" Archer asked.

"Getting dressed," she said. "Something's going on out there."

Archer started to protest, but the dog's cries were so desperate, he feared Rita was right. He wiped the sleep from his eyes. "I'll go," he offered.

He rose naked from the bed, and Rita cast down her eyes. He almost smiled, in spite of his sleepiness, in spite of the weird howling. After all they had done as lovers, she was shy about *seeing* him?

He made his way into the bathroom, pulled on his jeans, put on his shirt, buttoned it halfway up, but didn't bother to tuck it in. He didn't bother with socks, either, just stepped into his running shoes and was lacing them when Rita appeared at the bathroom door.

She wore jeans and a blue work shirt, its sleeves rolled up. "I'm going with you."

He wasn't talkative in the morning, and he didn't want to argue. And the damn dog was still keening and mourning as if the world were coming to an end.

Rita, whose imagination ran toward the dramatic, looked worried. "Maybe we're going to have an earthquake. They say animals act strange before an earthquake. Did you know that Arkansas is located over a bigger fault than the one under California?"

He raised his hand to quieten her. "No. No disaster dares happen until after I have coffee. But, God—what *is* it with that dog?"

He headed for the living room, with Rita at his side. She opened the door, and all they could see was the grayish white thickness of the fog. It was as if someone had packed the world in dense cotton. Somewhere near, the dog bayed out its sorrow.

Archer reached for her hand. "You got your shoes on?" he asked. "It's going to be damp out here."

"I put on my shoes."

"Wonders never cease," he said.

He found himself heading for Sig's yard and drawing Rita behind him. He narrowed his eyes against the fog. He could see only from six to ten feet ahead. Sometimes, fog gathered over the lake at night, thickening until it blanketed the shore and crept into the mountain valleys.

He heard the roar of a truck motor coming to life. He squinted. The truck's lights switched on. He could make out Sig Hobbler's pickup truck, then the shadowy figure of Hobbler himself.

"I heard the dog," Archer said. He and Rita weren't that far from the man, but the fog made Archer feel as if he were calling over a long distance. He couldn't make out Sig's face, only that he held a dark object in his arms. "Is something wrong?"

"Yeah," Sig answered with quiet bitterness. "Something's wrong." Archer stepped nearer, drawing Rita with him. His stomach gave a nasty pitch of surprise.

Sig held a dog—a dark, medium-size mongrel. It lay almost motionless in his arms. It whined and stirred feebly.

Rita's fingers tightened around his. He turned to her, saw her hand fly to her mouth. "Oh, Sig," she breathed. "What happened?"

"Somebody poisoned my dogs is what," he said with virulence. "Poisoned four of 'em. All but Trilly. For some reason Trilly didn't get none."

"Poisoned them?" Rita said in horror. "Oh, Sig—is that Blackie you've got?"

Archer saw the shadowy man clasp the shadowy dog closer to his chest. "Blackie's the littlest, and he's the worstest off. I can't talk. I gotta get these dogs to the vet. He's waitin' for us. Jesus, I'll kill the skunk who done this. I *will*."

"Sig—what can I do to help?" Rita asked.

Sig lowered the dog's body into the truck bed. "You can't help, Rita. You done made your choice."

Now what in hell does that mean? Archer wondered. He didn't like Hobbler's tone.

"I'll help you load up the dogs," Archer said without emotion.

"No!" Sig retorted sharply. "They's all sick. They'll snap at you."

"I can handle a sick dog," Archer countered, just as sharply. He saw a dark shape twisting on the ground. He bent, and took it, as gently as he could, by the scruff of the neck, then scooped up its body with his other arm. He laid the dog next to Blackie in the truck bed.

Hobbler was trying to soothe a panting dog that lay writhing on the ground. Archer could see it only dimly. But he could make out a fourth dog, almost motionless, lying near the truck.

He bent to it. Its sides were spasming, its head jerking convulsively. "I'm sorry, pup," he whispered to the dog. Carefully he lifted it and put it beside the others in the truck bed.

Trilly still howled as if her heart were breaking and the world were ending. "Do you want us to keep Trilly?" Archer asked, looking down at the sick dogs. "If somebody's put out poison . . ."

Hobbler was quiet for a tense minute. "Why should I trust you? After what you done?"

Archer shifted his shoulders tensely, trying to suppress a surge of aggression. "What do you mean? I didn't do anything."

"You cut Peavey's fence," Sig said with contempt. "You started all this . . . hatefulness."

Archer's spine stiffened at the charge. "I didn't cut his goddamn fence. I wouldn't touch it."

"Yeah?" Sig returned sarcastically. "Well, I know *I* didn't. And Joe—he's too worthless. He don't even own wire cutters. He don't own tools. He's too worthless. You're the one with all the fancy tools."

The accusation filled Archer's blood with chips of ice. He didn't answer it, he didn't deny it. He knew Hobbler was too angry to listen.

"I'm lockin' Trilly in the house," Sig said. "And if these dogs die, I'll find the man who done it and I'll kill him. I swear it."

"Sig, don't talk like that," Rita begged. She stepped forward and touched his arm. The fog was clearing slightly, and Archer could make out Sig's face as he stared down at Rita's hand. His expression was full of anger and confusion, and he looked as if he might weep. He glanced up for a moment into Rita's eyes, his own almost tearful.

Then he turned and for a moment stared wildly at Archer. He muttered something Archer couldn't make out, grabbed Trilly by the collar and dragged her into his house, still howling. When he came back out, he spoke to neither of them, just climbed in his truck and drove off.

Archer put his arm around Rita. She turned to him and pressed her forehead against his chest, hiding her face. He knew she felt badly about the dogs.

He held her tightly. A wave of foreboding swept over him. It was as eerie as Trilly's howling, which they could still hear, muted, from the house.

We should get out of here. We need to get out of here, he thought. *There's a bad moon on the rise.*

RITA *TRIED* TO MAKE Archer breakfast. Her effort was humble and far from successful—instant coffee and toast and peanut butter.

"I like my toast burnt," Archer insisted. "The body needs carbon. We're life-forms based on the carbon-chain molecule."

She knew he was just being kind again. "Maybe Sig's heard about my cooking," she said unhappily. "He probably thinks I'm the poisoner. I gave them my leftovers."

She set down her overdone toast, put her elbow on the table and her face in her hand. "Oh, God," she said. "I shouldn't joke about the poison. The dogs. The poor dogs."

He was silent a moment. Then he reached across the small table, touched her arm. "Hey," he said gruffly, "I know you feel bad. You were just letting off steam, that's all. Jokes do that sometimes."

"Black humor?"

"Exactly."

She shook her head tiredly. "Who'd poison the dogs? The poor dogs."

Archer rose and made himself more instant coffee. "Maybe they'll be all right. He had a vet waiting. Who'd do it? Well, you and I showed up, wondering what was wrong and willing to help. Who didn't?"

She looked up at him, took a bite of cold, blackened toast. "Peavey didn't. And Joe Johanssen didn't."

"Right," Archer said with irony and sat down across from her again.

"Peavey's *always* hated the dogs," Rita mused, pushing her toast away. "Joe resented them more all the time. And last night Buster bit him."

"Right," Archer said.

"And now Sig's accusing you of cutting the fence," Rita said, not quite believing the ill luck of it. "Why would he think you'd do it?"

Archer shrugged. "He resents me. And like he says, he doesn't think Joe's man enough. Who do *you* think did it?"

"Well, I know you didn't cut the fence," she said. "You wouldn't do such a thing. And I really hoped Sig didn't. I thought he listened to reason when I talked to him. So that leaves Joe. He had the strongest motive—the fence affects him the most. What do *you* think?"

"I agree." Archer stared into the black depths of his coffee. "Only I don't know Johanssen that well. Does he have the balls?"

It was Rita's turn to shrug. "I don't know. He's different when he's drinking—more aggressive. Oh, Archer, it's a mess."

He gave her a worried look. "Maybe I'm making it worse. I shouldn't be here this time of morning. They'll all know about you and me."

"They all know anyway," she said with resignation. But she knew that if Sig resented Archer, it was because of her.

"I feel better when we're together," he said quietly.

It was her turn to look away. "Yes. So do I."

"Nobody phoned you last night," he said.

She shook her head. *No. They knew you were here.*

"Nobody left any flowers. Or dead birds."

No, she thought. *They knew you were here.*

He was silent a moment. "We could go away for a while. Just get out of here. It . . . might be best."

The idea was tempting, but she couldn't accept it. "Where would we go?"

"I don't know. It wouldn't matter."

She put her hands around her coffee mug and gripped it tightly. "This is my home. It's all I've got left. That and my work. I have work to do here. So do you."

He bowed his head ruefully. "I figured you'd say that. You aren't the kind who runs away, are you?"

"I walked away from one thing in my life," she said, taking a deep breath. "My marriage. I don't want to make a habit of it."

"Yeah," he said, but there was a bitterness in his tone. "I suppose. You can't keep walking away, can't keep running. At some point you stop, and face it."

"Yes."

He drained his coffee and set down the mug. He glanced out the picture window. "The fog's thinning. The sun's coming out. I should get to work."

She nodded. "Yes. Me, too. I've got a window to do for this house in town. It's a huge project."

He gave her a restrained smile. He started to get up. She rose, too. She went to the window and looked at the sun catchers. She wasn't overly fond of the small pieces, but they kept food on the table, and some had charm.

She reached for one of the sun catchers—a milky white horse with a flowing mane and tail. It had been one of the most difficult of the sun catchers to make; the separate pieces were complexly shaped, delicate and hard to cut.

She moved back to the table and thrust it at him. "Here," she said. "Take this. Please."

He frowned down at it, but took it in his hand carefully. "It's . . . nice. Thank you. But why?"

"Because," she said, staring out at the foggy lake. "Because you didn't want to get involved in any of this, but you did. You did it for me. And every knight should have a white horse."

She didn't want to look at him because she felt too emotional, too vulnerable. For a moment he was silent. Then he said, "To be a knight all you need is the right damsel."

It wasn't a typical thing for him to say, so she tried to make light of it. "In distress?" she suggested. "Well, I'm certainly overqualified in that department lately."

"No," he said, stepping behind her. He bent and kissed her on the back of her neck, lightly and briefly. Too lightly and too briefly, she thought with yearning, but if he'd taken more time, they'd have ended up in bed again, she knew.

"No," he said quietly. "Just the right damsel."

Then he left her cabin, and she was alone. The crowded little room seemed impossibly empty without him.

ARCHER WALKED DOWN the incline to his own house. The fog was lifting from the slope, but still hung over the lake and the shoreline. He stared out at Patterson's dock. His eyes narrowed. The dock was *gone*.

First, amazement swept over him, then disbelief, then anger. It was gone. *How?*

He stalked toward the shore. Where the dock had been, now there was nothing in the shifting veils of fog. He looked down at the ground. Two thick metal stakes had once been driven deep into the earth. Attached to the stakes had been steel cables, and the cables had held the dock to the shore.

Where the stakes had been, there were now only holes gouged into the damp ground. The grass around them was trampled.

Archer swore. Somebody had jacked up the stakes and set the dock adrift. There was a moderate wind this morning, as there'd been last night, and it had probably lasted all night long.

The damned dock could have drifted half the night. It could be miles down the lake. It could have banged into another dock, a houseboat, a spill of rocks. God only knew how damaged it might be. Or where Archer would find it. Or how he'd retrieve it.

He stood, rubbing the back of his neck and gritting his teeth. He swore again.

He'd have to call the Corps of Engineers. The lake was a man-made one, created by damming the White River. The Engineers were in charge of it. He raked his hand through his hair. *Damn.* This was a complication he didn't need.

He heard footsteps, soft and rapid, behind him. He turned and saw Rita running toward him. He caught her in his arms, and they both stared at the foggy lake, at the place where the dock should have been.

"Oh, no," she breathed. "What happened?"

"I don't know." He felt a muscle twitch in his jaw. "Somebody pulled up the stakes."

"You're sure? It couldn't have been an accident?"

He shrugged in disgust. "It's possible. But not probable. No. We've got a wave of vandalism out here, is what I think."

In silence they stared out at the empty water, the drifting scarves of fog.

She was the first to speak. "Will you call the police?"

His muscles tensed at the word *police*. He wondered if she noticed. His stomach contracted more tightly, and the taste of gall welled up in the back of his throat.

"No," he said shortly. "I can't prove anything."

"But—" she began, putting her hand on his arm.

"No," he said more sharply than before. "Look, I'm going to call the Corps of Engineers. I've gotta track the damn thing down. It'll probably take me all day to get it back. There's a guy who builds docks, over by the marina. He's got a boat powerful enough to tow one. I'll have to hire him."

He was thinking out loud, trying to solve the problem of the dock so he wouldn't have to think about the police. But he couldn't keep from thinking of Rita.

Sighing harshly, he looked down at her. "Somebody's getting ugly," he said. "*Seriously* ugly. Look . . . I'll be chasing the dock. You—you take care of yourself, understand?"

She stared up at him, and he could see the alarm in her eyes. But her voice was steady, her expression full of resolve. "I will. I can. Don't worry about me. But, Archer, after the dogs and everything, don't you think we *ought* to call the police?"

"No," he said, adamant. "Come on. I'll walk you home."

She nodded, linked her arm through his. Together they walked slowly up the slope. "Who do you think it was?" she asked, staring down at the grass.

"Take your pick," he answered cynically. He didn't know which one. Peavey hated him, but Peavey hated everyone. Sig Hobbler believed he'd vandalized Peavey's fence. Joe Johanssen believed Archer had badmouthed him. And all three resented him over Rita.

For a man who had been determined not to get involved, he was getting in deeper all the time.

RITA WORKED DESULTORILY, making the pattern for her stained-glass window. The design was a complex one of grapes and vines and leaves.

She cut out the pieces with her usual precision, but found it hard to concentrate. Archer was gone. He had called the Corps of Engineers. The dock had been reported five miles away, badly banged up and wedged against an outcropping of rock. Archer had looked grim when he left.

Joe Johanssen had left for work. He'd gone to his car, head down, as if he didn't want to meet anyone's eye. Rita was alone at the cove with Peavey.

Peavey was in his front yard, attacking a grove of young mimosa trees with his chain saw. She turned the radio on, hoping to drown out the grating shriek of the machine.

But she couldn't help herself. Sometimes she went to the window, parted the blinds and stole a glance at him. He was cutting trees as if possessed. Sweat dripped from him.

He'd taken off his shirt, and he wore the style of undershirt she thought of as an old man's, the sleeveless kind. He had a pale body but was surprisingly well-muscled for a man his age. *Muscled enough to pry those dock stakes out of the ground,* she thought.

Around his head he'd tied a black bandanna. It gave him a surprisingly sinister look, like an aging Ninja. And once he'd looked up from his slaughter of trees and directly at her house. A look that might have been pain or ecstasy shone in his eyes.

Startled, she had let the blind fall back into place and looked no more—because the moment she saw that inexplicable glitter in his eyes, she realized what he was doing: *He was cutting down every tree in his front yard that stood between his house and hers.*

"Oh, God," she said to herself in despair. He'd have a perfectly clear view of her house—almost. Her yard was large, but its trees were few. Only the apple tree would be left standing between her and Peavey.

Her head ached. She rubbed her brow and sat at her worktable again. She took a sheet of mottled green glass and began cutting leaf pieces. She forced herself to think of the glass, not Peavey.

At shortly after one o'clock she was still cutting, and her stack of sharp-edged scraps was growing. The phone rang unexpectedly, startling her.

She answered and was surprised to hear the chirpy voice of Katy McInty, the real-estate agent.

"Listen, sweetie," Katy said in her brisk way. "I may have something for you. On this Peavey character. Got a pencil handy?"

Rita did.

"All right. Cindy, the secretary, remembers Harry saying that Peavey moved here from Lyttonville. You know Lyttonville?"

Rita knew. It was a small city thirty miles away. It was bisected by the state's busiest highway, and its main industry was chicken processing. Chicken trucks constantly rumbled in and out, and the odor of chicken always enveloped it.

"Well," Katy said, "Peavey's from Lyttonville. We've got an office there. Our company didn't handle the sale of his old house, but I had them snoop. I've got his old address. And the name of the people who bought his house. *And* their phone number. You can give 'em a dingle. Maybe they'll give you some poop on him."

"Katy, you're a *gem*," Rita said. "You're number one. I owe you a lunch for this."

"At least," Katy agreed cheerfully, and gave her a name and phone number: Mr. and Mrs. William B. Bitcon, 555-3637.

Rita thanked her again, hung up, then anxiously punched the phone buttons, hoping that someone in the Bitcon household would be home.

She was in luck. A woman answered mechanically. "Bitcon residence. Teresa speaking." In the background, children's voices mingled with the sound of a television.

Rita felt suddenly awkward now that she had made the connection, but she introduced herself and explained her situation. "I live out by the lake. There's sort of a little cluster of us—you know, we share the same road, the same water and phone and electric lines."

"Yes?" Teresa Bitcon sounded suspicious, impatient.

"Well," Rita said. "We have this new neighbor. He's been here about a month. His name is George Peavey, and I wondered if—"

"Oh, *God*, say no more," Teresa Bitcon cried. "So you got him, eh? I suppose somebody had to. But at least he's not our problem anymore—praise be."

"Problem?" Rita echoed, her attention pricking up. "He was a problem? Because he's certainly been a prob—"

"Problem?" Teresa Bitcon repeated with passion. "I'll tell you *problem*. This is the first house we ever bought, right? I look at this house, and I fall in love with it, okay? We offer the asking price. Everything should go smooth as silk. We didn't know we were dealing with Mr. Psycho."

"Mr.—Psycho?"

Teresa Bitcon launched into a long, complicated story of how difficult Peavey had been to deal with, how impossible it had seemed that they were ever actually going to close the deal. The tale was rife with incidents of Peavey's unpredictable temper and just plain spitefulness.

"My husband said after what we went through to get this house, he'll divorce me if I ever complain about it. He was ready to divorce me because I was the one that got us mixed up in the whole mess—God!"

"I take it the neighbors don't miss him," Rita said, probing.

"Listen, honey, when that old devil left, there was dancing in the streets. If I knew then what I know *now*, I never would have gone near him. No, ma'am."

"What's wrong with him?" Rita asked. "Why's he act the way he does? What's his story?"

There was a pregnant pause. The television in the background jangled with cartoon music. One child laughed. Another squealed.

"Listen," Teresa Bitcon said darkly. "There's something...not right about that man. Always has been. And he's been worse since his mother died. *She* could control him. Keep him on his medications and stuff. You know, gently walk him to the cracker factory when he got *really* out of hand."

"Cracker factory?" Rita said in alarm. "You mean . . . like a sanitarium or something?"

"*Yeah*, exactly. He's got this chemical imbalance or something in his head, okay? So he should take these pills to keep his chemicals straight. His mother saw he did, but she's not here now. He's got—my neighbor's got a name for it—it—borderline . . . borderline . . . What do you call it?"

"Borderline personality disorder?" Rita asked warily. The term was the politically correct way of saying someone was poised, none too surely, on the edge of sanity.

"Right. He's not sick enough to put away—or to keep put away. He can take care of himself—up to a point."

"Did he ever work?" Rita asked.

"When he was younger. He's smart—real smart—but he could never keep a job. Because he can't get along with people. His mother always took care of him. God, he's probably got her body stuffed and sitting in a rocker in the attic or something. I wouldn't doubt it."

Rita's alarm grew. "So he's living on what his mother left him?"

"Pretty much. She left him some kind of trust fund, so he could be independent. She told him never to sell the house. He didn't listen. He acted like the traffic in this town was created just to persecute *him*. If the air smells like chickens, it's to annoy *him*. If he picks fights with all the neighbors, it's because they're all against *him*. Nothing's ever old George's fault. Oh, no."

"He thought he'd be happier if he could get out of the neighborhood? The city?"

"Sure. 'Cause nothing's his fault, right?" Teresa said sarcastically. "But a guy like him? He'll never be happy. Not one person in the neighborhood was speaking to him by the time he left. Not *one*. And most of them were new neighbors. The old ones, he drove out."

"But—but—" Rita stammered. "Is he always just this awful, unpleasant person? Or can he be dangerous?"

There was another ominous pause. "Dangerous? Yeah."

Rita swallowed. "How dangerous?"

"First thing," Teresa said, "he's got a genius—like, this evil genius, see? For setting people against each other. Bill and I, we didn't know. We walked into it cold. He likes trouble. He gets attention that way."

"You said that's only the first thing," Rita prodded. "Is there more? Is there worse?"

"Yeah. Once he got in a fight with a neighbor, took a tire iron to him, tried to beat him. He got to take a little rest in the rest home for *that* one. They should have thrown his sorry butt in jail."

Rita swallowed again. "Did he hurt the man?"

"Yeah, he *hurt* him," Teresa said. "But that's not his usual style. No. When he gets rough, he picks on women."

"Women?"

"Yeah, like I said, if I knew *then*—his eyes always did give me the creeps, you know? He's got creepy eyes."

"What's—what's he done to women?"

"Look, I don't want to, like, alarm you, right? But I won't mince words. They put him away twice more—for rape. Once for rape. Once for attempted rape."

Rita's stomach lurched. "Oh, God."

"He's got a pattern, they say," Teresa said. "First he starts fixating on this woman. Then he starts calling her. That's how it happened both times. Just . . . these calls. And he *watches*. Both times it was a girl in the neighborhood. He kept calling them. At night, usually."

Rita felt even sicker, tension knotting her innards. She put her hand on her midsection.

"The first one—that's the one he actually raped—you know what he did? Only nobody realized why he was doing it at the time."

"What?" Rita managed to say.

"She lived next door to him. He got out in his yard and cut down all the *trees* in his yard that blocked his view of her house. Nobody figured that's why he was doing it until it was too late. Now is that sick—or what?"

Rita could make no reply. She sat, numb, gripping the phone and staring at nothing at all. From outside, she could hear the snarl of Peavey's chain saw.

10

"So what do they do?" Teresa continued in disgust. "He rapes this first woman, they put him in the hospital. For five years, right? Wrong. He's out in three. The second time, attempted rape? Back to the hospital—he's out in a year. That was—what?—four years ago. Now I ask you, what kind of system is that?"

Rita could make no answer.

"And that's not the guy's only problem. See, he's got these health problems—allergies—and they make him bitter. And he likes to sue people. He tried to sue the people next door for having a *pear tree*, for Pete's sake. He said it made him sneeze, it was a health hazard. One spring, he pulled up all a neighbor's tulips. Same thing."

"I—I—" Rita began. The chain saw suddenly stopped its whining buzz. Its silence seemed ominous.

"And," Teresa went on, clearly eager to vent her anger, "that's not all. Every once in a while, he'd decide he'd had it. Then he'd pull *another* kind of stunt. In my opinion, it was just to get attention. But the neighbors said you'd hear the sirens coming, and you knew good old George was up to his tricks again."

"Sirens?" Rita questioned, horrified. "You mean he set fires? He's a—a pyromaniac, too?"

"No, no, they say it'd usually start with this burst of hyperactivity, then—" A crash and a child's shriek pierced the background noise. Wails of pain quickly followed.

"What have you done to your brother?" Teresa cried in an accusing voice. "Oh my God, his *nose* is bleeding. Goodbye."

Teresa crashed the receiver down with such force that Rita winced. Her ear ringing, she set down the phone. She put her fingers to her mouth and gnawed on her thumbnail, a habit she'd broken years ago.

Realizing what she was doing, she jerked her hand away. "Don't panic," she said aloud.

The man who bought the house behind me is a convicted rapist. He called his victim up at night. He cut down the trees between his house and hers. He's calling me up. He's cutting the trees down. Don't panic.

She sucked in her lower lip and went to the window. Peavey had disappeared from his yard. So had all the young trees that had screened her house from his. He had made a haphazard stack of unevenly sawed logs. Firewood. Didn't he know mimosa wasn't good firewood?

She wasn't thinking straight, she rebuked herself. Firewood didn't matter. What mattered was Peavey. He had a borderline personality disorder. He was obviously not taking his medication. He was not responsible for his acts.

She thought of calling the police. But what could they do? They would tell her it was no crime for a man to cut down trees in his own yard. They would tell her it didn't matter what Peavey had done in the past; he had broken no laws here—yet.

She wished fervently that Archer was back. She decided the least she could do was warn the others who lived at the cove. She got out the telephone book and looked up the number of the health-food store where Sig Hobbler worked. She hoped she wasn't making a mistake.

He didn't seem happy to hear from her. He sounded distant. She asked how the dogs were. He replied that they were all going to make it, except maybe for Blackie. But Blackie, he said almost sullenly, still had a chance.

"If I find out who done this, I'll *kill* him," Sig threatened. "And I'll tell you something. I been in a war. I been in Nam. I've killed men. And by God, I can do it again."

Rita's head hurt worse. "Sig," she pleaded, "don't talk like that. We all have to be very calm. I've found out something—about Peavey. Listen."

She explained, as quickly and clearly as she could, what Teresa Bitcon had told her. She did not tell Sig about the rapes. She told him only that there had been violence, and that Peavey had been hospitalized—more than once.

Sig was silent for a long moment. "You don't have to be afraid of him," he said at last.

"Sig, that's—that's not the point," she said. "I'm afraid of the trouble he's making. He's not really in control of himself. So we have to be very, very careful that he doesn't provoke any of us into—"

"Rita," Sig said, and his voice sounded weary, "I told you once I'd take care of you. I...keep my word. But the man who hurt my dogs—"

"Sig, please. *Listen.* Don't take this into your own hands. Call the police."

"The police won't do nothing. 'Specially if none of them dogs die. The most the police do, they'll send out some fool deputy, like that kid last night, to *talk* to people. I can take care of my own."

She put her hand to her forehead. She'd forgotten how hard it was to reason with Sig, to make him understand.

"Sig, *please,*" she begged.

"And I ain't makin' no accusations—yet," Sig said grimly. "I don't know if it was Peavey. It could have been Joe. It could even be that feller...you took up with."

"It wasn't Archer. I'll swear to it."

"Yeah," he answered with sadness and bitterness. "I guess you can."

A hot wave of embarrassment swept over her. "We've all got to keep our heads. *That's* what's important. Goodbye."

She hung up, shaking her head. Sig was off in his own reality, and she didn't know if she'd reached him or not.

"Maybe I did make things worse," she muttered. Then she rubbed her brow again and said in disgust, "And now I'm talking to myself. Hello, Rita. How are you? Gone 'round the bend, like everybody else?"

She heard the chain saw start roaring again and straightened in her chair as if she'd heard a gunshot. She rose and went to the window.

Now Peavey was on the south side of his yard. He was attacking the big pine that he had fenced in. Today he had such wild energy, he seemed possessed. She realized sickly that this time he was probably going to bring the tree down.

And Joe would be enraged, Joe would be beating on his door again. Who knew what Joe might do?

Archer had warned her not to get involved, but what could she do? Joe Johanssen should know that Peavey was not a rational man, could be violent. For his own safety, Joe should keep his distance, no matter how Peavey provoked him.

She looked up the number of the post-office substation. Taking a deep breath, she pushed the numbers. Joe's supervisor answered, then put Joe on the line.

Joe seemed far more shaken by her news than Sig had been. "Rita," he said, his voice trembling, "I've gotta tell you something. Somebody was in my house last night. While I was asleep."

"What?" she said in disbelief. "In your house?"

"Listen, Rita," Joe said. "I had a couple of guns. They're gone. I can't even protect myself."

"Guns?" She was horrified. "How many?"

"Two," Joe said. "A .22 rifle and a shotgun. I always kept 'em in the gun rack. Anybody who walked up on my porch could look in the front window and see 'em."

Rita shook her head numbly. She remembered Joe's guns. He used them to kill snakes, which he feared and hated. Only last week Joe had shot a copperhead in his front yard. Then he had sat on his porch, drinking until his shaking stopped.

"Joe," she said, her throat constricted, "call the police. You have to."

He was silent. "No. I—I didn't have permits for 'em. I—I bought 'em from a guy in a bar one night, years back. He wanted the money for drinks. They got— They had the serial numbers filed off. I think they were stolen. I . . . wasn't thinking straight, I'd had a few too many. I don't want the hassle."

"Joe," she said desperately, "you've *got* to tell. A break-in? Stolen guns? This is serious."

"They didn't break in. They just . . . walked in."

"But *how?*"

"Oh, hell, Rita," Joe said miserably. "I didn't lock the door. I wasn't thinking straight then, either. Jesus. What am I gonna do? I'll buy another one. I gotta have some protection. Hell, that crazy Peavey could of took it. So could Sig. Maybe he thought I was gonna shoot his damn dogs or something—he's already got his own gun out. Oh, *hell.*"

"No," she said quickly, "don't buy another gun. We'd be better off if nobody out here had a gun."

"Well, Sig's got one, and maybe he's got three now. Or maybe he and Peavey both have guns now. This—this boy-friend of yours— He's probably got one, too."

"Don't call him my boyfriend," she said. The term sounded stupid and childish to her. "We're . . . friends."

Joe's voice went bitter. "You're more than 'friends.' And maybe he'd *better* have a gun. Maybe Peavey's gonna go after *him.*"

The suggestion shocked her. "After Archer? Why?"

"To get him out of the way. I saw him watching you two on the dock the other day. When you and that Smith kissed, I saw how Peavey acted. I don't even want to tell you what he did—"

"Oh, Lord," she said unhappily. She didn't want to hear, didn't want to imagine.

"He was pretty excited," Joe said sarcastically. "If you get my meaning. And if I were you, I wouldn't be quite so open about—"

"This conversation isn't about my morals," she answered. "It's about all of us staying cool and not overreacting to Peavey—or each other. Promise me, Joe, no matter what he does, you won't let him provoke you. You'll be playing right into his hands."

"Yeah, sure, the bastard ruins my life, and I don't get provoked, sure, sure."

"Joe—"

"Rita, I'm not stupid. I understand what you're saying. The guy is dangerous. All right, I'll keep my distance."

It was the best she could get from him. And she knew, deep inside, that he might not keep his word. Especially if he started drinking. And there was no doubt that he'd drink.

Feeling tired, she hung up the phone. She heard a loud, ringing crash and knew what it was. Peavey had brought the beautiful old tree down, at last. She closed her eyes.

She didn't want to look at him again, but she had to; it was as if he had cast an evil spell on her. She went to the window, parted the blind. The pine had indeed been cut, and so inexpertly it had nearly hit Peavey's fence. Its limbs still quivered from the impact.

She wondered, bleakly, about the animals that might have lived in the tree—the birds, the squirrels. Seeing it lying there was like seeing an old friend's corpse. She could remember that tree from her earliest childhood.

Then Peavey did an odd thing. He walked to the tree, staring at it. His shoulders slouched in fatigue, but a triumphant smile twisted his mouth. Then he kicked the tree, viciously and repeatedly, as if it were the body of a fallen enemy and he was desecrating it even more. He kicked and kicked, grinning the whole time.

She had to let the blind slip back in place and close her eyes again. Her heart was beating so hard that it hurt.

SIG ARRIVED BACK AT the cove at precisely five thirty-five, as he did every working night. Rita kept her blinds parted slightly so she could watch what was going on. Archer hadn't yet returned.

Sig had none of the dogs with him. He led Trilly out of the house on a chain. He let the dog relieve itself, then fastened the chain to his front doorknob.

He brought out a microwave dinner in a plastic serving dish and set it on the cable-spool table. He also carried his shot-

gun. He leaned the gun against the doorframe. Then he sat
in his broken chair and ate, Trilly chained safely at his side.
His eyes traveled from house to house, from Peavey's to Joe
Johanssen's, to Archer's, to hers.

Since Peavey had brought the tree down, he'd stayed inside, keeping to himself like a hermit crab. Joe Johanssen arrived at the cove shortly after seven. He got out of his car and
stared at the fallen tree. His expression was both angry and
aggrieved.

Then he reached into the back seat of his car and took out
a long package wrapped in brown paper. It was a gun, Rita
knew, and her heart sank.

Joe threw a defiant look in Sig's direction. Sig returned his
stare so coldly that Joe dropped his eyes, and climbed the
steps, his head down. He went into his house and didn't come
out again.

The evening was oppressively hot, and Rita hoped the heat
would keep Peavey and Joe inside. But Joe was drinking, she
was certain. If they were all lucky, maybe he'd drink himself
unconscious.

But if they were unlucky, he would booze himself into
righteous rage and then God only knew what would happen. She wished, for the hundredth time, that Archer was
back. Tension hung over the cove almost as palpably as the
fog had done that morning.

It was nearly dark when she saw a boat chugging up the
lake, a battered dock in tow. It had to be Archer, and she ran
outside and down to the shore.

As the boat drew nearer, she could see the light from the
rising full moon glinting on Archer's fair hair. She stood on
tiptoe and waved. He waved back.

But when the boat neared shore, Rita saw that Archer was
obviously bone weary, and the bearded man steering the boat
looked fatigued, too. Archer hadn't shaved, his clothes were
wet and muddy. One shirt sleeve was torn halfway off at the
shoulder, the knees of both jeans were ripped. His forearm
had an ugly red scratch almost a foot long.

He gave her a tired smile as the boat pulled up to her dock. He held a steel cable in one bruised and scraped hand. He made his way ashore, uncoiling the cable behind him.

He gave her a brief but fierce embrace, kissing her. His stubble grated against her jaw, but she liked it; it was *his* stubble.

"I shouldn't touch you," he said gruffly. "I'm a mess."

"What happened? You look like you've been in a war."

He released her. "I have. With this damn dock. It was wedged so tight in those rocks we needed five guys to get it out, and there were only two of us. Then the floats were ripped off one whole side—it's a long story."

"At least you're home."

"It's not over yet." He reached into his back pocket and pulled out a set of keys. "We're going to have to stake this thing. This is the key to the toolshed. Can you bring me the sledgehammer, baby?"

She smiled slightly because no man had ever before called her "baby." She unlocked the toolshed, marveled at the number and neatness of the tools, located the sledgehammer, and lugged it back to him. She was amazed at its weight, but he handled it easily.

He'd set a spike through the cable's eye, tapped it hard into place. Then he stood and pounded in the stake. Even tired, he was an extraordinarily strong man.

He wiped his brow. "This is a long way from done," he told her, regret in his eyes. "I'm sorry. You ought to go back. I'll be up as soon as I can."

She touched his arm, squeezed it. "I'll be waiting," she said softly. She walked back up the hill, sorry that he had put in such a punishing day.

Sig sat smoking on his porch. He looked at her with a vague, sad expression, but said nothing. Neither Joe nor Peavey was in sight, for which she thanked God.

The least she could do was feed Archer decently, for once. It was pleasant to think of something as mundane as food.

Using one of her grandmother's old cookbooks, she concocted a tuna-and-potato casserole that, to her surprise, looked *good*. She made an impromptu salad from the to-matoes Joe Johanssen had given her, mixing them with on-ions and a simple dressing, also from her grandmother's cookbook. To keep occupied, she even managed to put to-gether a coffee cake that neither burned nor fell apart.

Archer didn't appear until almost nine o'clock. He'd showered and changed into clean jeans and a blue T-shirt. He had shaved, his still-damp hair was combed into place, but he looked worn, and he was favoring his right leg.

She sat him down and fed him, finding it pleasant to hover and fuss over him. *God help me*, she thought in perplexity. *I'm getting domestic. This has got to stop.*

It did stop, when she sat across from him and began tell-ing him the day's events. Fatigue had etched Archer's face. Now anger and apprehension warred with it.

He slapped the table in frustration when he heard that Peavey had been put away at least three times for violent ep-isodes, then freed again.

"Damn the stupid law," he said with passion. "What kind of asinine system lets a guy like this run loose?" He swore and stabbed up his last bite of tuna casserole.

The news about Joe's stolen guns disturbed him even more. "Something's going to happen," he said from between his teeth. "Somebody's going to get hurt. I can tell it, I can feel it. I can almost *smell* it, dammit."

"I didn't know what to do," she said with a helpless ges-ture. "I thought I should tell Sig and Joe. That they should know about him—you know? Was it a mistake?"

He put his hand over hers. "No. You're right. You had to let them know. I mean, the guy's a walking time bomb."

"And he's got everybody at each other's throats, just like Teresa Bitcon said." She put her face between her hands. "He's clever, you know? Teresa said he was like an evil ge-nius. He's keeping everybody off-balance, suspecting every-body else."

"I wished you'd talked to this Teresa person more."

"So do I," she said, lifting her head and looking into his eyes. *They look so sad*, she thought. *So worried. And so tired.*

She squeezed his hand. "I tried to call her again. But they were gone. I got the baby-sitter. She said they wouldn't be back until after midnight. Maybe later."

He gave a long, rough sigh. He took her hand in both of his. His were so scraped and scratched that Rita ached for him. "Your poor hands," she said, and stroked his bruised knuckles.

"Forget my hands," he said, bending closer. "Rita, let's get out of here. Now. Tonight. I don't want you near that guy. And it's all getting too . . . explosive."

She looked into his eyes again, and wondered if he was right. But there was nowhere to go—not really. "I don't feel right . . . running away."

"I know you don't," he said. "But think about it. About the rapes. About the calls. About the trees. The trouble, the violence. Really think about it. Promise me?"

She gave him a melancholy smile and nodded.

"My God," he said, studying her face. "You're so beautiful." He gave her his crooked smile. "And know what? You can so cook. That was great."

I love you, she wanted to say. But she couldn't say that. "I've got to do these dishes," she said instead. She dropped her gaze and withdrew her hand.

She rose from the table, and he did, too. She started to clear the dishes. He began to help.

She shook her head. "Stretch out on the couch. This kitchen isn't big enough for two people. It's hardly big enough for me. Take it easy—you're beat."

He tried to insist. She was firm. He went to the old couch, threw himself on it, pulled one of the little crocheted pillows under his head.

She watched him with sympathy. His eyes were already closed, and his hair tumbled over his brow. Silence settled over the little house. There was only the hum of the air conditioner, the steady ticking of the cat-shaped clock.

She took her time doing the dishes, wondering if he was right; if the wisest thing wouldn't be simply to leave. But for how long? How long might this emnity and tension drag out? Days? Weeks? And they both had property to protect, jobs to do.

She dried the last dish and put it away. She wiped her hands, then went to the living room. She stared down at Archer.

He lay on his side, one arm dangling over the couch's edge, one folded beneath the pillow. "Archer," she said softly. She bent and touched his shoulder. "Let's go to bed. Let's just hold each other and sleep. You'll be more comfortable in bed."

He didn't stir. She spoke his name again, shook him slightly. Reluctantly, she let go of his shoulder and straightened. He was so soundly asleep, it would be difficult to wake him. And selfish.

Her hand tingled from touching him. Let him sleep, she thought. She wanted him beside her in the bed; she wanted his arms around her, the warmth of his body, the comforting flutter of his breath against her flesh.

But he was sleeping so profoundly that all the clichés fit; he was out like a light, dead to the world, down for the count. It was kindest to let him stay where he was.

Perhaps he would waken during the night and come to her bed. Until then, the only gift she could give him was to let him sleep.

She showered, and felt lonely in the shower stall. She regarded the soap regretfully. "You're no fun all by yourself, Mr. Soap," she said.

She put on a long, sleep T-shirt that depicted a striped cat playing the guitar and singing that he loved to eat mousies. She padded into the living room and took a last, yearning look at Archer. He hadn't moved. She plugged in a small stained-glass night-light, and went to bed alone.

She missed him. Without enthusiasm, she pounded her pillow into shape and settled against it. *Drat*, she thought, her emotions in conflict. *I've grown accustomed to his face.* She turned restlessly, hating the lonesome darkness. *I've also grown accustomed to his bod. And to his mind and his heart and maybe his soul.*

The little air conditioner in the bedroom rattled and rasped. She sighed and at last drifted toward sleep.

Archer might not be beside her, but he was in the next room, and with him there, whatever else she felt, she felt supremely safe.

SHE WAS AWAKENED BY a sound so loud and sharp it rang out even above the noise of her air conditioner. *Firecracker*, she thought groggily, forgetting that the Fourth of July was past.

She burrowed her face more deeply into the pillow. Almost immediately she sank back toward the depths of sleep.

But then she heard another report, just as loud, just as jolting. Trilly began barking and howling. The dog's cries were not sorrowful, as they had been that morning, but agitated.

A door slammed. *Her* front door.

She heard voices shouting, but she couldn't make out their words. She heard Archer's voice—she was sure.

That thought jolted her awake, and she sat up, disoriented. Archer wasn't beside her.

No, no . . . he was asleep on the living room couch, exhausted. No—he was outside, shouting something. . . . *Trouble. Trouble had been seething around them, everywhere. Had it finally boiled out of control?*

She rose, parted the blinds and peered outside, searching the scene for Archer, to understand whatever was happening. Trilly's barking grew shriller, more hysterical.

Rita didn't see Archer on the moon-silvered lawn, but suddenly she stopped searching.

Her eyes widened and she could see only one thing. Her heart seemed to jump up into her windpipe, shutting off her breath.

George Peavey's A-frame house stood like a dark triangle against the luminous sky. But, through the windows, she saw inconstant orange light dance and flicker.

His house was on fire.

11

RITA LEAPED FROM BED and ran through the semidark house. She accidentally smashed her shoulder against the opened front door but didn't feel the pain.

She raced toward Peavey's house. She stopped when she saw Archer standing tensely at Peavey's fence. The gate was open.

She caught his arm, looked up at him. "Has anybody called the fire department?" she asked.

"Yes." Points of fire danced in the windows. Black smoke seeped into the night, growing thicker.

She clutched his arm more tightly. "Where's Peavey?"

"Nobody's seen him. In there, maybe." He nodded grimly toward the house.

"Archer," she pleaded, tugging at his arm. They couldn't let Peavey die in the blaze. The volunteer fire department was good, but not good enough to get there immediately, and smoke could kill Peavey in minutes.

Archer swore. He shook her hand from his arm and ran through the gate and up to the porch. He kicked the front door of the house as hard as he could. It flew open easily. Smoke billowed out the door—a thick, dark cloud of it.

"Archer!" Rita screamed. "Be careful!"

She, too, ran to the house, but the heat stopped her at the door momentarily. Archer had already disappeared inside. She put up her arm to shield her eyes against the smoke, tried to steel herself to enter.

"Let the bastard burn!" Joe Johanssen cried from his porch.

Rita turned her back to the fire, took a deep breath and inched nearer to the door. But Archer was already stumbling back outside. He seized her, forcing her back. "Get out," he said. "It's an oven in there."

"But Archer—"

He half pushed, half dragged her back to the gate. "I saw him," he said. "I couldn't get to him. I think he's dead. Come on, get your hose. We'll do what we can."

She looked at him in horror. Even in the moonlight, she could see that smoke had stained his face. He coughed.

"Dead?" she asked, stunned. "Are you sure?"

"He's on the living room floor. He wasn't moving. Rita, I couldn't get to him. I tried—I couldn't. The flames drove me back. The room's an inferno."

"Oh, God," she said, stricken. He'd let go of her arm and was racing toward her coiled hose.

She ran after him. "We can't help with a garden hose." Her eyes were full of tears, and not just from the smoke.

Archer turned the water on full force and dragged the hose back up the hill. "Hey!" he yelled at Sig and Johanssen, who were both standing on their porches watching. "How about some help here?"

"Let him burn," Joe Johanssen said again. He sounded bitter and surprisingly sober.

Sig held the baying Trilly by the collar. He said nothing. The dog danced and fought against the restraint. She howled more dementedly. At last, Sig chained her.

He came down his steps, picked up his tangled hose, turned on the water. Then he turned his back on Peavey's house and began to hose down his own front yard.

"Sig!" Rita called out. But he ignored her. The fire's light played on his back. A window in Peavey's house shattered. Sparks issued from it and flew upward.

Rita gritted her teeth and headed for Joe Johanssen's garden hose, coiled around a holder. "Hey!" Joe shouted in protest when she turned on his water.

"We can't stand here and do *nothing*," she cried. She yanked a length of hose free and turned on the water.

"I did do something," Joe yelled back. "I called the fire department. Hey! That's *my* water you're using."

Rita ignored him and dragged the hose up the slope until she could stand close to Archer. They all had large lots at the cove and long hoses to water them.

"Hey!" Joe shrieked after her. "You're running up my water bill!"

Rita ignored him and trained the weak spray toward the burning house. It barely reached the front wall, but at least it might keep the fire from spreading to the yard.

Archer could get closer to the fire than she. He was poised tensely, silhouetted against the leaping light. He was, in fact, probably too close to the blaze, trying to hose down the steep roof. Rita couldn't believe how much smoke could billow from such a small house.

Her knees went weak with relief when she heard sirens. Trilly's baying grew more hysterical.

"Shut that damn dog *up!*" Joe Johanssen shouted.

Sig said nothing, kept calmly hosing his yard, his back to the fire.

Then a horde of vehicles came hurtling down the little road, sirens wailing. From them poured a mob of men in firefighting gear. There were police cars, too, and an ambulance.

A fireman seized her, thrusting her out of the way. "Stand back," he said. She was glad to drop the hose and obey. Trembling with exhaustion, she half backed, half staggered farther from the men. She stood under her big mimosa, leaning against it, watching numbly.

Archer was talking fervently and pointing at the house. Men in heavy gear donned oxygen masks and moved toward Peavey's door. They looked like space aliens to her, and like space aliens, had superhuman powers; they disappeared inside the smoke and flames.

Then Archer was beside her. He smelled of smoke and singed cloth. His shirt was dark with smoke and full of holes from sparks. Wordlessly, he put his arm around her and drew her close. His face was like stone, and he kept staring at the fire. She couldn't. She hid her face against his chest. She'd disliked Peavey—but just the same, she wept for him.

DAWN'S FIRST THIN LIGHT grayed the sky when the fire was finally declared safely out. The A-frame's brick exterior still stood, but its interior was half gutted, the living room ravaged and scorched.

Rita hadn't looked when they'd carried out what was left of George Peavey. She hadn't looked when the body was loaded into the ambulance. Then the ambulance lumbered up the road, its siren silent. There was no need for haste.

Rita clutched Archer's shirtfront more tightly. He held her closer, but didn't speak. She couldn't think and didn't want to think. She supposed, dully, that she was in a state of shock.

It didn't seem odd when a rugged-faced man in a summer jacket identified himself as Detective Horchow and said he wanted to talk to them. He had a uniformed officer with him, and Rita recognized him as the boyish-looking deputy of the night before.

She felt Archer's arms stiffen around her, his heart hammer harder beneath her cheek. She looked at him and saw his face had gone even stonier. He was wearing his emotionless mask.

But Rita asked Horchow to step inside. Archer said nothing. He seemed to hold himself taller and with a wary tension, as if poised for trouble. Rita told the men to sit at her little table; she fumbled about, trying to make coffee. Her fingers didn't obey. Her hands seemed to do all the wrong things, but she kept working, thankful for the distraction.

Horchow asked simple questions in a flat voice, as if he was bored. The young deputy took notes. Rita answered mechanically. Archer answered even more mechanically and, it seemed to her, reluctantly.

"So let me get this straight," Horchow droned. "You both heard two shots. You—" he nodded toward Archer "—were the first out of the house. The other men, Johanssen and Hobbler, both came outside shortly after you did."

Archer nodded, saying nothing. "Okay," Horchow said, sounding uninterested. "Then you—" he nodded at Archer again "—tried to go into the house to see about Peavey. You saw him lying in the front room, but you couldn't get to him.

You stopped the woman from trying to come in. You got a hose and tried to wet down the roof. *She* got a hose. Right?"

Archer nodded. Rita said, "Right." She set down mugs of coffee in front of the men. Her hands shook slightly.

Only Horchow tasted his coffee. He made a face of displeased surprise. "Okay," he sighed. "What did the others do? Hobbler and Johanssen?"

Archer didn't answer. Rita had just poured herself a cup of coffee. She stood at the counter. She remembered Sig and Joe's actions with bitterness. "Nothing," she said. "They did nothing."

"No," Archer said tonelessly. "Johanssen called the fire department."

Rita ran her hand through her hair. "Yes. I guess that's right."

Horchow cast her a mild look. "Would you sit down, miss?"

"Of course." She, too, sat at the table. She sipped at her coffee. It was terrible.

"Did they *say* anything? Hobbler and Johanssen?"

Rita bit back her words, remembering how Joe had yelled to let Peavey burn and Sig had only turned his back.

Archer spoke, choosing his words with care. "We all said, 'It's on fire.' We asked . . . if anybody'd seen Peavey. I said, 'Call the fire department.' Johanssen did."

Horchow leaned nearer to Archer. Rita winced. The little dining area was too crowded, and she was starting to feel claustrophobic. "Was anything else said? At any time?"

"I can't remember," Archer said, looking Horchow in the eye.

Horchow turned his attention to Rita. She saw Archer's gaze flick to her, too, full of suppressed intensity. *Be careful what you say,* he was telling her.

"What about you, miss?" Horchow asked. "Do you remember them saying anything?

Without knowing why, Rita was suddenly frightened. "Everything happened very fast," she said vaguely.

Horchow shrugged. His coarse features arranged themselves into an expression that said he couldn't care less. "Now we know," he said, "there's been a little trouble out here. You got called out here last night, didn't you, Fanshaw?"

The young deputy nodded without emotion. "Yes, sir."

Horchow nodded, too. He looked at Archer, then at Rita. Archer met his gaze, but Rita dropped hers without understanding why.

"But," Horchow told them, "you don't have to worry about implicating any of your neighbors. The fire, frankly, *was set*. We also found a suicide note—in the victim's mailbox. Addressed to 'Whom It May Concern.'"

Rita looked up, jolted. *The fire had been set? Peavey had left a suicide note?* She stared at Horchow, her lips parted in surprise.

But Archer's masklike expression didn't change. He blinked once, that was all.

"Yeah," Horchow said with no apparent concern. "He felt he was a misfit, everybody was against him, he couldn't go on, et cetera, et cetera. Typed it. Put it in an envelope. He *did* have a typewriter, didn't he?"

Rita had seen him writing in a notebook, that was all. "I— don't know."

Archer shrugged.

"Do either of *you* have a typewriter?"

"No," Rita said.

"No," Archer said without inflection.

"Did he seem particularly depressed, in a funk, lately?"

"Depressed?" Rita repeated, dazed. "No . . . not really."

Archer shook his head and said nothing.

"Was his behavior erratic, unpredictable—perhaps abnormal—in any way?"

Rita licked her lips. "Well, yes. It always was. He was . . . quarrelsome. A quarrelsome person."

Horchow turned to Archer, leaning closer to him again. "Would you agree with that, Mr. Smith?"

A muscle flicked in Archer's cheek. "Yes."

"I see," Horchow said. He got up. He paced into Rita's living room, his hands locked behind his back. He gazed idly at her worktable, her couch, the pictures on her walls. "Who did Peavey quarrel with?" he asked casually.

Rita glanced nervously at Archer. His eyes were telegraphing her the same message: *Be careful. For God's sake, be careful.*

She took a deep breath, then couldn't seem to exhale it. "Everybody," she said. "He quarreled with everybody. And he—he always started it."

"I see," Horchow said again. He stopped pacing and stared down at Rita's worktable. "He quarreled with you, Miss O'Casey?"

Rita let out her breath in a long, quivery rush. "Yes."

Horchow turned to face Archer. "He quarreled with you, Mr. Smith?"

"We . . . had words," Archer said, tight-lipped.

"Words," Horchow mused. "Hmm." He kept looking at Archer. He nodded. He sighed. "I don't want to get too personal, of course. But as I understand it, you were staying here, last night—correct?"

The muscle ticked in Archer's cheek again. "I fell asleep on the couch. I slept on the couch."

Horchow raised an eyebrow, looked at Rita's old couch, with most of its pillows spilled on the floor. "The couch," he said with the faintest trace of sarcasm.

"It's *true*," Rita blurted. "He was worn-out. Somebody'd pulled the stakes on his dock. It drifted away. It took him all day to get it back. He—"

"Oh," Horchow said with interest, turning back to Archer. "Somebody vandalized your dock? Who?"

"I don't know," Archer replied, squaring his jaw.

"Had a tough time getting it back?"

"Yeah," Archer said evenly. "I did."

"And I suppose that explains the . . . abrasions on your hands, that scratch on your arm."

Rita's heart went cold. Archer didn't answer. He and Horchow stared at each other like natural enemies taking each other's measure.

"That *is* how he hurt his hands," she burst out. "The dock was caught in some boulders. He came home like that."

"Uh-hmm, I see. Yes, thank you," Horchow said. But he didn't look at her. His gaze stayed locked with Archer's. "These 'wounds' of yours—they were bleeding a lot when you got back?"

Rita's mind whirled crazily, and the cold that had struck her heart now stole through her whole body.

"No," Archer said, setting his jaw more stubbornly. "I wasn't bleeding—particularly."

Horchow frowned, looking innocently puzzled. "So that doesn't explain why there's blood all over Miss O'Casey's porch, does it?"

Blood all over my doorstep? "What?" Rita cried. Her hand made an involuntary jerk and sent her coffee cup crashing to the floor.

Archer went pale.

"Yeah," said Horchow with another of his bored sighs. "There's just a whole lot of blood out there on that porch. I think you folks better come along to the courthouse with us. I think we need to get a more formal statement from you."

He nodded to Fanshaw, the young deputy. "You take the woman, Fanshaw. I'll take Smith."

The deputy stood. He put his hand under Rita's elbow. "Come with me, miss," he said.

And when she stepped outside, she was stunned to see that there *was* blood on the porch. Not as much as Horchow had led her to believe, but it was there, spattered across the doorstep, flecking the door itself.

And she saw something else she hadn't noticed before. Her apple tree was cut down. She couldn't believe it.

Only its stump still stood. The tree itself lay fallen in the grass.

"My tree," she breathed, not understanding. "My tree…"

She turned wildly, her gaze meeting Archer's. Horchow had his hand clamped tight on Archer's upper arm. "Archer," she said helplessly. "My tree . . . I never saw. . . . What happened . . . ?"

But only Archer's eyes answered her. *Be careful what you say,* they told her in anguish. *Be careful.*

Then they were being separated, put into different cars from the sheriff's department.

THE OFFICERS KEPT THEM apart. They also kept Rita isolated for an incalculable amount of time in a cell-like room. It had a mirror, and she wondered, frightened, if it was the sort *they* could use as a window, to spy on her.

She still wore her nightshirt with the singing cat on the front. The young deputy had let her put on a robe and slip into a pair of sandals. Now she sat alone, feeling trapped in a nightmare.

None of it made sense. The house couldn't have burned. George Peavey couldn't be dead. She and Archer couldn't be held like this, questioned by detectives. If Peavey had committed suicide, why were they being questioned at all?

And, idiotically, one irrational thought kept haunting her. Why had her apple tree been cut down? Why?

HORCHOW CAME AT LAST to question her. He brought another detective with him, a gaunt man named Mallenhoff. Mallenhoff offered her coffee, which she accepted, and cigarettes, which she refused. Mallenhoff, looking benign and sleepy-eyed, sat behind a desk and gazed at her mildly.

Horchow, no longer bored, was now truculent. She was amazed and put off-balance by his first question.

"What happened to your apple tree, Rita?"

She shrugged helplessly. "I . . . don't know. I didn't even notice it was cut down. Not until you were bringing us here."

He sneered. "Now, Rita, how could you not notice a thing like that? One of your neighbors says you're real protective of that tree. How could you *not* notice a *tree* was cut down?

She twisted her fingers together in her lap. "I— It was dark. The house was burning. All I could think was that a man could be dying. I wasn't thinking about . . . trees."

He leaned forward, thrusting his face into hers. "Did you threaten to shoot him once, Rita? You did, didn't you?"

She crossed her arms tightly, clenched her hands into her armpits. "I— He was throwing rocks at a dog. It was just . . . talk. Like when I used to get mad at my brothers, and I'd say, 'I'll kill you.' It was . . . talk."

"You're real nervous, Rita. Why? Did you kill him?"

He was so close she could feel his breath, hot on her face. "No!" she cried. "And you said he committed suicide. You said there was a—a note."

Horchow laughed and sat down on the edge of the desk. "I said a *typed* note, Rita. We couldn't find any typewriter in that house. No trace of one. But our men are looking for one. Will they find it in your house? Or your lover's?"

She suppressed a gasp of surprise. "I don't have a typewriter."

"What about a gun, Rita? That's how Peavy died. A shot-gun wound to the head."

"I don't own a gun." She wanted to go home. She wanted Archer.

"One was stolen from Joe Johanssen," Horchow said, almost slyly. "Did you steal it, Rita?"

"Of course not," she said earnestly. "Look, what is this? You can't believe I'm a *suspect*—"

"Johanssen's gun," Horchow persisted. "Did your lover steal it? Cooperate, Rita. It'll be a lot easier on you."

"No," she retorted. "Neither of us stole it. Listen, if I'm under arrest, don't I get a phone call or something? Aren't you supposed to read me my rights?"

"Don't get cute, Rita," Horchow said with a nasty twist of a smile. "We're just asking a few questions, that's all."

"They're pretty leading questions," she said, lifting her chin. "I don't like being treated like this. I—"

"Murder's a serious subject, Rita. What do you know about it?"

"Why do you keep talking about murder?" she demanded, glaring at him. "You said it was suicide."

"If it is, it's a *real* peculiar one," Horchow said. He reached for the pack of cigarettes Mallenhoff had set on the desk. He lit one. The smell nauseated her.

"For one thing," Horchow said, exhaling, "poor old Peavey not only got shot in the head, he had his throat cut. And his house set on fire. Now, even for a guy who wants to die, isn't that a bit of—excuse the pun—overkill?"

"I don't know anything about it," she said rebelliously. "He overdid everything else. Why shouldn't he overdo suicide?"

"Rita, Rita," Horchow said, shaking his head. "You're missing my point. His *throat* was cut. And you know what he used? You'll never guess what he used."

She turned to face him again. She spoke through clenched teeth, "How could I know? I wasn't *there*."

"What he got his throat cut with," Horchow said with satisfaction, "was a piece of glass. A big long piece of stained glass. But you wouldn't know anything about stained glass, would you, Rita?"

She felt as if the floor had been jerked from beneath her, and she was falling through space. She stared at him, speechless.

"Now why would he use a jagged old piece of stained glass, Rita, when a nice, sharp razor'd be so much easier?"

She realized that she was in a life-or-death contest with Horchow, and she had to reason with all the clarity at her command. Her mind raced. "I—I keep all my glass scraps in a special trash can. On the porch. So I can dispose of it safely. Probably everybody at the cove's seen me putting it out there. Anybody could have taken a piece."

"Rita," Horchow said with mock disappointment, "you're *still* not getting it, are you? You kept that glass on your porch? You've got somebody's blood all over that porch. I'll bet that before noon today, the lab boy's'll tell me it's the same type as Peavey's."

"I don't know anything about the blood," she said, trying to keep her voice from shaking. "Somebody's been putting strange things on my porch at night. Flowers. A dead bird—"

"Rita—" She was startled to hear Mallenhoff speak. He had a quiet voice, almost comforting.

"Just tell us," Mallenhoff urged. "Was this what happened? Peavey came into your yard at night, cut down your tree? You and Smith caught him? Things got out of hand. Somebody reached for the nearest weapon—a piece of glass. Things just got out of hand. Maybe it wasn't murder at all. Just . . . involuntary homicide. Even self-defense. But you panicked, tried to cover your tracks. Just *admit* it. It'll be easier—on both of you."

Rita uncrossed her arms and clenched her fists in her lap. "I didn't know the tree had been cut down. I—I don't even know if it was Peavey who cut it. He used a chain saw. A chain saw would have woke me up. A chain saw would have woke *everybody* up."

"But it wasn't a chain saw," Horchow said, bending close to her again. He stank of cigarette smoke. "It was a plain old hacksaw, from the marks. A man could get a tree down fairly quietly. It was a little tree. Real little."

Rita said nothing. She clenched her fists more tightly.

"Know what else?" Horchow asked with false brightness. "We couldn't find a hacksaw in that house, either. No sign of one. Oh, we'll keep hunting. But maybe somebody got careless. Maybe it isn't in the house—maybe somebody hid it. Did you hide that hacksaw, Rita?"

"I don't know anything about a saw," she snapped. "And stop calling me *Rita* every other sentence. And I'd like it if you took that cigarette out of your face. You didn't ask if I minded you smoking. Well, I've had enough damn smoke for one night."

"I'll bet you have." Horchow smirked. "And you've got a temper, too, don't you? Got mad enough to threaten to kill—just because Peavey threw a rock at a dog. Imagine. Just a rock. You think he poisoned all those dogs, Rita?"

Oh, God, she thought, *this is what they mean by a war of nerves. Calm down. Just calm down.*

"I don't know who poisoned the dogs."

"I'll bet you think he cut that dock loose, too—your lover's dock. I'll bet that got your temper up, too."

"I don't know *who* unstaked the dock."

"And Peavey took sexual notice of you, didn't he?" Horchow asked. "I'll bet neither you nor your lover liked that. And you were carrying on, hot and heavy, right under his nose."

She closed her eyes for a moment, took a deep breath. "I was not 'carrying on.' I'm an adult woman, and my private life is my own. I—I kissed Archer once in public. *Once.* That's not carrying on."

Horchow gave her a disbelieving grin that was unpleasant in the extreme. "Now we've got a little document that says you did carry on. That you *made* Peavey notice you that way. Let's see what you've got to say about it."

He snapped his fingers and made a gesture toward the quiet Mallenhoff. Mallenhoff opened a briefcase, took out a black book and handed it to Horchow. Its shiny cover was slightly charred, and so were the edges of its pages when Horchow opened it. A blackened corner fell off and floated to the floor. Rita watched it as if hypnotized.

Peavey's book, she thought helplessly. The little book she'd seen him writing in so furiously.

"This was in a metal drawer in the kitchen," Horchow said. "The kitchen didn't have much wood. The fire didn't take so well there. So let's just see what our friend Peavey had to say."

He started to read from the book. "Somehow she found out I have money. She offered me her body for money. These are the things she promised she'd do...."

He read a list of sexual favors so long and varied and perverse that Rita wanted to snatch the book from him, rip it to shreds. But she couldn't do that, because to touch the book would be destroying evidence or...

She couldn't think. She covered her ears. "Stop it!" she ordered, fighting back tears. "That's obscene. He made it all up."

"Just let me continue," Horchow said coldly.

"No!" Rita cried. "That's the most disgusting pack of lies I ever heard."

Horchow raised his eyebrows dubiously. "Oh? So you never kept your blinds open while you undressed, so he'd see you naked? He describes you naked. In detail."

"It's a lie," she insisted, pounding her knee with her fist. "He's a— He was a sick man, and he made it all up—"

"And you didn't take up with Smith to make him jealous?"

"I didn't 'take up' with Archer," she countered. "He and I . . . were attracted to each other, that's all."

"And you didn't leave the blinds open so Peavey could see you with Smith? He describes that in detail, too."

She felt humiliated and defiled. "No!" She had to wipe a tear away. Her hand shook with anger and disgust.

"And you didn't offer Peavey to have a threesome with him and Archer Smith?"

Rita wiped away another tear, but held her head high. "I don't," she said through clenched teeth, "even know how people *have* threesomes. I don't want to know. I'm not that kind of person. I never slept with anybody but Archer in my life except my ex-husband. And Archer and I only spent three nights together. The last one he was on the couch. And if you read one more word of that tripe, I—I'll throw up."

She had defended herself with such passion that Horchow seemed momentarily taken aback.

Mallenhoff spoke up quietly. "I think she's telling the truth, Frank. Ease up. Don't read any more."

Rita threw Mallenhoff a grateful look and wiped away her tears. She fought to regain control of herself.

Horchow rose and paced the room. Mallenhoff got up from the chair and came and sat on the edge of the desk, taking Horchow's place. Horchow turned and watched them.

"I think Smith probably did sleep on the couch—didn't he, Rita?"

"Yes," she insisted. "Yes. We're telling the truth."

"But in that case," Mallenhoff said gently, "you don't know what he did during the night, do you? I mean, he wasn't beside you, was he? He was in another room altogether. He might have gone anywhere, done anything. Maybe he heard something going on outside. Maybe he went out to check and found Peavey. Then one thing led to another. And you didn't even know. That could have happened, couldn't it, Rita?"

Her mind felt as if it were lunging drunkenly from one impossible idea to another. It was true that Archer had been in the other room. It was true that the bedroom air conditioner was loud and rackety, the one in the living room quiet. It was true he could have heard something she didn't, but if she agreed to that . . .

"No," she said stubbornly. "Archer didn't do anything like that. He *wouldn't* do anything like that."

Mallenhoff stared at her sadly. He didn't speak for a moment. "How well do you know Archer Smith?" he asked at last.

She squared her shoulders. "Well enough to know he'd never kill anybody. Never."

Mallenhoff looked sadder and swore a mild oath under his breath. He looked away from her. "Frank, you tell her. I can't. Damn. This is an ugly business."

He rose from the edge of the desk, and suddenly Horchow was there again. From somewhere he'd produced a manila folder. He tapped it.

"Rita, how much do you know about Smith's *past?*" he asked, narrowing his eyes.

She went silent, clenching her fists in her lap again. There were things she didn't know about Archer's background, but he couldn't ever have done anything really wrong; it had all been a terrible *misunderstanding* of some kind.

Horchow leaned toward her again, his gaze holding hers. "Rita," he said with sinister softness, "did you know that Archer Smith was convicted of killing a man? Of shooting him to death? That he served time in prison for it?"

The edges of her vision blurred and turned dark. Horchow went out of focus, became an unsteady shape. She had a cold, deadening sensation on the back of her neck, as if a ghost had laid its hand there, claiming her.

"No," she breathed. "No."

"Yes, Rita," Horchow said with that same softness. "Your lover is a convicted killer. St. Louis faxed us the details. You want to see the files?"

12

THEY HELD ARCHER FOR eight hours, questioning him, hammering away at his story, trying to undermine it. For eight hours he took it. They had to let him go at last, but they told him they'd see him again. Soon.

There was a cold-eyed deputy waiting to drive him back to the cove. The deputy didn't try to make conversation. Neither did Archer. He stared blindly out the window. He felt as if part of him had died, but maybe not enough, because the rest of him was sick. He felt as poisoned as one of Hobbler's dogs.

The police knew about him, about the killing in St. Louis. That meant that now Rita knew, too. They would spring the news on her to turn her against him. And she'd turn. How could she help it?

He couldn't blame her. He couldn't blame anybody except himself. The thought made him feel empty, hopeless.

The deputy drove down the rutted road to the cove, let him out at Patterson's house. Archer didn't thank him. He got out of the car, slamming the door. He walked up his stairs and didn't look back.

He'd seen the ruin of Peavey's house and had turned his eyes from it. Cops were swarming over the remains, searching, and it was fenced off with the yellow tape that marked a crime scene.

The cops would be everywhere before it was over—including at his door with a search warrant. And at Rita's, too, he supposed.

He unlocked the door. He went straight into the bathroom, leaned on the counter and stared at himself in the mirror. His face was grimy from the smoke, his eyes bloodshot.

His eyebrows were slightly singed, and so was the hair that fell over his brow. His clothes were filthy, full of holes from flying sparks. He looked like hell.

He stripped off his clothes and stuffed them into the wastebasket, even the shoes. He climbed into the shower, wanting to be clean. He didn't suppose he'd ever feel really clean again.

Afterward, he shaved, put on fresh clothes. He studied his image in the mirror and decided he still looked like hell.

He walked through Patterson's living room and into the kitchen. The house was furnished simply, with a lot of wood—mission-style couch and chairs, coffee table. Framed bland landscapes hung on the walls, along with a pair of mounted large bass that Patterson had caught and had stuffed. Sliding-glass doors led to the deck and overlooked the lake.

The lake was intensely blue today, but Archer didn't give a damn. He went into the small, tidy kitchen and opened the refrigerator. There were two beers inside; he took one and popped it open. It wasn't even five o'clock in the afternoon. So what? Maybe Joe Johanssen had the right idea. Life's rotten, buddy, so drink yourself blind to it.

He went back to the living room and sat down heavily in one of the chairs, stared out at the lake. He closed his eyes and pressed the cold beer can against his forehead. *We'll be talking to you again*, they'd said. *Stick around. Don't take it into your head to go anywhere. We'll be talking to you again. Jesus. Jesus.*

It was happening all over again. He couldn't believe it. He should never have come here. He should never have gone near Rita. "Rita," he muttered to himself, "I'm sorry."

Then he swore and stared out at the lake. The damaged dock was still in place, tilting drunkenly to one side. He tried not to think. He just sat, staring and wishing the dead part in him would grow, spread out to all his emotions, and mercifully kill them.

He sat that way for a long time. He should call Patterson, explain all this, tell him about the dock, too, but he couldn't. Not yet.

And then there was a knock at the door. He rose, forcing his face into an expressionless mask. It would be the police, of course. With their warrant. Let them come, he thought fatalistically. Let them tear the bloody place apart.

But it wasn't the police. It was Rita.

SHE GAZED UP AT HIM, her emotions warring. He looked mortally tired, but not beaten. His expression was blank, yet somehow defiant. She was angry, and she could tell he was going to deflect her anger with coldness.

She was also hurt, and he would probably try to ignore that minor fact. She'd had an opening speech prepared—curt, accusing and cutting. But something deep in his eyes made her forget it.

She'd wanted to keep her face as wooden and hard as his, but couldn't; that had never been her style. She was surprised to find tears rising in her eyes. She didn't say anything curt or cutting.

"Will you talk to me?" she asked.

He swallowed, but said nothing. His lips thinned. The wind off the lake stirred his blond hair.

She gathered all her reason and courage and repeated herself. "Archer . . . will you *talk* to me?"

He looked away, the lines beside his mouth deepening. "I ought to be asking you that question."

Impulsively, she started to put her hand on his arm. Then she remembered: *This man is a murderer. This man was in prison.*

But something in her could not accept such a thing so simply and without question.

He slanted a look at her outstretched hand. She started to draw it back, but slowly he raised his hand to hers, offering it, but not touching her.

Oh, Lord, she thought desperately. *If I take it, it'll mean I trust him, that I forgive him—with no explanation. It means he'll be back in my heart and in my bed.*

She couldn't. Life wasn't that easy or simple. She had to have an explanation. And even that might not be enough. She dropped her hand and turned her gaze away from him. "I'm sorry," she said.

"No," he said. "I'm sorry. I shouldn't have gotten involved with you. But you were— I couldn't stop myself because you were so . . ." He didn't finish the sentence.

They stood for a moment in awkward silence, not looking at each other. "You want me to explain," he said at last, weariness in his voice.

"Yes. I deserve that, at least." She raised her eyes to look at him. He still faced the lake.

"At least," he agreed. The muscles in his cheek made a complex movement. "Let's sit out here. I won't ask you to come inside."

Unshed tears burned her eyes. *No. I shouldn't go inside a murderer's house, an ex-convict's house.*

He gestured toward a set of wrought-iron chairs. Wordlessly she sat. He turned to face her, his back to the lake. He leaned against the railing, his hands clasping it on either side. He studied her face.

"How long did they question you?" he asked.

She folded her hands in her lap and stared down at them. "Hours," she said bitterly.

"They were . . . tough on you?" he asked.

"Yes," she said in the same tone. "They were tough."

"I'm sorry," he said. "It's my fault. If it wasn't for me, they wouldn't have—"

She raised her eyes to him again, her look challenging. "Archer, they said you murdered somebody. That you were in prison. They had a—a *file* on you. I didn't look at it. I didn't want to."

"I didn't murder him," he said without emotion. "I killed him."

Exasperated disbelief swept her. "What's the difference?"

"There's a lot of difference—once a court gets you. They convicted me of third-degree murder. Later a higher court overturned the conviction. But not until I'd done time. Seven months."

Such resentment flashed in his eyes that it startled her. She watched him warily for a moment. But she wanted the truth. "What did you do? What happened?"

He looked away. "It was a robbery. My folks owned this convenience store. A classic mom-and-pop operation."

She nodded, waiting for him to go on. He made a frustrated gesture. "One summer—four years ago—my father was in the hospital. He had cancer. His chances weren't good. I'd taken my mother's shift at the store one night, because he was—was having a bad time of it."

He paused and gazed sideways toward the woods. His Adam's apple worked up, then down. "Okay," he said, as if forcing himself onward. "I'm in the store. There's two customers. This . . . older couple. A man and a woman."

His hands tensed on the rail. He nodded, as if to himself. "This guy comes in. I'm at the counter. All of a sudden he's got a gun in my face. He wants money—a lot. I don't have enough to please him. He wants more."

He paused again, frowning into the distance. "Our store—this neighborhood—it had gotten tough. My dad had been robbed four times in six years. And that's how my cousin died. In a holdup. Dad started keeping a gun under the counter."

He crossed his arms. "This guy—he's big, see—you've got to understand he's *big*—six four, at least. He sounds dangerous . . . unpredictable. And he's waving this gun in my face. I give him my watch. He's not satisfied. He wants more. All of a sudden, he turns on this older couple. The *man's* the one who gets hysterical. He starts yelling. The guy tells him to stop. The guy is threatening to shoot."

Archer's voice had gone tight. "I reached under the counter. I got the gun. I thought he was going to shoot them. I shot. I meant to stop him, that's all—wing him. Instead I put a bullet through his spine. He lived for five days. And then he died. He . . . died."

Archer shook his head, as if he still didn't believe it.

He was obviously in such emotional pain that Rita felt a lump in her throat. His story bewildered her. "Archer...how could they convict you for a thing like that?"

He still wouldn't look at her. The corner of his mouth worked strangely. "I'll tell you how. His damned gun wasn't *real* is what. It was some kind of . . . toy replica or something. He *couldn't* have hurt anybody with it."

"But," she said, "how could you know . . . ?"

He shook his head. "Rita . . ." He took a deep breath. "He fooled me. The gun fooled me. His size fooled me. He was barely seventeen years old. I killed a *kid* holding a *toy*. Je-sus."

She stood and wanted to go to him, but something in his stance told her he didn't want to be touched. She rubbed her palms nervously on the thighs of her jeans.

"But . . . it was an accident. How could they convict you?" The breeze from the lake fluttered her hair so that she had to brush it back from her eyes.

"Look," he said stiffly. "They were making an example of me, all right? 'See what happens when people take the law into their own hands? When people start acting like vigilantes? Our children get killed.'"

"But you had witnesses. Surely they—"

"Rita," he said bitterly. "You don't know much about the law. We had a trial—it was declared a mistrial on a technicality. The whole thing started over again. It dragged on two and a half years. By the time we got to the second trial, the woman was dead. She was old, she died."

"Her husband, though," Rita protested. "He saw it—"

"He was a terrible witness," Archer said, his mouth twisting. "He was hysterical in the store. He was worthless on the stand. The prosecutor had him saying, 'Sure, no, the kid never threatened him, not really. He never threatened anybody.' And *he* could see the gun wasn't real. He was yelling to tell me not to shoot. The case had become . . . infamous. He didn't want to be implicated."

Once again she wanted to go to him, but the way he held himself told her to keep her distance. "Those—those television things they have in places like that," she said, "to tape robberies and shoplifters, didn't that—"

Archer shook his head cynically. "I'll tell you something about electronic devices, Rita. They *break*. It wasn't recording. Funny, huh? A real laugh riot."

"But . . ." she said, her tone pleading.

He turned and gazed out at the lake, his arms still crossed. "Hey, I got unlucky. That's all. A hot-dog prosecutor, a lousy witness, a broken taping device, a jury that didn't set standards for being bright. I got ten years."

"But . . ." she said again.

"My luck didn't get any better in prison," he said, his face going harder. "A couple of guys started calling me 'Blondie.' Saying 'Hey, good-looking.' You get the idea."

Her hands clenched spasmodically in horror. "You're not saying—"

"That's *exactly* what I'm saying," he said with vehemence. "Three of them jumped me in the laundry room. Threw a blanket over my head from behind, caught me by surprise, grabbed me—"

"No!" she protested, tears stinging her eyes again.

His nostrils flared. "I'm not all that big. But I'm strong. Stronger than they thought. I'd kill them before I'd let that happen. I nearly did kill one. I knocked him against a cement wall, gave him a concussion, broke his jaw."

"My *God*," Rita said.

He shook his head. "It didn't help my case. Then I had two episodes of violence against me. And I might still be rotting in there, except Patterson got interested."

"And Patterson . . . ?" She let the question trail off.

"He's a criminal lawyer. An excellent one. Somebody brought my trial to his attention. He studied it. He saw it was . . . a miscarriage of justice. He went to bat for me."

"Thank God," she said.

"He got the decision overturned. But by that time, there wasn't much left of my life."

She stepped beside him at the rail, keeping an arm's length from him. She cast him a sidelong glance. "You said that your parents . . . you lost them."

"My father died before I ever went to trial. My mother died while I was in prison. Heart attack. She went fast. She didn't have to suffer a lot."

Rita stared down at the railing. "You said you had . . . a girlfriend?"

"A fiancée," he said out of the corner of his mouth. "She couldn't take it. She stood it a couple of months after I was accused. She tried. But she . . . just couldn't take it."

She stole another glance at him. She could see that this conversation cost him greatly. Her own emotions were turbulent, conflicting.

"Your job?" she asked.

His mouth twitched. "I resigned. How could I coach kids when I'd killed one? It wasn't right."

"But you hadn't—"

"Rita," he said angrily, "you don't know much about basketball, either. They'd never let me forget it—the opposition. I'd damage any team that had me. The crowd would sit up in the stands and yell, 'Hey, killer! Can your team *shoot?*' Stuff like that. No. It was over."

"But none of it's fair," she said with passion.

"Life's not fair. Didn't anybody ever tell you?"

"I know, but still— I mean, how did you support yourself, pay legal expenses . . . ?"

"I worked for a builder until the trial. It doesn't matter. What happened . . . just happened."

"But all those awful things. You were *innocent.*"

Complex emotions played across his face. "No," he said. "I wasn't innocent. That's the worst part. Because, see, *I did it.* I killed a seventeen-year-old boy. I can still see him in my mind's eye. He was so tall. He could have been . . . a good basketball player. But he's dead—I did it."

He put his hand to his eyes and shaded them from her sight.

Rita felt as if her heart were being severed. The memories clearly racked him. And yet he had hurt her, too. "You let me think it was only a basketball scandal," she said softly. "Why?"

He didn't answer, only shook his head.

"You *misled* me," she continued. "Do you know how much that 'hurt? That—that awful Horchow told me, and I felt . . . dirtied, betrayed."

He said nothing.

Suddenly she felt a wave of anger at Horchow. She knew Archer's story was true; she could sense it. He had let her twist the facts to suit herself. But Horchow had twisted the facts, too, to manipulate her, turn her against Archer. And yet—as much as her heart ached for Archer—he could have *tried* to tell the truth. Why hadn't he?

"Did you think I couldn't understand?" she asked. "That I wouldn't forgive you?"

He didn't speak and she squeezed her eyes shut. No, of course he couldn't have told her. He had hardly been able to tell her now. Why would he think she could forgive him? Because he wouldn't forgive himself.

Oh, God, she thought. Her pride and her anger were cold companions, her doubt a sly and deceiving one. She loved Archer. She had trusted him before, she trusted him still.

She stepped close to him and put her arms around him. For a moment, his body stiffened and he didn't respond.

She laid her head against his shoulder, her forehead feeling feverish. "I understand why you didn't want to get involved," she said, locking her arms around his waist. "Not with Peavey. Not with me."

Suddenly his arms were around her, too, crushing her to him. "Rita," he said against her hair. "Rita. I'm so sorry. What have I done to you?"

"Oh, Archer," she said into his shoulder. "What have I done to *you*, getting you caught up in this? And what have you been doing to yourself, all these years?"

"I killed him. I *killed* him."

"It was an accident, a terrible accident."

He pressed his cheek against hers, hard. "Every day of my life," he said, his voice strained, "at some point, I look around and think, 'He can't see this day. He'll never hear music again. Or taste food. Or make love.' I did that."

"He did it to himself, too, Archer. All the blame isn't yours. You have to let go of it."

He took her face between his hands. He pressed his forehead against hers. "You know what's really ironic?" he asked. "His name was Jackie Smith. He was another John Smith. The same as me. When I pulled that trigger, it was like I killed myself, too."

"Then come back to life," she begged him, reaching up with her hand. She touched the corner of his mouth, her fingers trembling. "Please," she said. "Come back to life for me."

Something between a groan and a sob came from his throat. He raised her face to his and kissed her. He kissed her until she was faint with it, and he seemed nearly so himself.

"I won't make love to you again," he said unhappily, his lips touching hers. "Not until this is over. I won't compromise you. I don't want you to think I'm trying to love you into . . . being on my side."

"You didn't come to me. I came to you," she said, touching his mouth again. "I wanted to be snippy. I wanted to be cold. But I had to hear your side."

He laced his fingers in her hair. "I didn't kill Peavey, I swear to you. I was out like a light on the couch. I heard a shot. Then another one. I got up."

"I know, I know," she assured him, running her fingers across his lips. "I heard the same thing. I believe you."

"I went outside," he continued, looking into her eyes. "There was a lot of moonlight. Sig's dog started howling, low at first. I looked around. At first all I saw was the apple tree. And I thought, 'Peavey, you son of a bitch.' Then I looked up at his house. And I saw the flames. Not high yet. But I could see them through the windows. Then Sig came out. Then Joe."

"I *believe* you," she said with feeling. "But we still have a problem."

He nodded. "Yeah. At least, I do. Because with my past, I'm the number-one suspect."

"But you didn't do it," she said. "And if Peavey was murdered—and you didn't do it, and I didn't—then who did? Somebody here must be the killer. Who?"

They stared at each other and neither could answer. Beyond them, the lake stretched, a pure and innocent blue. Up the slope, the police sifted through the charred ruin of Peavey's house.

"They're going to try to pin this on me," Archer said, his voice bitter. "You know that, don't you?"

"I know," she said, and held him more tightly.

13

RITA WANTED TO GET AWAY from the cove, and Archer didn't blame her. She said she knew of a nature path over by the marina where they could walk through the forest.

Archer was tired, but restless, too. Ever since the police had questioned him, he'd been in the grip of a profound uneasiness, a state of floating dread. Only Rita eased it.

They drove to the marina, and she pointed out the beginning of the path. When they entered the shade of the woods, she reached over and took his hand so warmly and naturally that it gave him a sharp ache under his heart. That she could forgive him, after he had misled her . . . She was remarkable, extraordinary.

He looked down at her smooth face, her flowing hair, the glint of her big earrings. My God, she was beautiful. He wanted to smile at her, but couldn't.

"What do you think happened to Peavey—really?" she asked, squeezing his hand.

He shook his head, worried. "The police kept hammering at me that he couldn't have shot himself. That he wouldn't have held the gun at that angle—it was unnatural, peculiar. And that everybody said there were two shots. Why two? That sounds more like murder than suicide."

"Horchow kept going on about the stained glass. How did it get there? I just don't understand."

Archer, too, frowned. "I thought about that. Somebody had to plant it. To throw suspicion on you or me. Or you *and* me. I challenged the cops on it. I said, 'How do you know his throat was cut if he was burned? Are you sure?' They wouldn't answer. Maybe they couldn't. All I got out of them was that the glass was near his body. Or under it."

She shuddered. "It doesn't make sense. A piece of glass would make a terrible weapon. If you just grabbed it, you'd cut your hand all up."

Archer regarded his free hand with a look of disgust. "Mine *are* cut up."

"No," Rita disagreed. "I work with glass, I know it. You couldn't pick up a piece like that and use it for a weapon without getting a bad cut across your palm and your fingers—and the base of your thumb."

Archer let go of her hand and turned both of his palms up. There were no marks such as she described. She did the same. Her hands, too, were free of such cuts.

He felt a small wave of vindication. He slipped his arm around her shoulder, felt the silk of her hair against his flesh.

"Have you seen Sig or Joe?" he asked.

She nodded. "I saw Sig bring the dogs home. I used it for an excuse to talk to him."

"And?"

"And his hands aren't cut, either. I looked."

Archer lifted a brow. In his mind's eye he could see Joe Johanssen, his right hand swathed in bandages from the dog bite.

Rita must have read his mind. "Joe's hand was already torn up," she said. "With all those bandages, *he* could pick up glass, hold it that way. It'd be like wearing a glove."

Archer nodded, but wasn't convinced. "But anybody could have worn a glove. And a glove would mean it wasn't a spontaneous act—it was planned. That doesn't fit the scenario the cops were trying out. That I—or we—surprised Peavey at the tree, and this unexpected fight erupted."

"It's such a weird thing," Rita mused. "I mean, somebody cut his throat—or put the glass there, at least—shot him, set the house on fire, and wrote and planted a suicide note? It would have to be *very* premeditated."

His mouth twisted. "That's why they couldn't hold me. They couldn't make anything really stick. Or get me to change my story."

Somewhere in the trees, redbirds were calling—an incongruously cheerful, peaceful sound.

"They questioned Sig for three hours," Rita said. "And Joe for the same. Sig told me."

Archer's hard smile faded. "Don't get too friendly with Sig, Rita. He could have done it. Be careful."

An unhappy expression crossed her face. "I know he could. But I wanted to find out all I could."

"Joe could have done it, too," Archer said, staring into the shadows. "They both hated his guts."

Rita threw her hands out in exasperation. "That's what makes it so hard. He'd done something awful to everybody—I think. He must have poisoned Joe's dogs. He probably unstaked your dock. He gave everybody a reason to hate him."

Archer wished it was that simple. "Maybe not. Maybe somebody was planning this all along. Making it look as if Peavey was crossing everybody, so when he died, everybody looked equally suspicious."

Rita stared up at him. "Are you saying what I think? It could be Joe?"

He didn't like Johanssen, had never liked him. "Think about it. Who's got the strongest motive—and had it the longest?"

"Joe." He felt her shiver slightly, although the evening was warm. "Because of the fence and the vine. And then the tree. When Joe drinks, he can lose control."

"Yeah," Archer said with his upper lip twisting. "But he didn't seem so drunk last night. Did you notice? Like maybe he'd stayed sober because he had complicated business."

"Good Lord," she murmured. She pushed her hand through her hair. "I never thought to put it together that way. Of course, Joe could have poisoned the dogs—he didn't like them, either. *He* could have unstaked the dock."

Archer's lip curled even more cynically. "Yeah. He was mad at me. But Peavey'd been such a pain in the ass that whenever anything happened, he was the first person we thought to blame."

Rita looked up, aghast, at Archer. "Joe could have set Peavey up. Set everyone up. Made it look as if everybody had a motive to kill Peavey."

"Right," Archer said and squeezed her shoulder more tightly. "He could."

"And—and—" she stammered "—he *said* his guns were stolen. But that doesn't mean they were."

She caught on fast. God, he liked this woman, liked her so much he felt the pain under his heart again. But he tried to be flippant. "Precisely, my beautiful Watson."

"But what about the blood on my porch? Even the door? A policeman came in when they were questioning me. He said it *was* Peavey's blood. How'd it get there?"

"Yeah," Archer muttered. "That's what they told me, too. And that's the question they kept asking—how'd it get there? Damn good question."

"Well," she said earnestly, "how *did* it?"

He rubbed his forehead, stared off again into the darkening trees. "Maybe whoever killed Peavey attacked him in your yard. Maybe while he was cutting down the tree. They scuffled, got to your porch, the first blow got struck. But that's no good."

"Why not?" She snuggled closer to his side.

"Because it should have been noisy. I should have *heard* a fight that close. I don't think that's what happened."

"Then what?"

He watched a squirrel scamper out of their path. It looked ridiculously innocent in comparison to his thoughts. "I think somebody put blood there. Like, drained it out of him and spattered it there. To throw suspicion off themselves."

She put a hand to her midsection and pulled away from him slightly. "Don't say things like that. You're making me sick, talking like that."

She really did look almost ill. Archer wanted suddenly to take her in his arms. She was the only thing that kept him from feeling like a hollow man, possibly a doomed one.

"Rita," he said as gently as he could, "it's the only way I can explain it. Somebody *put* it there."

"But why us? Why would they do such things to *us?*"

He shook his head, feeling more cynical than before. "I think it was aimed more at me. Because . . . you chose me."

She put her hand to her face, covered her eyes. "If that's why this is happening, I'll never forgive myself. Never. Oh, God, we should have gone away like you wanted. We'd be out of it. We'd be safe. *You'd* be safe."

"Hey," he said. He stopped walking, took her by the shoulders. "Don't say such things. Don't feel such things. I...we... Don't. Don't cry. I couldn't stand it. You're the only good thing I've got."

She looked up at him. "I'm not crying," she said, but he saw the glint of tears in her eyes. "I just can't believe anybody could be this . . . hateful. Murder and lies, lies and murder. I hate it."

"I'm not too crazy about it myself." He forced himself to drop his hands away from her. He'd said he wouldn't make love to her again, and that, suddenly, was all he wanted—for the world to be reduced to the beautiful simplicity of making love to her.

He started to walk on. Rita stayed by his side. "Do you really think it was Joe?" she asked.

Archer jammed his hands into the pockets of his jeans. "Hell," he grumbled, shaking his head. "It could be either one of them. Sig *said* he could kill him."

Rita crossed her arms and hugged herself. "I believed him when he said could kill."

Archer squinted up through the trees. "I know Sig wouldn't poison his own dogs. But by then it seemed Peavey had done something to everybody except me. Maybe *Sig* unstaked the dock, just so it'd look like Peavey got to me, too."

She linked her arm through his and gazed at the ground. "Sig said he'd killed men in war. Of the two of them, he seems the one who really could kill somebody. But a murder this complicated? I just can't imagine it."

Archer kicked a stone aimlessly. "Sig's emotions were all tied up in those dogs. But Johanssen had both emotion *and* money at stake. And he knew it was Peavey's fault."

Rita shook her head dubiously. "But Sig said Joe's too cowardly to have even cut the fence. Could he have the nerve to murder?"

Archer gave a pessimistic shrug. "Sig could be wrong."

"What if he's right?"

"Then Joe didn't do it. And if he didn't, and you didn't, that leaves Sig."

Rita nodded, but didn't want to believe it. Sig was odd; he could be frightening, but there was something gentle in him. He was the sort of man who took in orphaned birds and squirrels.

There was violence, too, but Sig was too vague-minded to be devious. When his explosions came, they were direct, open and uncomplicated. And yet . . . he did get violent, he'd had explosions. She was ashamed to realize she was grateful.

She hugged Archer's arm more tightly, moved closer to him. "At least Sig's been in trouble with the law, too. You're not the only one."

"No," Archer said begrudgingly. "But I'm their best bet. They *want* me. I could see it in their eyes. They think they'll get me, too."

"No," she countered. "There's no such thing as a perfect murder. And this one's too—too weird. Whoever did it made a mistake somewhere. And the police will find it. They have to."

"The police," he echoed with contempt. "You don't know them like I do."

She looked up at his profile, severe in the fading light. "They're not all bad. The one called Mallenhoff was actually nice to me—really. He might listen to reason."

Archer's teeth were set on edge. "Rita, you've got too much faith in human nature. Mallenhoff isn't 'nice.' These guys play a game called Good Cop, Bad Cop. It's a trick to throw you off-balance. You think you can trust one."

She blinked in dismay. "No—" she tried to protest.

"Yes," he said emphatically. "And when they really want to mess with your head, they change roles. If they haul you in again, Mallenhoff might be so nasty that Horchow starts looking good."

He swore. "It's like the Gestapo. It's like being a prisoner of war. Pretty soon they almost make you *believe* you've done it."

"They can't question you again," she argued, stopping in the path and putting her hand on his shoulder. "And the look on your face scares me. You look like you believe that…that you're fated or something. It can't happen. They can't accuse you of this. It won't happen."

He set his jaw at a resentful angle. "Rita, this isn't never-never land. It's not a fairy tale. They look at my past. They've got Peavey dead. And if they can't find anybody better, they'll charge me."

"No," she protested, her hand tightening on his shirt. "Don't say that. Lightning can't strike twice. They won't put you on trial again, Archer."

"Damn right, they won't," he said stormily. "And you know why? Because I won't stand still for it this time. I'll put up bond, and I'll by God skip. I'll go on the run. I won't take the chance of going back to prison. Not again."

The look in his eyes was determined and wild. His words shocked her, but she knew he meant what he said. "You can't do that. You'd be a fugitive—you'd never have peace again."

"Do you think I have peace now?" he demanded. "I told you. They may think the others are interesting—but they think I'm their boy. They grilled them for three hours. Who'd they keep for eight?"

She put her hands on his upper arms, grasping them tightly. She tried to shake him, but he was too strong. "If you run, they'll be sure you're guilty."

He almost laughed. "Hell, they're pretty sure now, baby."

"You couldn't," she insisted, frightened for him. "It'd be suicide."

"No," he said with terrifying conviction. "I'll tell you what's suicide: going through it again. Going to prison again."

What about me? she wanted to cry. But she couldn't ask that. He'd never made any promises to stay.

He seemed to understand her thought. "I could take you with me," he said, putting his hands on her waist. "But it wouldn't be right. Look, if it comes to that, I'll take you with me...inside me, in my heart. I want you to know that if things go wrong, what I had with you was the most—"

She put her hand across his mouth. "No. Don't say things will go wrong."

Firmly he took her hand, drew it away, placed it against his chest. "Listen," he said fervently. "I'm to the point where I almost feel sorry for that SOB, Peavey. Once I looked into his eyes, and I saw something I recognized but couldn't remember. Maybe I didn't want to remember."

She stared at him, full of dread for him.

He pressed her hand harder against his chest. "Once, years ago, a rat got into my parents' store. It was doing a lot of damage and scaring my mother out of her mind. My father set this trap for it—an ugly trap, cruel. I was only a kid, but I hated the thing more than I hated the rat."

"Archer, you can't—"

"Shh," he said, bringing his face level with hers. "Listen. I went to the store one Sunday morning. My chore was to sweep it out. I was alone. I heard a noise in the storeroom. It was the rat. It was caught, but it wasn't dead."

She wasn't sure she could stand any more. "Don't. Please—"

"Rita...it was trying to chew its leg off. The look in its eyes—I can't describe it. That's how Peavey looked to me. Like a rat in a trap, crazy with pain. That's how I felt in prison. It's how I'm feeling now. I can't be trapped again."

"Archer..." She took his face between her hands.

He looked stricken. "The things I want to say to you," he said in a low, tight voice. "The things I want to do with you..."

"Say them," she urged, pressing her forehead against his chest. "Do them."

He gathered her to him, held her closely. "Rita, I feel it happening again. I know it's happening. This time I can't stand still. I can't let the trap close. I'll have to leave you."

"No," she said. "No." She lifted her face and kissed him.

"Rita . . . don't. Please, don't."

She kissed him again.

And in spite of all his high-minded vows, he found himself taking her in his arms, desperate with need for her. He wanted to stroke every inch of her body, kiss it, lose himself inside her. And he was kissing her, stroking her, so hard with desire it hurt. They fell to their knees under a wild mimosa tree and made love among the fallen blossoms.

"I'm sorry," he said afterward, touching her face. "I didn't mean to do that. I promised not to."

"If something happens," she said, her lips against the hollow of his throat, "don't run. It's the worst thing you could do. Don't run. Please."

He held her so tightly she couldn't breathe; so tightly it was as if he could never let her go. "I can't promise you anything," he said.

HE DIDN'T DO IT, he didn't do it, her mind kept chanting, during the drive home. *He made a mistake once. It was a terrible mistake, but an honest one. They can't keep persecuting him for it. They can't.*

But when they reached the cove, there were two sheriff's-department cars sitting next to the road by Archer's house. Her stomach twisted in fear. She sensed Archer's muscles stiffening, saw his hands tighten on the wheel. He swore.

"No . . ." She breathed the word like a prayer.

Archer's face had the hard, blank look of a man facing deadly odds but determined to fight. "There's two cars," he said tersely. "That means they're taking you, too. Stick to your story. You know the truth, don't let them shake you."

"Archer—" she said fearfully and touched his arm.

"They'll do the Good Cop, Bad Cop thing again. Don't let it fool you. Don't worry about protecting anybody except yourself. You're innocent. You haven't done anything."

"Archer, I'm scared," she said. "You don't think they're really here after me. They just want me to say something against you—don't they?"

"Just tell them the truth," he said, pulling up beside the cars. "Don't get smart, don't get cute. Don't flare up. Tell them the truth and watch out for yourself."

"It's not me I'm worried about," she said, clutching his sleeve. "It's you. . . ."

But he didn't seem to hear her. He was already opening the door. Two deputies had already gotten out of the cars at their approach.

She was amazed at Archer's facade of calm. He looked the deputies up and down with no apparent trace of fear. "Can I do something for you, gentlemen?" he asked. But she could hear the tension in his voice.

The larger, older of the two deputies stepped nearer to Archer. He had his right thumb hooked into his belt, his hand near his gun. "We want to bring you in for questioning again, John. And your girlfriend, Rita, too."

Archer nodded mildly, as if digesting the information and accepting it. He walked to the other side of the truck and opened Rita's door. When she stepped out, he put his arm around her protectively.

He stared levelly at the more aggressive deputy. "She had nothing to do with Peavey's death. I can guarantee you that. She's innocent."

"That may be so, John—"

"Archer," Archer said without emotion. "I go by Archer." His arm tightened around her, more possessively, more protectively.

"*Archer,*" the deputy repeated sarcastically. "Well, Archer, you and Rita have some new questions to answer. We'll just see how much the two of you know."

Rita tensed. The pressure of Archer's arm told her to be quiet, to let him do the talking.

"Know about what?" Archer asked, sounding almost bored.

The deputy hooked his other thumb in his belt buckle. He looked the two of them up and down with contempt. "About the typewriter they found dropped in the water just off your dock—Archer. We've had divers. They got lucky. Looks like the typewriter that wrote that 'suicide' note. They'll want to know why you dropped it off the dock—Archer."

Rita's head snapped back in surprise. Archer had pulled her closer still—whether consciously or unconsciously, she didn't know.

"And," the deputy continued sardonically, "they found a hacksaw buried near your yard. They're gonna want to know what you know about that. You come with me—Archer. Rita, you go with Officer Wolfe, here."

The typewriter that wrote the suicide note, Rita thought numbly. *Dropped off Archer's dock. The saw that cut down the tree. Buried nearby.*

She watched, disbelieving, as the deputy named Wolfe walked toward her, took her by the arm. He *looked* like a wolf, she thought dazedly. He had a pointed face and cold, pale eyes set at a slant.

She saw the other, older deputy take Archer by the arm, lead him toward the other car. Without protest, she went with Wolfe.

He put her in the back seat of the car—that was different from last night. A mesh separated her from the front seat and made her feel as if she were in a cage. There were no inside handles on the doors. She was being treated like a prisoner.

She didn't heed Archer's advice to think only of herself. "He didn't do it," she told Wolfe as he pulled onto the road. "He's innocent . . . innocent."

Wolfe didn't bother looking at her. "Yeah," he said without inflection. "That's what their women usually say, Rita."

"He's *innocent,*" she insisted, but she'd never felt as powerless in her life.

TO HER DISGUST, it was Horchow and Mallenhoff questioning her again. Horchow retained his hostile role. He thrust question after question at her, as if he were sticking pins into her.

She told the truth. She didn't know if Archer had a typewriter. She'd never been to his house before today. She knew nothing about the hacksaw.

She struggled hard to contain her anger and frustration. She struggled equally hard to keep Horchow from intimidating her. He was good at intimidation. And Mallenhoff was good at seeming sympathetic.

The turning point came when Mallenhoff, in his role of false friend, spoke as if on her behalf.

"Rita," Mallenhoff said in a too-gentle voice, "sometimes women think with their hearts, not their heads. Now try to be logical, can you? Everything points to Archer Smith. You know it. We know it."

His words made her so angry that the air of the small room seemed to fill with a red mist. *I'll show you what logical is, you son of a bitch,* she thought. *I'll show you how to think.*

"All you've got is circumstantial evidence," she said with such utter coldness that Mallenhoff's sleepy eyes opened wider. "All you've got is a stupid theory so complicated it's impossible. And you're calling him guilty because he was convicted once before—wrongly. You can't prove a thing. And you *know* that."

"Rita," Horchow said, "you're getting sassy. Being defensive. Scared? Why?"

"I'm tired of this," she said with passion. "Why would he do such a stupid thing? Drop the typewriter off his own dock? Then *bury* the hacksaw? Bury it in such an obvious place you could find it in one day? Use a piece of glass for a weapon? It's idiotic. He's being framed—and you're falling for it."

"Rita, Rita, Rita," Mallenhoff said mournfully. "You're thinking with your heart, not your head."

I'm the only one in this room thinking at all, you fascist, she thought. But she lifted her chin defiantly and said nothing.

In the end, they could charge her with nothing. They had to let her go. But they still held Archer.

SHE REALIZED ONLY WHEN they led her out of the interrogation room that she and Archer were not the only ones the police had called back.

Joe Johanssen was being led from another room by another deputy. Like her, he was taken downstairs. They were put into separate cars and driven back to the cove. The car he was in followed hers all the way.

When the cars arrived at the cove, she was let out. So was Joe. Nobody spoke. Joe went into his house, his head down. She went into hers.

She closed the door and leaned against it, taking a deep breath. She felt like a hunted animal that had escaped but was still in danger. *Archer's the one in danger*, she reflected. *I've got to help Archer.*

She heard the slamming of the deputies' car doors, heard motors start and the cars turn around and head up the road. She waited until their sound faded completely.

Then she took another deep breath and went back outside. She half walked, half ran to Joe's house. She pounded on his door.

He took a long time to answer, and when he did, his face was wary, full of reluctance.

He had a bottle of beer in his bandaged hand. Rita wanted to close her eyes and pray: *No. Don't let him drink. This man may be a killer, don't let him start drinking again.*

But she was desperate. She had to have information—at any price.

Some men like to think women are stupid and helpless, she thought. *Use it.*

She smiled rather sickly at Joe. "Joe," she said. Her voice was shaky, and she let it be. She looked into his eyes as if he alone could save her. "What's happening to us? I feel so ... confused. And ... and helpless."

He looked her up and down. There was caution in his gaze, even calculation, but she thought she saw a spark of hunger, as well.

After a moment he licked his lips and looked into her eyes. She tried to seem as guileless and dependent as possible. Once more she thought, *This man may be a murderer.*

But Joe finally opened the door. "Come in," he said, like a spider inviting a fly into its web.

14

Rita was willing to play only *so* stupid.

She ducked her head, pretending to blush. "I—I don't think I'd better," she said. "You know. Would you sit on the porch and just . . . talk to me?"

He looked her up and down again. She stole a glance and saw him take a long pull of beer. "All right," he said at last. He gave her a look of distrust, but he came out on the porch. Gingerly he lowered himself into one of his deck chairs. As demurely as possible, she sat beside him.

"So," she said, letting her voice tremble. "They called you in again, too? Joe, they can't think *you* killed Peavey. You'd never do anything like that."

Liar, liar, she thought, her heart speeding in agitation.

But he took the bait. "They took us all in," he said bitterly. "They've still got Sig. Your boyfriend, too, huh? Well, maybe you and I seem more innocent than the others. Maybe not."

She realized, with a wave of dismay, that she was alone at the cove with Joe. But that didn't seem as important as the news of Sig.

They're holding Sig, too. Archer wasn't the only one they suspected.

She let her surprise show on her face. She tried to seem even more defenseless. "They're still questioning Sig?"

Joe glared at the shell of Peavey's house. It was a dark hulk in the moonlight, and the crime-scene tape that fenced it off fluttered gently in the breeze.

Joe exhaled in disgust. "I'd just got home. There were cops everywhere. It was like an anthill of cops. They were digging in Sig's yard. They found the hacksaw. I saw them do it."

Her scalp tingled with surprise. She slid him a reticent look. He was taking another long drink of beer. "They found the hacksaw in *Sig's* yard?"

"Right next to the road," Joe said, sounding disgusted. "Why didn't he have the brains to throw it in the lake, too? He's got a boat. Why didn't he go out to the middle and drop the whole shebang in? Jeez, he never did have any brains."

"Joe," she said in shock that was only half feigned. "You really think Sig did it? That *he* killed Peavey?"

"Hell, yes," Joe said with vehemence. "I've lived next door to the SOB for four years now. He's got a screw loose. Anybody touch one of those stinking dogs, he'd kill, all right. He's just enough of a wing nut."

He drained his beer. Rita squared her jaw in determination. "Do you have another of those?" she asked. "I could use one."

"I could use another one myself," he said with angry resignation. "Who's gonna buy this house *now*? Now we got a murder charge hangin' over everything. Who's gonna buy a house next to a goddam killing ground?"

Rita gripped the arms of her chair tightly and watched him as he rose and lumbered inside. He didn't *talk* like a murderer. He talked like the Joe she knew—self-centered and worried most about his own problems.

She took a deep breath, trying to marshal her thoughts. Joe was back in a moment, bearing a freshly opened twelve-pack of beers. He sat down, giving her one and taking one for himself. He opened his and took a long gulp.

"Why—" she said carefully "—why do you think it's Sig?"

Joe glowered at the moon. If he was acting, he was doing a fine job, she thought.

"I told you," he said with contempt, "that boy's a few bricks shy of a load. As soon as Peavey touched those dogs, he was a dead man."

She opened the beer for appearance's sake. "You think Peavey poisoned them?" she asked. Then, although she hated herself, she batted her eyelashes slightly.

Joe's chest puffed out. "*I* sure as hell didn't do it. I didn't want him coming after me with that shotgun. Well, he and Peavey were two of a kind. Good riddance to bad rubbish. But will *anybody* buy this house now?"

He shook his head unhappily. "A murder victim. A psycho killer. Great neighborhood. Criminy, I got the worst luck in the universe."

She pretended to sip her beer. She tried to think hard and logically, the way none of the men believed her capable of thinking. "They're holding . . . Archer, too. Why? I *know* he didn't do it."

Joe tossed her a measuring glance. "You shouldn't of took up with that guy, Rita. Nobody knows anything about him. There must be something in his past. You should stick with people you know."

She gritted her teeth and fought off a shudder of repulsion. "Maybe. But even *you* think it's Sig. Why hold Archer?"

Joe narrowed his eyes. "Maybe they think they did it together," he said bitterly. "They're confused, is what—the cops are. Why'd they drag me in again? Why you?"

"I don't know," Rita said. She pretended to take another drink of beer. Joe took a bona fide chugalug. *Drink up,* she silently urged. *Drink enough to talk your lips off. But not enough to chase me around the cove. I'm not up to that tonight.*

"You know why they keep pulling me into it?" Joe said in a knowing, superior voice. "They're so confused, they're toying with a goddam conspiracy theory, is what. They're playing with the idea that we *all* killed him. Together."

Truly surprised, Rita could only stare at him. Joe gave her a wise wink. "But they can't pin anything on *me*. Except a couple of unregistered guns. And I came clean about that right off. I'm nobody's fool."

Rita sat very still, the beer can a cold weight in her hand. "I . . . came clean, too," she said, as if she were making a great confidence to him. "I admitted there'd been trouble between Peavey and me. I actually thought of cutting a hole in Peavey's fence myself. But I didn't. Tell me, Joe—just between the two of us—did you do it?"

The beer he'd been swallowing went down the wrong way, and he sputtered. He looked at her with resentment. *"No,"* he said emphatically. "You want to know the truth, Rita? I wasn't even *conscious* the night that fence got cut. Peavey got me so mad I drank too much and passed out. I'm not proud of it, but it's the truth."

She gazed up at the moon. "I wish I *had* cut it," she lied. "I'd be proud if I'd had the nerve."

Joe finished his beer and reached for another. "I don't have wire cutters—nothing like that," he muttered. "Ask the police. They searched this place. They searched us all. Hell, if I wanted his stinking fence down, I wouldn't cut a slit in it. I'd of got in my car and drove it down, dammit."

God help me, I believe him, Rita thought. *Let him keep talking. And not turn amorous.*

She shrank against the back of her chair, trying to look smaller and weaker than she was. "Did Sig have a type-writer? I was only in his house once. I don't remember one."

"Humph," Joe grunted. "He coulda had anything in that junk pile. Coulda had a hundred typewriters."

Rita pondered this. She phrased her next question carefully. "They kept asking and asking me about a typewriter. I said I didn't have one. What did you say?"

Joe drank, then wiped the foam from his lips. "I told 'em the truth. I don't have a typewriter 'cause I can't type. And if I *did* have one, and did write the stupid suicide note, I wouldn't be dumb enough to drop it off a dock. Hell, I'd of put it and the hacksaw into Peavey's house—so nobody'd suspect anything."

Rita pressed her lips together, thinking furiously. What Joe said made sense. Why *hadn't* the killer planted the saw and typewriter inside Peavey's house? Because he hadn't had time to think of it? Or because he simply wasn't thinking clearly?

"You're right," she agreed. "That's right, Joe."

"I read a lotta murder mysteries," he said with pride. Then he belched softly. "I figure these things out." He squinted at

Sig's house malevolently. "You know what? I think Sig might of cut that dock loose, too. Hoping your boyfriend'd think it was Peavey. Maybe he even cut down your apple tree. Yeah. Ever think of that?"

She blinked in surprise and gripped her beer more tightly. "Sig?" she asked. "Well . . . to be honest, *yes*. I thought about him letting the dock loose. But my tree? I never thought of that."

Joe sank more deeply into his chair. "Sure. Make you both think Peavey struck at you, too. Then we're all mad at him— right? We all got motives. Sig spreads the suspicion all around—everywhere."

Joe's speech was growing slurred. By the moon's light, she could see his eyelids fluttering, trying to stay open. He'd had little sleep last night; none of them had. The beer was having a narcotic effect.

"Joe," she said, frantic to learn as much as she could. "*Why* are you so sure it's Sig?"

"Because," he said drowsily, "who wazza one doin' violent stuff from the start? Him. Cuttin' that fence. Sittin' out there with his shotgun."

"But how can you be *sure* he cut the fence?"

"To get me in trouble," Joe mumbled. "All he cares about is his stupid dogs. Who didn't like his dogs? Me 'n' Peavey. So he steals my guns and kills Peavey. Tries to blame everybody else. Whadda mess. Good God, who's gonna buy this house now? I got the worst luck in the world."

He took one more drink. Then he set the can on his stomach, holding it with both hands. "My *property* values..." he mourned, barely audibly. Then his eyes closed, his head dropped to one side and he was asleep.

Rita stared at him in frustration. He began to snore quietly.

Gently she took the beer can from him and set it on the floor of the porch. Then she rose, uncertain what to do next. She glanced at his screen door. His living room lights burned brightly. He'd left the door unlocked. Just as he said he had the night he claimed the guns had been stolen.

I shouldn't go inside, she thought, but couldn't take her eyes from the screen door. *It'd be immoral, illegal and an invasion of his privacy.*

But then she thought of Archer. How long had the police had him this time? Almost five hours. She drew a long, shuddery breath and stepped inside Joe's house.

It was half bare—his wife had taken much of the furniture. It was surprisingly neat; Joe was a tidier person than she was.

She looked about the room. The gun rack stood against the wall, empty. A tiny desk was placed against the opposite wall, next to the plaid sofa. Joe's phone sat on it, atop the phone book. His bills were arranged in a letter holder. There was a beer mug holding pens and pencils, a stamp dispenser, and a small box of stationery.

She opened the box. The paper was note-size and had his name and address printed in the corner. There wasn't room on the desk for a typewriter. The only other blank paper she found was a lined pad in his desk drawer. It was stamped with an advertisement for his realtor.

She gritted her teeth. She hadn't seen the suicide note, but certainly it couldn't have been written on Joe's stationery or a sheet from the realtor's pad. Such evidence would have pointed straight to him.

She searched the house quickly but thoroughly, with criminal boldness. She even looked in his clothes hamper, searching for bloodstained clothing. Surely if you blasted a person at close range with a shotgun, you'd get bloody—wouldn't you?

But her search yielded nothing. He had a small toolbox, but it was nearly empty. It held a hammer, two screwdrivers, a pair of pliers, that was all. It was too short and narrow to contain a hacksaw.

She slipped back outside, glanced down guiltily at Joe. He snored loudly now, his mouth open, his legs spread apart.

She started down the steps to her own house. She saw four of Sig's dogs on his porch, whining by the big wooden bin in which he kept their sacked dog food. They were pawing at the bin, and one stood on its hind legs, straining to reach the hidden food.

She sighed in exasperation. The poor dogs were hungry. And there was no one to feed them, except her. She squared her shoulders and went to Sig's deck. The dogs danced around her eagerly, their claws chattering against the floorboards.

She was using an old metal scoop to ladle food into the dogs' bowls, when a sheriff's-department car drove up.

She straightened, her heart beating wildly with hope. *Archer, come home to me. Let the nightmare be over.*

But the car stopped before Sig's house, and it was Sig who climbed out, looking more gaunt than usual in the moonlight. He looked her up and down, his face expressionless. He climbed his steps, his back straight, but with weariness in his gait.

Rita put the scoop back in the bin. A sharp pain pierced her heart, a duller one drilled into her stomach. The police still held Archer.

She looked up into Sig's shadowy face. "You're back."

He nodded.

She turned away, biting her lip. She felt empty, full of foreboding. She could feel him watching her.

"You was feeding my dogs," he said. "That was nice of you, Rita. You're a nice woman."

She faced him again, her expression bitter. "I'm not a *happy* woman. They've still got him—Archer. They must think he did it."

She wanted to go on, to say how impossible it was for Archer to be guilty, but her voice failed her. It was going to break, and then she would cry, and she refused to cry because she had to be strong.

"Maybe he did do it, Rita," Sig said quietly. "Maybe you should accept that."

"No," she said. "He couldn't have. I—I *know* him."

Sig sighed. He raked his hand through his graying hair. "Rita, I *didn't* kill Peavey. And the police know. I'm—what do you call it—?"

"Cleared?" she echoed in a choked voice. "How? Why did they keep you so long?"

He shook his head and gazed up at the moon. "Cleared. I'm cleared. They kept me 'cause I done some bad stuff in the past, like shooting when those kids threw firecrackers at my dogs. They let me go on account I can't spell so good."

She stared at him without comprehension.

He shuffled his feet, looked down at the feeding dogs. "They read me these words to write. It was the words to the suicide note, I guess. I . . . couldn't spell 'em good."

She balled and unballed her fists. "The n-note. What did it say?"

He shook his head in disgust. "It was all crazy. It was talking about things I never heard of. Exit—essential. Exit—essential dee-spair. Crazy stuff."

"Existential despair?" Rita asked. "Was that what it said, 'Existential despair'?"

Sig shifted his weight uneasily. "Maybe. Hell, Rita, I couldn't write nothin' like that." He gave a contemptuous laugh. "Neither could Joe."

But they think Archer could, she thought in distress. *Archer's been to college.* She knew the term *existential despair* from her own freshman philosophy course. It meant a hopeless belief that life was absurd and without meaning.

She turned to stare across the yards to where Joe slept, sprawled in his lawn chair. *Joe, then,* she thought. *It has to be Joe. There's nobody else left.*

"I know what you're thinking," Sig said in a slow voice. "You think Joe done it. No. They let him go first. He don't got the guts, Rita. Once you been in a war, you can look into a man's eyes and tell it—can he kill? Joe's a coward. But your friend—he ain't."

She drew in her breath so sharply it hurt. "Don't say things like that. Joe . . . could have cut that fence. He *can* be destructive."

Sig shook his head and swore softly. "He don't have that much nerve. I told you that."

She drew herself up tall. "Then *you* cut the fence. Maybe you and Joe worked together. He wrote the note—you killed Peavey. And now the two of you are trying . . ."

He put his hand on her shoulder. The gesture sent tremors of fear through her. She shouldn't have spoken so recklessly, accusing him that way. Now he was touching her, and she had no one to help her.

Archer, I want you, her mind cried.

"I didn't," Sig said bending close to her, "cut that fence. I gave you my word I wouldn't. I gave you the wire cutters. Your boyfriend must of done it."

"No!" she retorted. "Why would he? He didn't want to get involved. He wouldn't have gotten involved at all—if it hadn't been for me."

Sig bent closer. "Rita, you took up with that feller and you hardly knew him. People ain't always what they seem. Like me. Did you ever look at me, Rita? Really look at me?"

"Leave me alone," she almost sobbed. She struck his hand away from her shoulder. He stepped back, as if she had frightened or hurt him.

"You don't *know* him," she said angrily.

Sig stood silent for a moment, studying her. "They told me something," he said at last. "Your boyfriend, he won't take no lie-detector test. I said I would. Joe said he would. Your boyfriend won't. Now what's that tell you?"

He won't let them trap him again, she wanted to scream. *It tells me he won't play their game. He's fighting—that's all*.

"I seen he had something . . . dangerous in him," Sig said in his slow voice. "I seen it in his eyes. I never thought he'd hurt you, though. Or do any of this. I'd of kept him away from you—if I'd known."

"*You* were the dangerous ones," she accused. "You and Joe and Peavey. Archer stepped in because—"

"Rita, you don't know him. You're talking crazy. Trust me. I'll watch out for you—"

"Stay away from me," she ordered. "I don't trust you."

He tried to reach for her again, but she shouldered her way past him, fled down the steps and to her own yard. She couldn't help herself. The tears spilled over, ran hotly down her face.

She stopped on her porch. Even in the moonlight she could see the blood on her doorstep. She ran her hands through her hair, weeping harder.

The blood, the damning bloodstains. How had they got there? Between the evidence of the bloodstains and the sunken typewriter, Archer was trapped. Caught like a rat in a trap.

She pressed her fingertips against her throbbing temples. She glanced, tearfully, back toward Sig's house. He hadn't followed her. He stood amid his tail-wagging dogs, staring in her direction.

She held her head higher. Maybe she was right; Sig and Joe had worked together to kill Peavey. Maybe they would come after her tonight, because she suspected them.

Let them try, she thought bitterly. *If they do, then they'll show their hand. They'll prove Archer's innocent.*

But she was confused. Why would neither of them admit to cutting the fence? It was such a petty thing, compared to murder.

Oh, hell, she thought in despair, did it matter who cut the fence? Maybe Peavey had done it himself, just to make them all suspect each other. Maybe she'd walked in her sleep and done it herself. Anything was starting to seem possible.

The wind rose, and something angular and white tumbled across the corner of the porch and came to rest against the side of the house. She stared at it without knowing why.

She should go inside, get out of Sig's sight. *Let him watch,* she thought, strangely calm at her center. *Let him watch if that's what it takes to have him make his move.*

Slowly, almost languidly, she walked to the white thing rustling in the flower bed. It was part of a book, she saw, its pages fluttering in the silvery light. It's edges were charred. It must have been in the fire.

With the same dreamy slowness, she reached for it. It was caught among the tall leaves of the tulips that had long since bloomed. She had always loved the tulips. Her grandmother had planted them years ago....

The pages were the front part of a book; its cover was gone. In the faint light she could read the title page, even before she took the little sheaf from the tulip bed.

Tulips, she thought.

Caught like a rat in a trap.

Her hand stopped, as if she'd been bewitched and turned to stone. She read the title again.

Tulips, she thought again in awe. *Tulips.*

A rat in a trap.

Thunderstruck, she knelt before the book, motionless. She watched its black-edged pages riffle in the wind. A series of thoughts plunged through her mind, and she watched them falling into place like the pieces of a puzzle.

"My God," she whispered to herself. Tears sprang to her eyes again. "Tulips," she breathed.

Her hand shaking, she picked up the remnant of the book. She stood and turned to stare at Peavey's house. The crime-scene tape fluttered, fencing it off, and signs warned her to stay out.

She ignored them. She was conscious that Sig still watched, but she walked slowly to the tape. She stared down at it a moment, then stepped over it.

Picking her way through the rubble, she walked to the blackened, gaping rectangle that had once been the front door.

Moonlight poured into the ruined house through the door and windows and a burned hole in the roof. She stood, scrutinizing the living room. She looked at it a long time.

Then, at last, she saw what she wanted to see, what she had prayed to see. It stood, charred but still intact, half obscured by pieces of the fallen roof.

And then she understood. If she could just get more information—just a little more.

Her phone was ringing when she entered her house, still clutching the book. With a mixture of hesitance and hope, she picked up the receiver. *Archer*, she thought. *Tell me you're coming home and it's all right.*

But it wasn't Archer. The voice belonged to a stranger. He said his name was William Patterson, from St. Louis, and he was Archer's lawyer.

"Yes," she said, full of sudden foreboding.

"He called me," Patterson said grimly. "He got only one phone call. He asked me to call you."

"Yes?" She closed her eyes. She knew what he was going to say.

"Miss O'Casey," Patterson said slowly, as if he hated saying the words, "tonight Archer was arrested for first-degree murder. He—he said to tell you that he'll be fine. That he can take care of himself."

She kept her eyes shut. She said nothing. She pressed the broken book against her chest and held her breath.

"I'm coming there," Patterson said. "I'm leaving immediately. I'll arrange for bail to be posted."

He said if he got out on bail, he'd run, she thought. *And he will.* She said nothing. She held the book tighter.

"Miss O'Casey? Are you there? Listen, the important thing is not to panic. We'll work this out. Things will be fine. I assure you that I'll do everything in my power...."

She nodded, and an odd feeling, almost like serenity welled up inside her. She thought of the tulips. She thought of a rat in a trap.

"Yes," she said quietly, even, calmly. "Things will be fine."

15

RITA AND PATTERSON walked into the county courthouse shortly after one o'clock the next day.

Patterson was a small, wiry man with thinning white hair and a formal manner. His face seemed ordinary, bland, even uninteresting—until one looked into his eyes.

Patterson's irises were a startlingly clear amber color. This made his gaze as golden—and as alert—as that of a fox. A quick and relentless intelligence shone in his eyes.

Today both his face and Rita's showed weariness. They had caught but little sleep the night before. Patterson had arrived at the cove shortly after midnight. He had flown in in his own Cessna plane and had rented a car.

He'd knocked at Rita's door because she'd told him she'd wait up for him. He'd appeared on her threshold like an elderly wizard, but bearing the magic tools of technology: a cellular phone, a portable computer and fax machine, even a compact dot-matrix printer.

He'd invited her to come discuss the case at his house, which was larger and more comfortable. They'd spent the night talking, drafting letters, laying out strategies—and phoning. Patterson was a demon for phoning. Sometimes one would steal a nap on the couch while the other kept working.

Now they strode into the courthouse. Patterson's eyes were shadowed by fatigue, but he radiated an aura of cool and perfect confidence, and Rita, with less success, tried to do the same.

She'd dressed in a demure skirt and a blouse with a button-down collar. She felt uncomfortable, but knew she had to dress this way for the occasion. She'd even put on high-heeled shoes. She'd pulled her hair back as tightly as she could and fastened it with a gold barrette.

Patterson was natty in an expensive summer suit. He carried an ancient briefcase that bulged alarmingly. He and Rita walked up the stairs to the detective division.

Rita looked at the drab, familiar walls and shuddered. Somewhere, down in the depths of the courthouse basement, in the county jail, Archer was locked behind bars and going through hell. Every time she thought of him her heart withered as if it would die.

Patterson walked, without hesitation, to a door whose frosted-glass window was stenciled Chief of Detectives. He did not knock. He pulled it open as if he owned the place, and marched inside. Rita swallowed hard and followed him.

The chief of detectives was named Fitzgibbons. Patterson had found out the man's name, character, strengths and weaknesses during the night's long work session.

Patterson had learned much about a great many things. He pursued information doggedly and had no qualms about phoning in the middle of the night to demand it. He was by turns so commanding and persuasive that he usually got it.

Fitzgibbons sat at his desk in a short-sleeved shirt, his tie loosened. He had been dictating into a tape recorder. When he saw Patterson and Rita, he frowned and switched it off. He had a graying crew cut and a bulldog face that clearly said, *Who the hell are you people?*

"What is this?" he demanded.

"I'm William Hartford Patterson, attorney, of Patterson, Truman, and Vanderbilt. I represent John Archer Smith, whom you are holding under false arrest. This is Miss O'Casey, who has evidence to offer on my client's behalf."

Patterson swung his heavy briefcase onto Fitzgibbons's desk so that it landed with a reverberating thud. He unfastened its closing straps. "Miss O'Casey, by the way," Patterson said, speaking quickly and with calm authority, "was questioned about this case. Certain of her civil rights were severely violated."

Fitzgibbons's dark eyes went cold and glazed at the words *civil rights*. He stiffened in his chair. Rita watched with bitter satisfaction.

"But that," Patterson said, rifling through his papers, "is a matter I will pursue later. What I demand *now* is the release of my client."

Fitzgibbons held up one big hand, a signal for Patterson to slow. "Whoa," he said condescendingly. "Your *client* is under arrest. You want him out? Post bond. The judge sets it this afternoon."

"Wrong," Patterson said, not slowing a whit. "I want my client released, not out on bond. I also want to see the arresting officer. I want my client to be present."

"Now wait a minute," Fitzgibbons said militantly. "You don't barge in here giving me orders, pal. You—"

"I have a writ," Patterson said, unfazed, "from Judge Rodham that my client has a right to be present." He slapped an official-looking document on Fitzgibbons's desk.

Fitzgibbons frowned more formidably, but he also looked uncomfortable. "How in hell did you get a writ from Rodham?"

"That's immaterial," Patterson said with a loftiness that Rita admired. "I also have a writ demanding the arresting officer be present."

Rita almost smiled as Patterson slapped down the second document. He was master of intimidation and the unexpected move. He had labored all morning to get the writs, and now he produced them like rabbits out of a hat.

Fitzgibbons was clearly caught off-balance. "My arresting officer is home in bed," he objected.

"Wake him," Patterson retorted. "I have *writs,* sir. Or will you violate a judge's direct orders?"

He's good, Rita thought with gratification. *He's really good*.

With a look of disgruntlement, Fitzgibbons picked up the writs and read them.

Patterson glowered down at Fitzgibbons as if the other man were a hopelessly guilty defendant. "According to Black,

Nolan, and Connally, false arrest may be grounds for suit and punitive damages. At the heart of the tort is . . ."

Patterson plunged on, as if reciting an incantation. Rita held her breath as Fitzgibbons pored over the writs.

At last Fitzgibbons reached for the phone. He punched the buttons with undisguised ill-humor. He scowled up at Patterson and Rita. "Hello," he growled into the mouthpiece. "Horchow? I don't care. I want you here, and I want you now. Why? Trouble on this damn Peavey case, is what."

He crashed down the receiver and glared at Patterson. "He'll be here as soon as he can. Wait outside. I've got work to do."

"Indeed, you have," Patterson said frigidly. "Now, what about my client? I have a writ—"

"You'll see your client when Horchow gets here," Fitzgibbons snapped nastily. "Now—out."

Patterson shut his briefcase with cool efficiency, picked it up and offered Rita his arm. He cast Fitzgibbons a superior glance and walked her from the room. He almost left a trail of frost in the air.

When the door closed behind them, she looked into his fox-yellow, intelligent eyes. "You're a wonder," she breathed.

"No, my dear," he said with an amused half-smile. "I am merely brilliant. *You* are the wonder."

"We'll see," she said worriedly. She had great faith in Patterson. She had faith in what she herself had discovered. But was faith enough?

HORCHOW CAME STAMPING up the stairs, unshaven, his beefy face ruddy with displeasure. When he saw Rita his lip curled. He didn't speak. He knocked at Fitzgibbons's door and was admitted.

Rita watched the clock on the courthouse wall tick away. Fitzgibbons and Horchow isolated themselves for almost twenty minutes. Rita grew twitchy and more worried than before.

Patterson, calm, read a copy of *The Yale Law Review*.

Then, when her nerves had almost reached the shattering point, she heard heavy footsteps on the stairs. She whirled on her wooden bench and stared toward the sound. She stood, her heart pounding crazily.

She drew in her breath when she saw Archer between two uniformed deputies. He still wore the clothes he'd had on the evening before, and his jaw was stubbled. His hands were cuffed before him, his ankles manacled. The expressionless deputies held him, one by each arm.

Archer made his way, shuffling and clanking, toward Fitzgibbons's door. Archer's face was more masklike than the deputies', but there was something dangerous deep in his shadowed eyes.

His gold hair hung over his brow, and he carried his chin at an angle that said he was cornered, but set for a fight. His gaze met hers, then swept to Patterson, then back to her.

Her eyes locked with his. She started to step toward him but one of the deputies warned her off. They half led, half pushed Archer into Fitzgibbons's office, then closed the doors again.

Rita's breath had turned ragged, the way it did just before she cried. Archer was chained like an animal. She had seen the desperation and rage in his gaze, his doubt that there was any hope. She forced herself to maintain control.

The door, shut again, remained shut. "What are they *doing* in there?" she begged Patterson. She didn't understand this cruel delay.

"They play their games," Patterson said calmly. "I play mine."

He kept reading. *He must have ice in his veins*, Rita thought miserably, while she had merely human blood in hers, and it was pounding hard enough to give her a headache.

But at last the door swung open, and Patterson and Rita were admitted without welcome. Fitzgibbons sat at his desk, looking no happier than before.

Archer sat in a folding chair against a bare wall. His face was steely, but again Rita thought she read something wild flickering in his eyes. She sensed his growing determination to escape this situation, no matter how recklessly, or at what cost. The two deputies flanked him.

Archer met Rita's gaze momentarily, then looked away.

Horchow sat in a cushioned chair at Fitzgibbons's right hand. His expression was as antagonistic as Fitzgibbons's.

Fitzgibbons nodded curtly for Rita and Patterson to sit in the two metal folding chairs before his desk.

Patterson shook his head and remained standing. So, by instinct, did Rita.

"Now," growled Fitzgibbons, "what's your game? You one of these high-priced lawyers that go around getting criminals off? Is that your gig? Nice business."

Rita simultaneously flinched and felt a prick of anger.

"My 'gig,'" Patterson said, unruffled, "is justice. Which, in Mr. Smith's case, we do not have."

Fitzgibbons crossed his arms, which were large and hairy. "We arrested Smith on probable cause. There's sufficient circumstantial evidence. We made sure of that."

Patterson heaved his briefcase up on Fitzgibbons's desk again with unexpected force. "You do *not* have probable cause," Patterson said with sarcasm. "You do *not* have sufficient circumstantial evidence. You have a few suspicious facts. There's a profound difference—gentlemen."

"Take that up with the prosecutor's office," Fitzgibbons ordered with a dour shake of his head.

"This case will never get to the prosecutor's office," Patterson countered acidly. "Did you check the background of this 'victim'?"

Rita's heartbeat sped to an even more violent pace. Archer was watching them now, a wary interest in his eyes. But he kept his expression distant, cold.

"My men are checking on Peavey's background, yes," Fitzgibbons snarled. "It'll be a thorough job. We're shorthanded right now, but every effort is being made—"

"Every effort is being made to railroad an innocent man because of *your* sloppy investigative techniques." Patterson threw out the accusation with enough force to make Horchow jump slightly. Even Fitzgibbons looked startled.

"This woman—" Patterson said dramatically, turning to Rita "—this lone *woman*, hounded by you as she's been, has had time to check. She's *made* time to check. She's made it her *duty* to check—when it should have been yours."

Archer's eyes met Rita's again. She tried to smile, but was too nervous.

"I know what you have against my client," Patterson said, warming to his cause. He had turned from a mild-looking little man into a human buzz saw of argument, sharp and unstoppable.

"We—" began Fitzgibbons.

"You," Patterson sneered, "have the *flimsiest* of circumstantial evidence. A typewriter dropped off a dock—you don't know if my client ever touched it. A piece of glass beside the corpse—a piece that anyone might have taken, planted. A sprinkling of the victim's blood by the door of the house where my client slept. Blood that could have gotten there by any number of means."

"He wouldn't take a lie-detector test," Horchow challenged. "The other two would."

Patterson looked so angry that he frightened even Rita. "That is not probable cause!" he cried. "He has the *right* to refuse it. The test is not reliable. The test is not admissible in court. The test has no bearing."

"Now, listen," Horchow said truculently. "We've cleared Sig Hobbler. The Johanssen man looks clean. It's your friend here who—"

Patterson banged the desk so hard it shook. "*All* my client has against him is a prior conviction that was overturned. You assume he's guilty on the basis of his past. This is unconstitutional. This is persecution of the basest sort. It is barbaric, intolerable. And I will personally see that you—" he stabbed his finger first at Fitzgibbons, then at Horchow "—and this department *pay*. I will have your *jobs*. I will see you *barred* from law enforcement for the rest of your lives."

Fitzgibbons half rose from behind his desk. A huge man, he should have dwarfed Patterson, but did not. Patterson's moral outrage was too overwhelming.

"Listen," Fitzgibbons said hotly. "Somebody killed Peavey, and your ex-con here—"

"Yes!" Patterson cried dramatically, throwing his arms upward and outward like a preacher. "Someone killed Peavey. And the answer should have been obvious all along. *If* you'd done your work."

Fitzgibbons shook a finger at Patterson and Rita. "We *have* done our work, dammit. Somebody killed a man, and we—"

"*Precisely,*" Patterson said in triumph. "Someone did kill him. But not my client." He turned to Rita. "Tell them, Miss O'Casey. Tell them who their murderer is."

Rita felt a surge of fright, like a person suddenly pushed to the center of a stage. But Patterson had rehearsed her, and done so rigorously.

"Last night, I saw something in my flower bed. It was a book—part of a burned book."

Patterson withdrew it from his briefcase and laid it before Fitzgibbons. The big man eyed it as if it were a snake.

"It was in the tulip leaves. And I'd been thinking that you had poor Archer caught like a rat in a trap."

She swallowed. She glanced at Archer, who stared at her, his gaze unreadable. "And it all came together for me then. Archer said once that Peavey's eyes reminded him of a trapped rat's—of an animal crazed with pain."

"What is this crap?" Fitzgibbons demanded, with a disbelieving shake of his head. "Rats and tulips—this is crap. You people are crazy."

"Be quiet," ordered Patterson in a tone so dangerous that Fitzgibbons blinked. "Let the woman speak."

"Sig said that the suicide note mentioned 'existential despair.' Sig couldn't spell it. But Peavey could. This book came out of his house. Look at the title—look."

She held her breath as Fitzgibbons glared at the title page again. The soot-stained page bore the words, *The French Existentialists: A Primer.*

"It's—it's about existentialism," Rita said. "And it's his book. His name is up in the corner. It's partly burned off, but it's there. And he's—he underlined in it. A lot. You can see for yourself."

Reluctantly, Fitzgibbons opened the fragile pages. They were marked by underlining in red.

"Nothing about this killing made sense," she said, squaring her shoulders. "If the killer surprised Peavey at the apple tree, why didn't he throw the hacksaw in the fire? Why didn't he put the typewriter in, too?"

"Cut to the chase," Fitzgibbons said sharply.

Rita took a deep breath. She didn't look at Archer because she was afraid to. What if she failed him?

She leaned forward, bracing her hands on Fitzgibbons's desk. She met his eyes. "Peavey killed himself. He planted evidence almost everywhere to make other people look guilty. Then he wrote the note, put it in the mailbox. He went back to his house, started the fire and killed himself."

Fitzgibbons rolled his eyes in disgusted disbelief. He swore. "Get serious, lady, this ain't 'Murder She Wrote.'"

"No," Rita countered. "I think it's Murder *He* Wrote. It's the only explanation that makes sense. Archer said he'd seen *pain* in Peavey's eyes. Archer was the only one who noticed—the rest of us were too busy disliking the man."

"This is bull—" Fitzgibbons began.

"No," Rita interrupted angrily. "Listen. I talked to Teresa Bitcon, the woman who lives in Peavey's old house, his old neighborhood. Peavey *had* to be unhappy. He was a seriously ill man, he didn't have a friend in the world—"

"Lady, he was a crackpot, but that don't give anybody the right to blow his head off."

Rita emulated Patterson and slapped the desk. "*Listen*," she ordered. "That's just what I'm talking about. He wasn't a—a crackpot. Don't call him names. He was mentally ill. He had problems. He was lonely, confused, driven—"

Fitzgibbons swore. "Get out the violins," he muttered. He swore. "You people all *hated* him."

"Nobody understood," Rita retorted. "And if we had, what could we have done? We aren't doctors. Somewhere along the line, the system failed George Peavey. He—he was one of those people that fell between the cracks."

Fitzgibbons swore again.

Rita shook her head scornfully. "I called Teresa Bitcon back. She'd started to tell me something before, about Peavey doing something that made the neighbors hear sirens—"

"So you learned Peavey had set a fire or two," Fitzgibbons sneered. "You blabbed it to all your neighbors, and somebody got the idea to turn Peavey into toast. Namely lover boy, here."

Rita leaned across the desk more aggressively. "My first thought was that he set fires. But Teresa had to hang up. Then it hit me, so I called her back. Peavey would reach a certain state of disturbance—and he'd try to kill himself. He did it more than once. The sirens belonged to *ambulances*. This man had a *history* of suicide attempts, dammit."

"So you say," Fitzgibbons challenged. "But you can't prove—"

"We *can* prove," Patterson countered with obvious relish. He drew a sheaf of faxes from his briefcase. "These are notes from Mr. Peavey's psychiatrist. The man had six documented suicide attempts. Six. This was the seventh. Only this time, it worked."

He threw the fax sheets before Fitzgibbons, who looked at them in confusion. "How did you—how did you— We were checking for a psychiatrist, but—"

"Perhaps," Patterson almost hissed, "you weren't persistent enough. Or perhaps you don't know how to look. I do, and I'm persistent."

Rita was still afraid to look at Archer. "Teresa Bitcon said Peavey's specialty was estranging people and setting them against each other. I think he hated seeing other people happy when he was so unhappy himself."

"Mr. Peavey," Patterson said from between his teeth, "was severely manic-depressive. *Very* severely. His mood swings could be controlled to a great extent by medication. But at times he wouldn't take it. He would hide his pills, lie about taking them."

He stabbed his finger at the pile of faxes. "It's all here," he said. "With his mother gone, he obviously went off his medication. He stopped seeing his doctor. In short, he was *destined* to spiral out of control."

Horchow had started sweating. Sweat filmed his lined brow, moistened his upper lip. Fitzgibbons looked uncomfortable.

"Manic depression is a cruel illness," Patterson said. "In a manic phase, the victim can become paranoid, combative, dangerous to others and himself. He can also become hyperactive—and stop sleeping almost completely."

Rita swallowed, still too fearful to look at Archer. "Peavey was obviously in a manic phase at the lake. He thought he was making a fresh start. He didn't understand what was happening to him. And there was nobody to help."

"Psychiatrists," Patterson said with venom, "don't go chasing after absent patients. Their time is too valuable."

Rita added, "Mr. Patterson talked to the psychiatrist. A patient in a severe manic phase is at great risk for suicide. Dangerously high risk. But he can still be thinking according to a private, twisted logic."

She licked her lips. "Peavey made enemies of us all. He built a spite fence and cut down Joe's tree and wisteria. He poisoned Sig's dogs. He unstaked Archer's dock. He cut down my tree."

"Miss O'Casey," Fitzgibbons said, his lip curling, "Peavey was shot at a highly unnatural angle for a suicide. It's much more likely that someone else—"

"Horchow told me that, too," Rita interrupted, pointing at the detective. "But 'unnatural' doesn't mean 'impossible.' Peavey could have purposely put the gun at an odd angle—to throw you off. He'd done everything else. Why not that, too?"

Horchow shifted uncomfortably in his chair. Fitzgibbons looked sullen. "So you're claiming—"

"It makes sense," Rita said earnestly. "Peavey cut down my tree. He wrote the note. He buried the hacksaw in Sig's yard, to throw suspicion on Sig. He dropped the typewriter off Archer's dock. He put bloodstains on my porch."

"Now that's a cute trick," Fitzgibbons said. "He goes over and bleeds on your doorstep. Is that where he cut his throat? Then walked home and shot himself?"

"Peavey had *allergies*," Rita argued. "When I looked at my tulips, I remembered Teresa saying he'd pulled up a neighbor's tulips. He claimed they bothered his allergies. That's why he . . . defoliated his yard. Allergies."

Fitzgibbons pushed himself back from his desk in disgust. "So *what?*"

"So my brother had them," she answered, her chin high. "And he had to have *shots*. And every time you take that shot, you have to test to make sure you haven't hit a vein. If you do, blood comes into the syringe."

Fitzgibbons gave a mocking laugh.

"If you take allergy shots," she retorted, "you get used to needles. Peavey could have drawn out his blood. Several syringes full. Then spattered it on my porch."

Fitzgibbons rolled his eyes again. "I don't believe this. You don't even know if he took shots. You don't know if he had any needles."

"*Au contraire, mon cher gendarme,*" Patterson said with utmost mockery. He reached into his briefcase and pulled out another sheaf of faxes. "We do know. A statement from his allergist, Dr. Potter of Lyttonville. A statement from his neighborhood druggist. He took shots. He'd bought syringes for years. He bought them by the boxful."

"There wasn't that *much* blood on my doorstep," Rita insisted.

"About 40 cc's," Patterson said confidently. "Or four syringes' worth."

Fitzgibbons only shook his head and looked angry.

"None of us had a typewriter," Rita said. "But Peavey did."

"Now how do you know *that?*" Fitzgibbons almost spat.

"Because he had a typing stand," Rita replied. "One of those metal ones. It's still there, in his living room. In the rubble. And I'll bet it's just the right size to accommodate the typewriter you found."

"Now just a damned minute," Fitzgibbons objected. "You don't *know* he had a typewriter. What is—"

"We do know," Patterson retorted with satisfaction. He withdrew another fax from his briefcase. "A statement from the only typewriter repairman in Lyttonville. Peavey had a Smith-Corona electric portable. Exactly what you found, perhaps?"

"Oh, my God," groaned Horchow and put his hand to his eyes.

"How did you *get* all this?" Fitzgibbons exploded, his bulldog face turning red. "It's impossible you got all this stuff since yesterday. You can't— It isn't—"

"It's not impossible," Patterson said icily, "if one is willing to think and to work. I also have a very dedicated staff in St. Louis. They're willing to work for me, all night long if necessary."

Fitzgibbons swore and pushed his chair farther back. He kicked the corner of his desk. "You musta been gettin' people outta bed all night long, you . . . fanatic."

"I don't mind getting people out of bed," Patterson said with a smile, "if they have information I want. And I can usually get it. A few magic words, such as *subpoena* and *obstruction of justice*, do wonders. And all the major hotels in Lyttonville have fax facilities for business travelers."

Rita finally dared to steal a glance at Archer. He sat, his head high, his face wary, as if afraid to hope. He didn't meet her eyes, but he nodded, as if he knew she was looking at him but didn't trust himself to look back.

Horchow still sat with his hand covering his eyes. He seemed humiliated. Fitzgibbons let out a long sigh of exasperation. "Okay, Sherlock," he said from between clenched teeth. "We found the stained glass right under him, next to his collarbone. It sure as hell looked like it could cut his throat. You're saying it didn't?"

"Your word choice is interesting," Patterson said. "It 'looked like it could have.' But I suppose the body was too burned to tell if his throat actually was cut. Correct?"

"The medical examiner couldn't ascertain," Fitzgibbons admitted sullenly.

"Rita," Patterson said, "show the gentlemen how one might seem to have died with a piece of glass in—or near—one's throat."

He reached into his briefcase and withdrew a carefully wrapped object. She took it and stripped away the tissue that protected it. It was a long bladelike scrap of glass.

She picked it up carefully. She kept her eyes locked with Fitzgibbons's. "Like this," she said, and slid the blade into her button-down collar. She let go. The button held it in place.

Fitzgibbons looked at her with blank dismay.

"One more thing we began to wonder," Patterson said crisply. "Sig had been implicated by the buried saw, Archer by the typewriter, and both Archer and Miss O'Casey by the bloodstains. Why didn't anything point to Joe Johanssen?"

Fitzgibbons's lip twitched nervously.

Rita took the glass from her collar and set it gingerly on his desk. "And you were missing something. Joe said he had *two* guns stolen. You found one of them in the house, beside Peavey. But nobody's ever talked about the other one."

Patterson sighed and shook his head. "We deduced that it was probably hidden somewhere that would implicate Joe. He and Sig were good enough to help us look. It had been buried—under his garbage can. We uncovered it—but left it there. For *your* men to take as evidence. I think we've done enough of your work, thank you."

Horchow had raised his head and now stared glumly at the floor. "This is insane," Fitzgibbons grumbled. "Why would the wacko implicate everybody? It's nuts."

"Your terminology is politically incorrect," Patterson said sharply. "You're talking about a sick, unhappy man. He struck out at them all because he envied them all. And because the only ease he knew for his unhappiness was to make others unhappy, too. George Peavey committed suicide. He tried to make it look like murder. He almost succeeded—thanks to you. Now—release my client."

"Yes," Rita insisted. "I want Archer. Give him back."

Patterson turned and gave her a stern, questioning look. Her cheeks grew hot, and she looked away, but she knew she had, as usual, blurted out exactly what she felt. *I want Archer. Give him back.*

"Unlock him and get him the hell out of here," she heard Fitzgibbons say tonelessly.

She kept her face turned away. She didn't want to see Archer in chains again, not ever. Her head was spinning and she felt half faint with relief.

But there was still the question of whether Archer had been so burned by this arrest that he would retreat into himself again, go away, try to forget it all, including her.

But then, suddenly, she found herself in his arms, and he was kissing her hair, her cheek, her jaw, her lips. His arms held her tightly, hungrily.

"Get them out of here," Fitzgibbons ordered. "I don't wanna see this. Out, *out!*"

Patterson took Archer by the shoulder, but could barely wrench him away from Rita. Somehow he steered the two of them out of Fitzgibbons's office and into the corridor. Archer still held Rita possessively, still kissed her cheek and throat almost compulsively, as if he couldn't stop.

Patterson pulled the door shut behind them. "You'd think I'd get a little credit," he grumbled.

Archer laughed, turned, grabbed the little man, embraced him and kissed his cheek. "Patterson, I think I love you."

Patterson struggled mightily and freed himself. He stepped backward with an indignant look. "Archer," he warned sternly, "don't *ever* do anything like that again."

"I think I love you, too," Rita said, throwing her arms around Patterson's neck and kissing him full on the mouth.

"Well, now," Patterson said, when she let him come up for air. "That's altogether different. That's a little bit of all right. You may do that again."

Archer grinned as Rita kissed Patterson again, as emotionally as before.

THREE DAYS LATER, Archer and Rita were in Rita's tiny kitchen, feeding each other chocolate-covered strawberries. Rita sat on the counter, next to the chilled plate of berries. She had one arm looped around his neck. She licked the chocolate from her lips and smiled at him.

He stood between her legs, and she had her legs twined lightly around his thighs. He had one arm draped around her shoulders. "Want another strawberry?" he asked.

"No," she said, looking up into his eyes.

"Me, either," he said. He put his other arm around her, and she twined both hers around his neck. They leaned their foreheads together.

"I was afraid you'd come out of that jail and I'd never see you again," she said, rubbing her brow against his.

"I was afraid I might do just that," he said. He pulled her nearer. "I felt crazy in that cell. I swore if I got out, I'd put so much distance between it and me, I couldn't measure it. If I had to run for it. Even if I didn't."

"I'm glad you didn't." She hugged him more tightly.

"I couldn't," he said. "As soon as I saw you again, I knew I couldn't. Not now. Not ever."

Ever, she thought, with a happy little quake inside her. Archer had never before spoken as if they could have a future. For the past three days, he had been affectionate, passionate—and almost happy. But not quite. He had been like a man coming out of shock. Tonight, at last, he seemed himself again.

He put his hands on either side of her face. "Once, I told you if I was free to say the things I wanted to say . . . do what I wanted to do . . ."

She remembered that walk through the forest, when suspicion still hung over him like an executioner's ax. "I remember," she said, half sadly. So much bad had happened to him since then.

"Well—" he lifted her face to his "—now I *am* free. Thanks to you. You set me free, Rita—in more ways than one."

"Archer," she said, smoothing his hair back from his forehead, "Patterson did all the work. He was remarkable. All I had was this idea. *He* proved it."

He shook his head. "I couldn't get over it. Neither could Patterson. I mean, I know he almost works miracles. But how could you look at a burned book in a tulip bed and suddenly know that Peavey killed himself?"

Her hand moved to his cheek, stayed there. "It just happened. I sort of knew what existentialism was." She looked away in embarrassment. "See . . . I nearly flunked philosophy in college, and I never *could* understand existentialism. I still don't. I just knew it was in the book and it mixed me up."

He laughed. "God, you're something. You solve this whole thing, then get shamefaced about a bad grade in college? Hey, that bad grade may have saved my life. Look at the big picture."

She smiled shyly and looked at him again. "You helped, too, Archer. Because you're the only one who saw that Peavey was in pain. That he was like somebody in a trap. And what really bothered me was there was no way to explain the blood on the doorstep."

She frowned slightly at the memory. "It was so weird. I saw the book's title. I'd been thinking of what you said. I'd even been thinking, 'What if Peavey cut the fence himself?' I saw the tulips and remembered the allergies. And I remember my brother learning to give himself a shot, and the blood coming up into the syringe, and it was—all there. What if he'd killed *himself?*"

"Patterson said he might never have put it together."

"He's still the one who proved it."

"I asked him," Archer said, his thumbs stroking her jawline. "Why did it come to you like that—in a flash? Do you know what he said?"

"No," she answered softly, wishing he'd kiss her.

"He said, 'I think it happened because she loves you.' He's a smart man, Rita. He's hardly ever wrong. Is he right? Do you love me?"

A small wave of dismay swept her. Archer didn't want to be loved—did he? If she told the truth, would he tell her it was impossible between them?

But she couldn't lie. "Yes," she said, and realized that tears suddenly shimmered in her eyes.

"Rita," he said with a pained swallow, "I love you, too. I wasn't ready for love, but it didn't matter. I love you. I want to marry you and live with you and have lots of kids. Will you have me? An ex-con who still has nightmares sometimes?"

"Oh, yes," she said, staring into his eyes. "I love you so much. I'll wake you up when the nightmares come. I never want to be apart from you again."

He gave a little laugh. He kissed her—lightly, self-consciously. "I want to name our first son William Hartford Patterson Smith. What do you think?"

She kissed him back. "Let's name them *all* William Hartford Patterson Smith—even the girls."

"He's coming back this weekend." Archer smiled. "I think he wants to see an engagement ring on your finger. Let's put it there."

"Let's," she said and raised her lips to be kissed again.

"Want to make love in the shower again?" he whispered.

"Yes," she said, her face pressed against his throat. "Mr. Soap wants to tell you welcome home."

He lifted her from the counter, kissed her and carried to where Mr. Soap waited to make it a cleaner, friendlier world.

Temptation

Lost Loves

'Right Man...Wrong time'

All women are haunted by a lost love—a disastrous first romance, a brief affair, a marriage that failed.

A second chance with him...could change everything.

Lost Loves, a powerful, sizzling mini-series from Temptation continues in June 1995 with...

**Gold and Glitter
by Gina Wilkins**

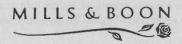

MILLS & BOON

This month's
irresistible novels from

Temptation

WHAT MIGHT HAVE BEEN by Glenda Sanders

Lost Loves mini-series

One night of passion had cost Richard Benson dearly. He had got a girl pregnant and had dutifully married her—but it was another girl, Barbara Wilson, he loved. Now, single and with a daughter in tow, Richard was back in town, hoping to recapture what might have been.

SCANDALS by JoAnn Ross

Grief-stricken over the death of his brother, cynical, hard-nosed Bram Fortune did the unthinkable—he sought comfort in the arms of his brother's fiancée. They parted the next morning, and then Dani came back to him—she was pregnant with *his* child.

TROUBLE IN PARADISE by Lisa Harris

Archer Smith was looking for peace, but this was shot to ribbons when he saw his neighbour, sexy Rita O'Casey. He wasn't the only man watching her, and there was trouble brewing.

A TRUE BLUE KNIGHT by Roseanne Williams

Tomasina Walden avoided cops so, when she heard that Detective Brogue Donovan was planning to move in next door, she told him the house was haunted. Rather than scare him off, her ghost story seemed to bring out his protective instincts...

Spoil yourself next month
with these four novels from

Temptation

GOLD AND GLITTER by Gina Wilkins

Lost Loves mini-series

When Michael Spencer came to work for Libby Carter, she
tried to quell her unwanted attraction to his rugged, sexy looks.
He had obviously been hurt badly in the past and he was a man
who was used to moving on...

LADY OF THE NIGHT by Kate Hoffmann

Annabeth Dupree wasn't a call girl although it was true that
she had inherited a bordello! How could she convince
everyone—including Zach Tanner—that she wasn't the bad
girl they thought? Especially when the look in Zach's eyes told
her he was starting to *like* this bad girl...

MOLLY AND THE PHANTOM by Lynn Michaels

The princess and the jewel thief. Two greater opposites
couldn't be found, except that Princess Molly needed the
dashing, devil-may-care Chase Sanquist's help. He intended to
steal the Phantom, the centrepiece of her crown jewels—and
she wanted him to do exactly that.

THE BOUNTY HUNTER by Vicki Lewis Thompson

Tough and independent, Gabe Escalante was a man of justice
and was closing in on a dangerous criminal. Dallas Wade was
the next intended victim and suddenly Gabe wanted to be more
than her bodyguard. It could prove to be a fatal mistake.

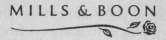

GET 4 BOOKS AND A MYSTERY GIFT

Return this coupon and we'll send you 4 Temptations and a mystery gift absolutely FREE! We'll even pay the postage and packing for you.

We're making you this offer to introduce you to the benefits of Reader Service: FREE home delivery of brand-new Temptations, at least a month before they are available in the shops, FREE gifts and a monthly Newsletter packed with information.

Accepting these FREE books and gift places you under no obligation to buy, you may cancel at any time, even after receiving just your free shipment. Simply complete the coupon below and send it to:

HARLEQUIN MILLS & BOON, FREEPOST, PO BOX 70, CROYDON, CR9 9EL.

No stamp needed

Yes, please send me 4 free Temptations and a mystery gift. I understand that unless you hear from me, I will receive 4 superb new titles every month for just £1.99* each postage and packing free. I am under no obligation to purchase any books and I may cancel or suspend my subscription at any time, but the free books and gifts will be mine to keep in any case. (I am over 18 years of age)

1EP5T

Ms/Mrs/Miss/Mr _____

Address _____

_____

_____ Postcode _____

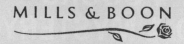